GOD REST YE,
ROYAL GENTLEMEN

GOD REST YE, ROYAL GENTLEMEN

RHYS BOWEN

THORNDIKE PRESS
A part of Gale, a Cengage Company

LIBRARY OF CONGRESS CIP DATA ON FILE.
CATALOGUING IN PUBLICATION FOR THIS BOOK
IS AVAILABLE FROM THE LIBRARY OF CONGRESS.

ISBN-13: 978-1-4328-9122-0 (hardcover alk. paper)

Published in 2021 by arrangement with Berkley, an imprint of Penguin Publishing Group, a division of Penguin Random House, LLC.

Printed in Mexico
Print Number: 01   Print Year: 2022

Dedicated to my good friend and doyenne of the mystery world Barbara Peters.

And with thanks to Michelle Vega and my wonderful team at Berkley Prime Crime, my brilliant agents Meg Ruley and Christina Hogrebe and also to John, Clare and Jane, who are my first readers and give great suggestions.

CHAPTER 1

November 25, 1935
Eynsleigh House, Sussex

I'm looking out of my window on a misty November morning. A deer and fawn are standing at the edge of our woods and a couple of hares just raced across the grass. It's hard to believe that this lovely place is now my home and that my life is now so settled. I also still can't quite believe I am a married woman with a wonderful husband. Sometimes I want to pinch myself to find out if I'm dreaming. But then I don't want to wake up!

" 'Christmas is coming, the geese are getting fat, please to put a penny in the old man's hat,' " sang my housemaid, Sally, in a high, sweet voice as she brandished the feather duster over the portraits in the long gallery. I have never actually seen the value of feather dusters. All they seem to do is to make the dust fly off one surface to land on another nearby. That was certainly happening at the moment, but then, Sally was getting into the spirit of the season and dusting like an orchestra conductor in time to her singing.

She was a trifle optimistic about Christmas coming. It was still a month away, an idea just looming at the edge of my consciousness. But the song brought a sudden realization that I'd have to do something about getting ready for the holiday season. Now that I was mistress of a great house it would be up to me to see to decorations, invite guests, buy presents. . . . Golly, I thought when I realized what might be expected of me.

Until now Christmas had been a cheerless affair at my family castle in Scotland, with my sister-in-law, Hilda, Duchess of Rannoch, commonly known as Fig, only allowing one log on the fire at a time, in spite of the fact that gales were habitually felling trees all over the estate. Now, for the first time, I could have the holiday I had always dreamed of — in my own house with my new husband, and maybe family and friends. I pictured sitting by a roaring fire with my nearest and dearest around me and went through to the study to find paper and pencil to make a list of people to invite. Darcy was sitting at the desk and looked up in surprise as I came in.

"Hello — I didn't hear you coming."

"Sorry, am I interrupting something?" I asked.

"No. Just some odds and ends I promised I'd clear up for the Foreign Office." He gave me the wonderful smile that still melted me like ice cream on a hot day, even after four months of marriage. "Did you need me?" he asked.

"No, I just came to get some paper," I said, "but Sally was singing about Christmas coming and it dawned on me that it was up to me to arrange things. I'm sure we can find a suitable tree on the estate and Mrs. Holbrook will know where decorations are stored, but we should invite people, shouldn't we? This house is far too big for just the two of us."

"A house party, you mean?"

"Gosh, that sounds a bit grand and formal, doesn't it? I was thinking more of people like Mummy and Max, Granddad, Belinda and your father and Zou Zou. Our nearest and dearest."

"I notice you haven't mentioned your next

of kin." He looked up at me with a wicked grin.

"My brother, you mean?" I paused, collecting my thoughts. "Much as I love Binky and my nephew and niece he'd have to bring his wife with him. Besides, the Duke of Rannoch has responsibilities around Christmas. He has to dress up as Father Christmas and hand out gifts to the crofters' children, and preside at the gillie's ball on New Year's Eve. And Fig's awful sister, Ducky, will be bound to join them. And her even more awful brother-in-law, Foggy, and utterly dire daughter, Maude." I paused then added, "And Fig would be too cheap to pay for train tickets anyway."

"I take it that's a no," he said, making me laugh. "But what about your royal relations? The king and queen should give the party some class, shouldn't they?"

I gave him a severe look. "You are teasing," I said. "You know perfectly well they always go to Sandringham for Christmas, and besides, the king isn't well. And he hates staying in other people's houses."

"Well, there is always the Prince of Wales, and don't forget Mrs. Simpson." He was still smiling.

"Over my dead body," I retorted. "She is the last person in the world I would want to spend a holiday with — apart from Fig. Or should that be 'with whom I should want to spend a holiday'?" I paused. "In any case I'd die of nerves if I had to entertain anyone of rank, even if they would come."

Darcy looked down at the papers on the desk again.

"What about your father?" I asked. "Do you think he'll come?"

"I don't think you'll get my father to leave Ireland twice in one year," Darcy said. "You know he hates to travel. He hates mixing with people he doesn't know. And besides, it's steeplechase season. He'll have horses in the big races around Dublin."

"I'll take it that's a no," I said, repeating his words.

"I just know my father too well," he said. "But there are other people we could invite. My aunt Hawse-Gorzley, for one. We both had Christmas at her house once."

I shot him a horrified look. "Oh Darcy. Think of all the awful things that happened that Christmas. Someone died every day."

"Apart from that it was quite jolly, wasn't it?" he said, making me give an exasperated laugh.

"Darcy! I'd expect the guests to be dropping like flies if she was here."

"It wasn't my aunt's fault that people were

11

being killed around her," Darcy pointed out. "And they did catch the murderer."

"All the same," I said, "that is a Christmas I'd prefer to forget."

"Didn't I propose to you on that occasion?" He was looking up with a challenging smile.

"That part wasn't so bad," I retorted and helped myself to writing paper.

As I was on my way out he called after me, "We'll have to invite the neighbors, you know. It's the done thing for the lady of the manor to entertain."

That brought me up short. I still hadn't quite come to terms with the knowledge that I was now not only a married woman but also supposed to be a leading light in local society.

"Oh crikey," I muttered. "A festive dinner, you mean? Boars' heads and flaming puddings and things?" My thoughts went immediately to Queenie, who was the only cook we had. She had been filling in quite well, but if it came to flaming anything . . .

"I don't think it has to be a formal meal," Darcy said. "Maybe just for a wassail bowl and mince pies."

"I think I can manage that much," I said. "I mean Queenie can manage that much.

She has a surprisingly light touch with pastry."

Darcy frowned. "Speaking of Queenie — it really is about time we found a proper cook. I know she's not bad at what she does, but her food is strictly of the nursery variety. If you really do want to invite people for a house party I'm not sure they'll be thrilled with shepherd's pie and spotted dick. And God knows what she'd do to a turkey. Probably explode it."

"You're right." I chewed on my lip. "I've been meaning to do it for ages. In his last letter Sir Hubert asked me whether I'd found a good chef." In case you've forgotten, Sir Hubert was the true owner of this lovely estate. He had been one of my mother's many husbands and had made me his heir, allowing us to live at Eynsleigh while he was off climbing mountains.

"Any chance he'll be home for Christmas?" Darcy asked.

"I'm afraid not. The last letter was from Chile and he was even talking about getting a boat across to Antarctica to go exploring there. I wish he didn't live so dangerously."

"You can't make a leopard change his spots," Darcy said. "If your mother hadn't turned him down for a second time he might have stayed closer to home."

13

"It was because he kept going off exploring and climbing things that she left him in the first place. I believe she really does love him, but you know Mummy — she likes to be adored all the time. And she does like Max's money."

Darcy frowned. "I don't think I'd be too happy in Germany these days, however rich I was. The more I hear about Hitler and his henchmen, the more worried I get."

"Surely he's all bluster, isn't he, Darcy?" I asked. "Big speeches and parades to make the Germans feel better."

"If you want my opinion, the man is a dangerous lunatic," Darcy said. "I believe he plans no less than world domination — and your mother's Max is helping the cause by turning his factories to making guns and tanks."

This was a subject that was worrying me — one I tried to push to the back of my mind. I didn't want to admit that my mother was now deeply entrenched among the Nazis or that she might be in danger. I told myself that for all her aura of frailty she was a tough little person and could always take care of herself. I switched to a more pleasant topic.

"You'll have to do what Binky does and play Father Christmas to the local children, won't you? Doesn't the lord of the manor have to do that?"

"I suppose so. That will be fun," he said. "Good practice for when we have some of our own."

I wished he hadn't said that. It was another subject that was worrying me. We had now been married over four months and there was still no sign of a baby. I know the doctor had told me that these things take time and I should just stop worrying and let nature take its course, but there was that tiny sliver of doubt that kept whispering that there might be something wrong with me. I was absolutely sure there was nothing wrong with Darcy. His private life had been as colorful as my mother's before he met me.

"So I'll write to invite Mummy and Max, shall I?" I asked as Darcy turned his attention back to the papers on the desk. "And Belinda, Zou Zou and of course Granddad."

"It's your house," he said easily. "Invite who you want, as long as we have a cook that won't set fire to the house."

"Queenie hasn't done that yet."

"There's always time." He grinned. "I think a house party would be splendid. The more the merrier. It would be good practice for our entertaining skills."

"What about some of your friends," I said. "Anyone you'd particularly like to invite?"

"Most of my friends are still unmarried and likely to be off having fun skiing or on a yacht over Christmas," he said. "You said you'll invite Zou Zou. She's my friend too. Maybe she'll want to bring a couple of others along."

"If she doesn't go over to Ireland to be with your father."

He grimaced. "That relationship doesn't seem to be going anywhere, does it? My stupid father is too proud to pop the question because he feels he has nothing to offer her. She's a princess and he's a mere baron. And she has oodles of money and he has none."

"And I think she likes her freedom. She enjoys flying off to Paris in her little plane, doesn't she? And her house in London. I do hope she comes, Darcy. She's the life of any party, isn't she?"

"She's a wonderful person. Quite unique," he agreed. The way he said it reminded me that his relationship with Zou Zou might not have been entirely chummy, but it would have been childish to mention that. And she was a wonderful person, who, like my mother, just happened to be a magnet to men.

"Off you go then and write your invitations," Darcy said. "I think Christmas Eve to the New Year should be about the right amount of time to have guests, don't you?"

"Perfect," I said. I went off happily to the morning room and settled myself at the table in the window. It was my favorite spot when the sun was shining, which it was today. It faced the rear of the house, with a view across the grounds. Manicured lawns with a rose garden, now pruned to bare stalks for the winter, stretched to a wild woodland beyond, today laced with strands of morning mist. Dewdrops sparkled on the frosty grass. It was a perfect day to go out riding and I wished we had horses. My own horse was still at Castle Rannoch in Scotland and of course Darcy and I had no spare money to buy mounts, both coming from families who had lost their fortunes long ago. I paused for a moment, wondering how I could bring Rob Roy down from Scotland. That would be a long, and expensive, journey and one for which I couldn't ask my brother to pay. My brother, the current Duke of Rannoch, was as penniless as I was.

Then I decided that a dog might be the next best thing. One can have lovely walks with a dog. Perhaps I'd ask Darcy for one for Christmas. I pictured a black Lab puppy bounding at my heels.

I went back to the task at hand. "Dear Belinda. We are planning a little house party for Christmas and do hope you can join us if you are not going to your father's house."

"Dear Zou Zou. We are planning a little house party over Christmas and do hope you can join us. P.S. We're inviting Darcy's father. Perhaps you can persuade him to come."

"Dear Mummy. We are planning a little house party for Christmas and would love it if you and Max could come over from Germany to join us. It would be so jolly if you were here."

"Dear Granddad, I do hope you will come and stay over Christmas. I miss you and it would be perfect if you were here." I knew better than to mention the words "house party" to him. Any trace of posh or formal would make him shy away, since he came from a humble background and felt ill at ease among the upper classes. (In case you don't know my family history, my mother was a famous actress who married a duke, so I had one grandfather who had lived in a Scottish castle and one who lived in a semi-detached in Essex. I adored him.)

I addressed the envelopes, put on stamps

and had just deposited them on the tray in the front hall for the postman to collect when Mrs. Holbrook appeared. "Oh, there you are, my lady," she said. "I wonder if you'd come down to the kitchen for a moment."

Alarm bells sounded in my head. "Oh dear. Nothing's wrong, is it?"

"Not at all, my lady. It's just that it's pudding day."

"Pudding day?"

"Yes, November twenty-fifth. A month before Christmas. Always been pudding day in this house. The day the Christmas puddings are made. And it's always traditional for the lord or lady of the house to come and give a stir for good luck."

"Oh, right." I gave a sigh of relief. Not a disaster at all. "I'll fetch Mr. O'Mara. Perhaps he'd like to be part of this."

I hurried back to the study. Darcy looked up, a trifle impatiently this time. "What is it, Georgie?"

"Mrs. Holbrook has invited us to come and stir the pudding."

"What?"

"It's pudding day, apparently, and the lord and lady of the house are supposed to give the puddings a stir for good luck."

"I really need to get this stuff off to the

19

post," he said. "Do I have to be present to ensure good luck?"

"I suppose not. . . ."

He saw my face and pushed back his chair. "Of course I can spare a few minutes. We have to make sure we have good luck next year, don't we?" And he put his arm around my shoulders, steering me out of the room. He really is a nice man, I thought with a little glow of happiness.

Down the hallway we walked, past the dining room, through the baize door that led to the servants' part of the house and down a flight of steps to the cavernous kitchen. On rainy days I expect it could be rather gloomy unless the electric lights were shining. Today the windows, high in the south wall, sent shafts of sunlight onto the scrubbed tables. Queenie was standing at one of them, her hands in a huge mixing bowl. She gave us a look of pure terror as we came in.

"Hello, Queenie. We've come to stir the pudding," I said.

"Oh yeah. Bob's yer uncle, missus." She sounded distracted. I noted she now called me "missus" instead of "miss." I suppose it was a small step forward. After several years she had never learned to call me "my lady." Or perhaps she knew very well and was just being bolshie about it. I sometimes suspected Queenie wasn't quite as clueless as we imagined.

"Is something wrong?" I asked.

" 'Wrong'?" Her voice sounded higher than usual.

I walked toward the pudding bowl, with Darcy a step behind me. Inside was a big sticky mass of dough and fruit. It looked the way puddings were supposed to look, from my limited experience.

"It's just that you had both hands in the bowl when we came in. Doesn't one usually stir with a spoon?"

"What? Oh yes, right." Her face had now gone red. "It's just I was looking for something."

" 'Looking for something'?" Darcy sounded puzzled, but then he hadn't had close contact with Queenie for as long as I had.

Her face was now beet red. "It's like this, you see. A button was loose on my uniform again. I meant to sew it on but I forgot and I was giving the pudding a bloody great stir when all of a sudden — ping — it popped clean off and went flying into the pudding mixture and I can't for the life of me find it again."

"Queenie!" I exclaimed. I knew I should

21

be firm with her and scold her for not keeping her uniform up to snuff, but it really was rather funny.

"What exactly is this button made of?" Darcy asked. "It's not celluloid or something that might melt when it's cooked, is it?"

"Oh no, sir. It's like these others." She pointed at the front of her uniform dress, where there was now a gaping hole revealing a red flannel vest. "I think it's bone."

"Well, in that case nothing to worry about," Darcy said breezily. "If someone finds it — well, people are supposed to find charms in puddings, aren't they?"

"Silver charms," I pointed out.

"We'll tell them it's a tradition of the house, going back to the Middle Ages," Darcy said. "It's a button made from the bone of a stag that was shot on Christmas Day."

"Darcy, you're brilliant." I had to laugh. "Just as long as someone doesn't swallow it or break a tooth. Please keep trying to find it, Queenie. Only use a fork and not your fingers."

"Would your ladyship like to stir now?" Mrs. Holbrook asked. She handed me the big spoon. I took it and stirred.

"You're supposed to wish, my lady," Mrs.

Holbrook reminded.

"Oh, of course." I stirred and you can probably guess what I wished for.

Then Darcy stirred and I wondered if he was wishing for the same thing. Mrs. Holbrook opened a little leather box and handed us the silver charms. "You'll want to drop these into the pudding," she said.

"Oh yes. What fun." We dropped them in, one by one: the boot, the pig, the ring and silver threepences.

"And the bachelor button," Darcy said, dropping in a silver button and giving me a grin.

"Thank you, sir. Thank you, my lady," Mrs. Holbrook said. "I'll help Queenie look for the unfortunate button, don't you worry. We'll find it between us."

As we came up the stairs from the kitchen Darcy put a hand on my shoulder. "Now do you agree that we need to get a proper cook before Christmas?"

CHAPTER 2

November 26
London

> Off to London to see Zou Zou. What could
> be nicer? I do hope she can help me find
> a cook or, better still, find a cook for me.
> She knows everybody. Although I'm not
> sure we can afford the sort of cook she
> might find. . . .

When we were getting ready for bed last
night Darcy mentioned casually, "I think
I'll have to go up to town in the morning."

"Oh?" I tried not to sound too interested.

He looked up from untying his shoes.
"The letter that came in the afternoon post
contained a couple of things that need sort-
ing out in person, I fear."

I now tried to show that I wasn't alarmed.
"That doesn't mean you'll have to go away,
does it?" (I should probably mention, for

24

those of you who haven't met Darcy, that he doesn't have a proper job but he takes on assignments for a nebulous branch of the government. In other words I suspect my husband is a spy!)

"I don't think so," Darcy said. "Don't worry. I plan to be home for our first Christmas together as a married couple, whatever happens."

"That's good news." I gave him a bright and confident smile. "I'm so looking forward to it. And planning it with you will be half the fun."

He took off his tie and draped it over the back of a chair. Some of you may be asking yourselves why Darcy is undressing himself in our bedroom and not being undressed by his valet in his own dressing room, as is right and proper for a man of his social standing. Well, the answer to that is that he doesn't have a valet. He's always been an independent sort of chap and besides, he's never had the funds to employ a valet. He might be the son of a lord, just as I am the daughter of a duke, but neither of us inherited money. Actually now I do have a maid, a little local girl who is sweet and willing and amazingly accident free, which is a miracle after years of Queenie's mishaps. Yes, Queenie was my maid before she became the cook. But most nights I don't need my new maid's help to undress. It is hardly taxing to take off a jumper and skirt, is it?

"You know," Darcy said, adding his shirt to the pile on the chair, "you could always come up to town with me in the morning. Go and see Zou Zou and ask her advice on finding a proper cook. She knows everybody."

"Good idea," I said. "I haven't seen Zou Zou in ages and I can give her the Christmas invitation in person. And I could also pop down to Essex to see Granddad and make sure he'll join us."

"Not until you've been to an agency and hired a cook" — Darcy wagged a finger at me — "or we'll have more strange unidentifiable objects in the Christmas dinner."

"Oh golly, yes." I had to laugh. "That was a bit much, wasn't it?"

"Face it, Georgie. The girl is a disaster, isn't she? We should probably send her back to my aunt and uncle, who seemed to like her for some reason."

"Yes," I said, hesitating. I knew full well that Queenie was a disaster some of the time but she was a good sort and had been jolly brave on a couple of occasions when I had got myself into a bit of a pickle. That was British understatement — when I was almost killed. So I did owe her something and she did make a really good spotted dick!

"But even if we have a real chef, he'll want an assistant cook, won't he?"

"Now who is getting a little too fancy?" Darcy asked. "You'll be telling me we need a butler and I need a valet next."

"You seem to be able to undress yourself remarkably well," I remarked as I noted that he was now standing in just his pajama bottoms with a bare chest — and looking jolly handsome, by the way. "Better than I can," I added. "I seem to have the clasp of my bra caught in my jumper."

"Always willing to help." Darcy came over and skillfully removed both jumper and bra. After that neither of us had anything to talk about for a while.

The next morning was classic November weather: a beastly fog through which we drove at a snail's pace to the station and then the train crawled, equally cautiously, toward Waterloo. Darcy set off on his own mysterious errand while I caught the tube to Victoria. When I emerged from the Underground station I saw that the white mist of the countryside had been replaced by the dirty brown fog of the city. I recoiled at the sooty smell in my nose and metallic taste in my mouth. Golly, I don't know how people can live in cities! I made my way to Eaton Square and knocked on Zou Zou's door. It was opened by her French maid, Clotilde.

"Oh, my lady," she said in surprise. "We were not expecting visitors on such a terrible day. I don't believe my mistress knows you are coming. She is still in bed, I am afraid. . . ."

"She is not ill, I hope?"

The hint of a smile twitched on her lips. "No. She stays in bed when she sees no reason to get up. Please, go into the drawing room and I will tell her you 'ave arrived."

I was divested of my overcoat and went into a delightfully warm room, reminding me of the first time I had met Zou Zou, or rather Princess Zamanska as I then knew her. At that moment I was at my lowest, sure that Darcy and I could not be married. And she had taken me under her wing.

I heard her voice now. "Who was it, Clotilde? I hope you sent them away. I have no desire to be sociable today."

Then Clotilde's lower response and then a shrieked, "Lady Georgiana? Why on earth didn't you say so? Tell her to come up immediately and tell Cook I feel strong enough for some coffee and one of his delicious croissants."

Clotilde returned. "Zee mistress says she would be delighted to receive you in her boudoir." She started to lead me to the staircase.

"It's all right. I know the way." I gave her a smile. "I did stay here once before my wedding, remember?"

"Of course, my lady. 'Ow is Mr. O'Mara? Very well, I 'ope?"

"Flourishing, thank you." I continued up the broad staircase and tapped on Zou Zou's door. Almost instantly she called, "Darling, come in, please."

She was sitting up in bed with her luxuriant dark hair cascading over her shoulders, wearing a pink silk robe trimmed with some sort of fluffy pink feathers. Her face was usually perfectly made up with luscious red lips, but this morning she was as nature had made her — which was still close to perfect. I was never sure how old she was. At least forty, although her skin was still without a wrinkle. She reached out an elegant white hand to me. "Georgie, darling. Just the tonic I need for a beastly day. Honestly when the weather is like this it's simply not worth stirring. If I could be allowed to fly my little

29

plane, I'd be heading for the South of France as fast as I could." She patted the sheet beside her. "Come and sit down and tell me everything. Is there a special reason for this visit or are you just being kind to an old, old friend?"

I perched beside her on the bed, smiling. "You are not old, darling Zou Zou. And there is a double reason for my call. The first is to invite you to join us for Christmas. I thought we'd have a little house party, as it's our first Christmas at Eynsleigh and such a big house ought to have lots of people in it, shouldn't it?"

"Oh dear." Zou Zou gave a little sigh. "I'm afraid I won't be able to join in the fun, although it does sound heavenly. I'm having Christmas lunch with friends and then I'm popping across to Ireland for the big race meeting on Boxing Day."

"Oh, so you'll be seeing Darcy's father. How lovely for him." I tried to hide my disappointment.

"Wouldn't miss it for the world, darling. We've several horses entered at the race meeting. I'm hoping for great things. Thaddy's been working miracles with them. He's so good at it, you know."

So there was hope for those two. I really shouldn't begrudge them their time together. "So that brings me to my second request," I went on. "I've been meaning to hire a proper cook. We've been getting by with Queenie's cooking for too long, but I can't have people for Christmas and feed them bangers and mash, can I?"

Zou Zou gave that delicious throaty chuckle. "But I'm not lending you my chef, my darling, if that's what you wanted. He is more precious than rubies and he stays right here."

I flushed. "Oh no. I wouldn't dream of suggesting such a thing. I wanted your advice on how to set about finding a good cook. I wouldn't even know where to start or how to know the good ones from the bad ones."

Zou Zou patted my hand. "The best way, of course, is to snap one up when someone dies. But failing that, one of the good agencies. They vet very carefully. I'd try the Albany. They know their stuff."

I chewed on my lip. "But won't their chefs be top-notch and thus too expensive for us? We have some of Sir Hubert's money set aside for paying a cook but not a first-class chef."

"You could always advertise in *The Lady.*"

"That's a good idea," I said. "I'll try your agency first and, if not, I'll put the ad in

The Lady."

At that moment there was a tap on the door and Clotilde entered, bearing a tray on which there was a coffeepot, two cups and a plate of pastries. She placed it on a side table, deftly poured coffee and hot milk into the cups and handed one to Zou Zou.

"Sugar, my lady?" she asked.

"One, please."

She dropped the cube into the cup, stirred and handed it to me. Then she placed the plate of croissants between us along with a small plate and napkin each, then gave a little bow before retreating. When would I ever have a servant like that? I wondered — then reminded myself that Zou Zou had the funds to pay for the best. It must be nice.

We ate and drank in silence, Zou Zou dipping her croissant into her coffee and me trying desperately not to shower crumbs across her pristine eiderdown.

"So who else are you inviting for Christmas?" she asked. "Anyone fun?"

"I'm not sure yet," I said. "My friend Belinda, of course. My mother, if she'll come from Germany. Maybe some of Darcy's friends."

"Oh my dear. I'm not sure how many of them are house-trained," she said, giving me a wicked grin. "But some of his relatives, maybe. He does seem to have oodles of them, doesn't he?"

"I haven't met most of them," I said. "He did suggest his aunt Lady Hawse-Gorzley."

"I don't know her."

"Devon family, on his mother's side," I said. "But we spent Christmas at her house once and people got killed with monotonous regularity. It's sort of put me off."

"Well, it would do," she agreed. "I expect you'll come up with a jolly set. What about all those girls who came out with you?"

"I've rather lost touch," I said, not wanting to admit that their lifestyle had seemed a lot grander than mine — their fathers having not lost their money in the great crash of '29. I slid cautiously to my feet. "I really should be going if I'm to visit your agency. Come down to see us before you go to Ireland."

She took my hand and squeezed it hard. "I will, darling girl. And I'll bring a hamper from Fortnum's to make up for deserting you over Christmas."

I took my leave and came out into the damp and dreary fog. Actually the weather matched my mood. Zou Zou would have been the life of my little party. On the train up to London I had wondered if it was too early for the decorations on Oxford Street

33

and Selfridges' windows and realized it probably was. And now I had to face a terrifying domestic employment agency. I made my way out of Eaton Square, up Grosvenor Place, successfully negotiated Hyde Park Corner — which was tricky in the fog — and turned up Park Lane. The fog seemed to be lifting a little as I found Curzon Street and peered at the house numbers until I found the agency. My nerve almost left me when I saw the steps leading to an impressive front door.

"Buck up, Georgie," I said to myself. "You are the employer here, not some poor girl from the country come to find a job." I mounted the steps and pressed the doorbell. It was opened almost instantly by a young man with a neat little mustache and a smart charcoal three-piece suit. "Can I help you?" he asked in an attempt at a posh accent.

"I hope so. I'm Lady Georgiana and I need a new cook." I had been going to say I was Mrs. O'Mara, but decided this was a moment when a title was needed.

His expression changed instantly. "Welcome, my lady. Please do come in. Allow me to escort you to our Miss Probus, our senior advisor, who will be most happy to assist you." There was so much bowing and scraping that the words "Uriah Heep" came to mind. I was wafted through to an inner office where sat one of those terrifying women who seem to inhabit such places. They always appear to be far superior to their clients and doing one the greatest favor if they actually manage to find a staff member to suit.

"Miss Probus, this is Lady Georgiana," he said, still in his gushing voice. "She needs a new cook."

The woman's haughty expression did not flicker. "Please take a seat, your ladyship, and we'll see what we can do for you. Is this a cook for your London house or your country estate?"

"Country estate," I replied. "Eynsleigh in Sussex. Although only my husband and myself are in residence right now I do plan a Christmas house party."

Her eyebrows, clearly drawn with brown pencil, shot up. "You require a cook in time for a Christmas house party?"

"That's right."

"Oh no, no, no. Dear me, no," she said. "I'm afraid that's quite out of the question. We could assist you in the new year, but I'm afraid everyone has already snapped up our cooks for their Christmas house parties. We are much in demand, you know. People come to us as early as September." She spread her hands in a gesture of despair. "I don't know what to tell you, my lady. I think you'll find all reputable agencies will have the same story. Any chef worth his salt will have already been booked."

I came out feeling annoyed and a little guilty. I knew I should have been looking for a cook before this, but I kept telling myself that Queenie was good enough while there were just the two of us and I had plenty of time. Now what was I going to do? Maybe find a local woman to come and help out? But again any local woman who was a good cook would have been snapped up for somebody's Christmas celebration. I thought of trying other agencies but I didn't think I could face any more dragon ladies who looked down their noses at me. No, I'd have to put an advertisement in *The Lady* and just hope that something showed up.

I decided the only thing to do right now was to go and visit my grandfather. If anyone could cheer me up, he could. And he was not likely to be out on a day like this, knowing that he suffered from a weak chest. So I walked back across St. James's Park, where trees loomed eerily through the fog, and came at last to the St. James's tube station. I was quite tired and hungry by the time I stepped aboard the District Line train bound for Upminster. It was a strange journey of swirling grayness all the way and I had to peer hard to make out the street signs as I walked up the hill from the Upminster Bridge tube station. But there, at last, was his own dear little front garden, looking sorry for itself at this time of year. I rapped on the door and eventually heard the shuffle of feet. It was opened a few inches and a raspy voice whispered, "What do you want?"

"Granddad, it's me," I said.

The door was immediately flung open wide, to reveal my grandfather, unshaven and in his dressing gown and slippers.

"Blow me down, love, I didn't expect to see you today," he said. "Come inside, quick, before the bloomin' fog gets in." He almost yanked me through the door, closing it with a bang. "Now, what about a nice cup of tea, eh?"

I followed him into the kitchen. "Are you not well? I see you're still in your nightclothes."

He looked up from filling the kettle at the sink. "To tell you the truth, love, I have been a bit poorly. The old chest, you know. It's all this ruddy fog."

He put the kettle on then spooned tea leaves into an old brown teapot. "So what brings you out on a day like this? Not for a jaunt, I'll be bound. Nothing wrong, I hope?"

"Not at all. I was up in town for the day and I'd finished my business so I thought I'd pop down to see you and invite you in person to come and spend Christmas with us."

His old face lit up in a big smile. "Well, that's very kind of you, ducks. Are you sure I wouldn't be in the way?"

"When would you ever be in the way, Granddad? You're my favorite person in the world — apart from Darcy. It would make Christmas very special if you were there to share it. Say you'll come."

He hesitated. "Well, I won't say no. I was thinking to myself it would be a bit quiet this year, seeing as how Hettie died. We always used to have a little celebration together with her family." He looked up again. "But only if you're sure. You ain't having no posh people, are you? You know I don't fit in with your sort."

"I'm only inviting Belinda and maybe Mummy —"

"Not that German bloke. You know I can't stand Germans."

"Granddad, he's really quite nice. Besides, he can hardly speak English so you won't have to say anything to him. And he was only a child in the Great War, so you can't blame him for Uncle Jimmy's death." I kept silent about Max's factories now seeming to make articles of war. "Anyway," I added, "I don't suppose they'll come. Things are very lively in Berlin in the winter."

"Humph." He made a disparaging noise. "All that marching and flag waving. Gives me the willies. No good will come of it, you mark my words."

The kettle shrieked. He poured boiling water into the pot. "Now how about some grub? It's just about dinnertime, isn't it?"

I didn't correct that assumption. To upper-class people dinner is eaten at night. To working class in the middle of the day.

"I am a bit peckish," I confessed, "but only if you have enough?"

"Not have enough for my granddaughter?" He shuffled over to the larder, looked around, then brought out a tin of baked beans. "I don't have nothing fancy, I'm afraid. I haven't been out to the shops lately, but I always find baked beans on top of toasted cheese goes down a treat."

It did. Isn't it strange how the simplest things give the most pleasure? We ate together and then an idea came to me. "If you don't have much food in the house why don't you come down to Eynsleigh with me? It's clearly not doing you good staying on here with the fog. You'll get fresh country air. We can walk around the estate on fine days and Queenie can fatten you up."

"So you didn't get yourself another cook like you were going to?"

I made a despairing face. "Oh golly, Granddad. I should have done, I know. But I've just been to an agency in London and they told me I'd be unlikely to find a good cook over the Christmas season, as they are all already snapped up for house parties."

"Oh well, I expect Queenie will manage," he said, patting my hand. "She's not that bad, is she? Not what you'd call a fancy cook, but . . ."

"Granddad, she is all right with things she knows, like shepherd's pie and meat hot pot, but I don't know how she'd handle something complicated like a Christmas dinner if we have guests. You know how accident prone she is."

Granddad chuckled. "Set fire to the whole ruddy kitchen when she lights the Christmas pud, I expect."

"Don't! That's exactly the sort of thing I'm afraid of. What am I going to do, Granddad?"

"Don't worry, ducks. Something will

come up. That nice housekeeper of yours will know a local woman to come and help. It won't be fancy foreign muck, but good enough for Christmas dinner."

"You're right," I said. I reached out and took his old wrinkled hand. "So you will come with me right now?"

"Now?"

"Yes. Why not? You said yourself that you're running low on food and haven't liked to go out and shop. I'm meeting Darcy at Waterloo at four and we'll drive home from the station."

His eyes met mine. "Struth," he muttered. "Are you sure?"

"Of course I'm sure. If I had my way, I'd want you with us all the time. Can I help you pack some clothes?"

"Oh no, ducks. You make yourself comfortable. Have another cup of tea and there's biscuits in the barrel."

Half an hour later we set off, Granddad insisting on carrying his own suitcase, because, as he pointed out, "I ain't done for yet!" while I carried a string bag with various bits of food he didn't want to throw out, including a new packet of bourbon biscuits, a wedge of Cheddar cheese and half a dozen eggs. I suggested he give them to a neighbor but he insisted on bringing them. It was clear he wanted to contribute his share to our pantry.

I found myself smiling as the train took us back to Sussex. The fog had dissipated here, just clinging in strands to fences and walls. Green fields sparkled in bright sunlight and horses tossed their heads, taking off as the train steamed past. I had my first guest for Christmas. All was right with the world after all.

CHAPTER 3

December 3
Eynsleigh, Sussex

Who said "The best laid plans of mice and
men . . ."? My glorious Christmas party
seems to have run into a hitch or two.

Having put my advert into *The Lady* magazine and snagged my first guest for Christmas I was quite hopeful that all would be
smooth sailing from now on. But no replies
were forthcoming from *The Lady* while letters came back in quick succession from
Belinda and my mother.
Belinda's said:

Darling Georgie,
You are so kind to think of me at Christmas and of course I'd have loved to
spend it with you, but I've already made
plans to go down to Cornwall. Still try-

ing to get my hands on my grand-mother's house, you know, and still deciding if I want to modernize my cottage. Jago is being so helpful. . . .

I'll bet he is, I thought. And going down to Cornwall has nothing to do with the cottage. Anyway, I was glad she might have found a decent chap at last.

And the letter from my mother said:

Darling Georgie,

What a sweet idea. It sounds divine. But you know we can't leave Berlin over Christmas. Max has to do his duty and spend Christmas Eve with his mother (while I stay well away!). And we've been invited to the Goebbels' country lodge the next day. I can't stand the man personally, but Max says he's getting to be quite powerful so we have to keep in with him. Oh, how I do long for a lovely English Christmas! Do pull a cracker and eat a mince pie for me, won't you?

Your loving mother

So it appeared that my house party was still limited to one. I gave in to Darcy's suggestion and invited the Hawse-Gorzleys. Only to receive a letter back from Lady

Hawse-Gorzley by return of post.

> My dear Georgiana. How kind of you to think of us — especially after the frightful Christmas you had here once! Unfortunately we have already made plans. You heard, I'm sure, that Bunty has become engaged to the lord-lieutenant's son Peter. We've been invited there over Christmas so that the two families can become better acquainted. I expect your party will be most jolly if orchestrated by the wicked Darcy! Do give him our love.

"Oh golly," I said, handing the letter to Darcy. "It looks as if my brilliant Christmas plans will be down to my grandfather and us."

"Never mind," he said. "We'll have a buffet supper for the neighbors, a bit of carol singing. You can volunteer to help with the Christmas pageant at the church." He looked at my face and had to laugh. "You have got me, you know," he said in a soft voice. "Our first Christmas together."

I let his arms come around me. "I know," I whispered. "I'm a lucky girl. But I can't exactly play sardines with you and Granddad, can I?"

"Think what might happen if I found you in the linen cupboard." He squeezed me tighter.

"Stop it!" I was laughing. "Your aunt said you were wicked and you are."

"A leopard can't change his spots, you know."

"Speaking of leopards, at least we aren't among those awful English settlers in Kenya," I said, remembering several embarrassing or even dangerous incidents during our honeymoon. "We're perfectly safe at home in England. A lovely peaceful Christmas together."

I later regretted saying those words. There is also another saying, "Be careful what you wish for." Because on December the eighth a letter arrived.

"From your brother," Darcy said, bringing in the morning post and handing me an envelope embossed with the family crest.

"That's nice of him to write to wish us a happy Christmas," I said as I opened it. The handwriting was not my brother's.

"Oh crikey," I exclaimed. "It's from Fig. What does she want?" My eyes scanned the page, then I muttered, "Oh no!" and gave Darcy a horrified glance.

"What is it?" he asked. "Bad news?"

"The worst," I said.

"Something's happened to your brother?"

"Much worse than that."

I began to read:

My dear Georgiana,

We send you our very best wishes for the festive season. As you know we always spend Christmas at the castle — family tradition. However, this year something unforeseen has happened. The boiler decided to burst, right when the weather turned frigid. The repair company says they can't supply a new one until the new year, so we've no alternative than to shut up Castle Rannoch and come down to London.

"What wrong with that?" Darcy asked as I had paused.

"It goes on." I took a deep breath before continuing.

Knowing that you have that lovely big house to yourselves — which we still have not seen, by the way — I suggested to Binky that it might be much more jolly if we came down to you for a proper family Christmas. I take it you will be home and not flying off to some exotic destination? If it's convenient I thought we'd arrive about the twenty-first and stay until after New Year's Eve. I expect you have enough servants, but if not, we will be bringing Hamilton and Mrs. McPherson with us, as they have no family to go to and we could hardly leave them in a cold castle. If we bring them to you, we won't have to pay to heat Rannoch House when we are not in residence!

Do let us know what sort of hampers and things we can order from London to add to the festivities. Binky and Podge are SO looking forward to seeing you again. Binky said it will be just like old times.

Your affectionate sister-in-law,
Hilda, Duchess of Rannoch

There was a long silence.

Then Darcy started to laugh. "You said you wanted a house party." He chuckled. "And now you have one."

"But Fig — ten days of Fig!"

"It has solved your cook problem for the moment," Darcy pointed out. "You've always said that Mrs. McPherson was a marvelous cook."

"She is," I agreed. "And she's patient enough to teach Queenie a thing or two.

But ten days of Fig!"

Darcy put an arm around my shoulder. "While I agree that she is the most depressing person who has ever existed, think of your little nephew and niece. Won't it be good to have children in the house over Christmas?"

Immediately I pictured Podge and Addy's little excited faces on Christmas morning and nodded. "Yes. You're right," I agreed. "It will be, as Fig says, a lovely family Christmas."

We set about making preparations. Mrs. Holbrook had a bedroom prepared for Binky and Fig, opened up the old nursery and had beds made up for Nanny and the rest of the servants they would be bringing with them.

"Will there be a maid and a valet, my lady?" she asked.

"Oh, I'm sure there will," I said. "Fig never goes anywhere without her maid."

"I thought I might put the butler in a proper bedroom in the west wing, over near your grandfather," she said, looking at my face to see if this was the right thing. "I'm thinking he's an old man and our servants' rooms on that top floor are not the most congenial."

"Quite right, Mrs. Holbrook." I gave her

an approving smile. "He must be at least seventy but he won't retire. He has no family and he's been at Castle Rannoch his whole life. And it will give my grandfather someone to talk to. He feels out of place here."

"I know he does, bless him. (She had become rather fond of my grandfather.) But if I know butlers, your Hamilton will think it's above his station to get on familiar terms with any of your guests, however humble."

I had to laugh. "I know. You're right. Isn't this whole class thing silly, when you think about it?"

"Silly, my lady?" She looked suspicious now. "It's how things are always done. If you had servants thinking they were as good as their masters, what kind of world would we be living in then? Chaos. That's what it would be. Look at Russia. They threw out their aristocrats. Made everyone equal, so they said. And then that Stalin behaves worse than any aristocrat ever did."

I nodded. "That's true. Anyway, we'll leave the old men to get along, shall we?"

Food was ordered. A Father Christmas outfit was found in the attic for Darcy (a trifle moth-eaten, but who looks closely at Father Christmas?) and I had a fun day

50

selecting and wrapping little presents for the local children. Zou Zou came down one day, laden with the promised Fortnum's hamper, a crate of champagne, boxes of crackers and a sprig of mistletoe "because you never know. . . ."

"You know," I said to Darcy as I snuggled against him under the covers on a freezing cold night, "I'm beginning to look forward to this after all. We are going to have a splendid Christmas in our own home."

Chapter 4

December 12
Eynsleigh, Sussex

Another example of "best laid plans . . ."
This morning's post brought another letter. Oh crikey. What are we going to do
now?

"Some Christmas cards have arrived."
Darcy came into the dining room with the
morning post as I was tucking into kidneys
and bacon. I had been for a walk around
the grounds with Granddad and the cold
weather had certainly given me an appetite.
I could feel my cheeks still stinging. I looked
up from my food. "Oh lovely. Who from?"

He glanced at the postmark of the top
envelope. "Norfolk," he said. "Who do we
know in Norfolk?"

"Apart from the king and queen at this

time of year? Does it have a royal crest on it?"

"No, it doesn't." He opened it. It was not a card but a long letter. He turned it over, frowned and looked up at me with an astonished expression. "Good God. It's from my aunt Ermintrude," he said. "When did she ever write to me?"

"Wasn't she the one who sent us that awful painting for a wedding present?"

"The very same. She's an eccentric. Thinks of herself as quite an artist. She probably wants to hear that we've given her painting pride of place."

"But she doesn't live in Norfolk, surely. She lives in Yorkshire, you said."

"She did, last time I communicated with her."

"So what's she doing in Norfolk?"

His eyes were scanning the letter, the frown on his forehead getting deeper by the second. "It seems she's moved there," he said. "She was finding North Yorkshire too bleak and remote as she moves into old age. So when Queen Mary mentioned that Wymondham Hall had become vacant and suggested she might move there —"

"Wait," I interrupted. "Queen Mary invited her to move there? What does she have to do with your aunt?"

He held up a finger. "Ah, she goes on to mention that. 'You may not know that I was a lady-in-waiting to the queen when I was a young woman and when my husband was serving in the army. We two struck up a friendship that has lasted a lifetime and the queen has said it would warm her heart to have me living nearby again.' "

"Gosh." I was almost speechless for a moment. "Your relatives never cease to surprise me. Is she your father's sister or your mother's?"

"She's my mother's sister. Oldest sister, I believe."

"I see. And I didn't know she had been married. I always thought of her as an eccentric spinster when you described her."

Darcy shrugged. "Frankly I don't know that much about her. She married some chap who had a family seat in a remote part of Yorkshire and she's spent most of her life up there. We visited once when I was a young kid. Very bleak, like Wuthering Heights, I seem to remember. He died years ago. Maybe in the Spanish flu epidemic? Or was it some sort of accident? I'm not sure."

"So why is she writing to us now? Is she upset because we sent the thank-you letter for the wedding present to Yorkshire and it missed her?"

"Worse than that," he said, echoing what I had said about Fig's letter.

"How worse?" I asked cautiously.

"Listen to this."

Dear Nephew,

You may have heard that I have relinquished the house in Yorkshire (much too big for one person to rattle around in) and accepted the queen's kind suggestion that I take up residence at Wymondham Hall at the edge of the Sandringham estate.

"Then the bit about being a lady-in-waiting. Then she goes on."

It seemed to me that this Christmas should be a time for a celebration, after years of lonely isolation in Yorkshire. As you know, your late uncle and I had no children, so there was never much gaiety on the estate. This year I had a sudden urge to be surrounded by young people and laughter again. And since I have yet to meet your young bride (having not been invited to your wedding) I should like very much if you would care to join the little house party I am arranging. I know it is late for such an invitation and you have probably have plans for an Xmas celebration of your own. However, I hope I can persuade you to bring your guests to Norfolk and join me. My house is not a mansion but is comfortable enough. I can offer you six bedrooms, a nursery and ample rooms for servants.

"Not exactly tiny then," I commented.
"The Yorkshire one was vast. Whole wings of bedrooms," Darcy said, then went on reading.

When I mentioned my little plan to Her Majesty, she perked up immediately, saying how happy she would be if her dear Georgiana was close enough for a visit during the Christmas celebration. It won't be much of a festive time for them this year. The king's health is rapidly declining and I fear it will only be a matter of time. The queen speaks most fondly of your bride, Darcy. I think it would be a comfort to her to have her close at hand during what will be a difficult time for them.

This time I swallowed back the word "golly." I knew the queen had asked me to do small favors for her and always seemed pleased to see me but to speak of me in such terms was quite unnerving. I looked up at Darcy. "What do you think?"

"It rather sounds as if it is a royal summons, put through the mouth of an intermediary," he said.

"Do you think so? The queen would really like me there but doesn't want to invite me herself because that would be too formal?"

"That's what it sounds like to me."

"So we should go?"

"I think we probably should go," he said, weighing the words. "And it is an answer to your prayers, isn't it? Binky and Fig as a small part of a bigger house party, as opposed to Binky and Fig and just us."

"Now that you put it that way, you're right," I said. "But what about all the stuff we've ordered? We've a turkey coming from the butcher in the village. Queenie's made Christmas puddings, albeit with a button in one of them. . . ."

Darcy had been reading on down the page. He looked up again. "It seems that is mentioned too. She says, 'I now have a smaller complement of servants than I did at the house in Yorkshire. I'm reduced to a butler, footman, head housemaid, cook, personal maid, and gardener. Two women from the nearby village come in to do the heavy work and I can probably acquire more for a house party but it would help if you bring an undercook, your personal maids and valets, as well as perhaps some food to add to the feast, since my cook is no longer used to catering to large numbers." He grinned. "We can take that enormous turkey you've ordered plus Queenie's Christmas puddings — including one with a button in it."

"But an undercook?" I frowned. "We couldn't bring Mrs. McPherson to be an undercook. That would be an insult. She's been in charge of her own kitchen since I was born."

"You're right. I suggest she stays here with Hamilton since your sister-in-law is too cheap to keep the London house open. They'll have a good time with Mrs. Holbrook and our servants."

"Yes," I said, then my smile faded. "But that means I'll have to take Queenie to be the assistant cook, doesn't it? Oh gosh, Darcy. I hope that will be all right. I mean, she is quite a good cook, but things do seem to happen to her, don't they?"

"I'll speak to her, if you like. I'll warn her strongly to be on her best behavior," he said. "But knowing Queenie, she loves to eat, doesn't she? She'll be in heaven preparing food for a big party."

"I hope so," I said. "Just as long as she doesn't eat it all herself, and the queen doesn't come to visit. We can't risk a disaster with royals in the vicinity." The kidneys had now congealed on my plate into an unappetizing brown mess. I pushed my plate away. "Well, I suppose we had better write and accept her kind invitation. I hope Binky and Fig are happy about it. Knowing Fig and her snobbishness, she'll be delighted to be within the reach of the royal family." I stopped, my mouth open, as I'd just realized. "My grandfather, Darcy. What do we do about him? He won't feel comfortable at a party near Sandringham, will he? But it would be rude to leave him behind."

"Why don't you ask him?" Darcy said. "Give him the choice. You know he gets along well with Mrs. Holbrook. He may enjoy spending Christmas with her and your Scottish servants."

"Yes, he may prefer that, but I don't want him to think we are just tossing him aside. And I'll miss having him near us for Christmas." I got up, leaving the dining table and walking over to the fireplace where a large log was glowing. "Whatever next, Darcy? I should never have wished for a party in the first place, should I?"

CHAPTER 5

December 22

Off to Norfolk to stay with a strange aunt.
Not the Christmas I had planned. I hope
it's all right.

Darcy was quite right. My grandfather's
face fell when I told him about Aunt Ermintrude's invitation. He shook his head.
"Oh no, ducks. That sort of thing ain't for
me. Not hobnobbing with the gentry. I
wouldn't know where to put meself, and
you wouldn't know where to put me either."
He covered my hand with his own. "But
don't you bother about me, ducks. I'll just
head on home. I'm used to my own company. I'll be fine."

I put my hand on his arm. "No, Granddad. Please don't go. Why don't you stay on
here? You get along well with Mrs. Holbrook
and you'll be company for her. Also my

brother's butler and cook are coming, so you'll eat well. Mrs. McPherson is a splendid cook. You'll be spoiled!"

"Well." He gave me a hopeful little smile that melted my heart. "That doesn't sound too bad, does it? As long as that butler doesn't treat me like the dog's dinner."

"I will personally have a word with Hamilton and I'm sure the two of you will get along well. He's your age, you know. You can moan together about the state of the world."

I had also been right about Fig's reaction. I had telephoned her a few days before they were due to come down to us.

"A change of plans?" she asked sharply. "What do you mean? You're brushing us off? At the last minute?"

I explained the letter from Darcy's aunt and then added, "We could hardly refuse because it did sound like a roundabout invitation from the queen."

"I see." There was a long pause. "Well, if your presence would bring comfort to the queen at a difficult time, then of course we must go." Another long pause. "I must say it will be a novelty spending Christmas at Sandringham. Or as good as at Sandringham . . ."

I could actually hear the wheels turning in her head and imagined her saying to her friends, "Well, of course, we spent Christmas at Sandringham. The queen does so rely on Georgiana. . . ."

Queenie was equally delighted. "Yeah, I don't mind coming along and helping out," she said. "Just as long as that cook don't try to boss me around." I realized she was never going to turn into a deferential servant however hard I tried.

"You must try to call me 'my lady' if the occasion arises and also be exceedingly polite to Darcy's old aunt. She is also to be addressed as 'my lady,' do you understand?"

"Bob's yer uncle, miss," she said, then giggled and put her hand to her mouth. "There I go again, don't I? My old dad used to say I must be twins because one couldn't be so daft."

I stifled the sigh that rose in my throat. Was I really out of my mind to consider taking her to Lady Aysgarth? I could recall so many disasters, and every time I thought Queenie had improved, something happened to prove me wrong. And yet she really was a good cook and it was out of the question to bring Mrs. McPherson. I'd just have to do a lot of praying.

As it happened it was lucky that we had

decided to take Queenie. When I told my new lady's maid that we would be going away for Christmas and she should make sure all my evening wear was cleaned and pressed, she looked up at me with horror. "Going away, your ladyship? But you wouldn't be taking me with you, would you?"

"Of course. I'll need my maid to dress me and take care of my clothing."

This produced an open mouth and then floods of tears. "Oh, no, my lady. I can't go away for Christmas. I simply can't. It's my old mum, you see. She's been poorly and I'm her only child still living and if she didn't have a chance to see me over Christmas, well, it would break her heart."

"But, Maisie, I explained to you when you took the position that a maid usually travels with her mistress."

"I know, but my mum wasn't quite so bad then. Don't make me go, your ladyship. I beg you." She looked up at me with tears welling in her eyes. "Please, your ladyship, I know you could sack me for this, and I understand if you have to, but my mum comes first. If she passed away over Christmas and I wasn't there to say goodbye, well, I'd never forgive myself."

Even Scrooge could not have resisted a

statement like that. My expression softened. "Very well, Maisie. You've been a hard worker and a quick learner and I'd hate to lose you now. I expect I can manage without you this time, but in future if we travel, you will be expected to come with me."

She actually took my hand and I thought for a horrid moment that she was going to kiss it, but luckily she thought better of it.

"You won't regret it, my lady, I promise you. I'll make sure everything is in perfect order before you go and I'll work twice as hard when you come back."

"I suppose I can do without a maid," I said to Darcy when I told him about this. "After all, you can do up the buttons I can't reach, can't you?"

He frowned. "But I can't press and clean and polish, can I? What if we go out walking and you get mud on your shoes? Or spill something at dinner? I think Aunt Ermintrude will expect you to bring a maid with you. Can you find another girl from the village?"

"Not train her in time," I said. "Think of the awful disasters with Queenie when she tried to clean my velvet evening dress." I stopped, thinking. "We are taking Queenie with us and she does have some idea about a maid's duties. I suppose I could enlist her if necessary when she's not needed in the kitchen."

"Highly irregular," Darcy said.

"Well, you come up with a better idea," I snapped, instantly regretting it. "I'm sorry, Darcy. This whole escapade has made me very nervous. I'm going to a strange house, taking my socially awkward sister-in-law and my questionable cook and I'll probably have to go and visit the king and queen. Now I really wish that we'd decided on Christmas by ourselves at home."

Darcy put his arms around me. "Chin up, old thing. It will all be fine. We'll have a splendid time, you'll see."

I gazed up at him. "Promise me one thing," I said. "Don't you dare go running off at the last minute, leaving me to face your aunt Ermintrude alone."

"I promise," he said and kissed me.

I realized I had been letting this whole business upset me. Having only been responsible for myself for most of my life I was now supposed to be in charge of a host of people, and I was feeling rather overwhelmed by it. Why couldn't Darcy and I have taken a little flat in London and lived happily but simply? I thought. Then I remembered; we had looked at lots of flats in London and the only ones we could afford had been absolutely awful.

Binky and Fig arrived at Eynsleigh. Since we were due to leave on the twenty-third I relented and invited them down earlier so that they could at least have time to enjoy Eynsleigh first. They came on the eighteenth and were suitably impressed. Fig made lots of comments about lucky Georgiana having fallen on her feet this time and how nice it was to have a house with enough heat. Binky was impressed with the grounds and the kitchen garden. The children loved the big rocking horse in the nursery and Podge found Sir Hubert's old train set. So all that went without a hitch. Except maybe my grandfather. When Fig came into the long gallery to find him sitting by the fire, having tea, she gave a little twitter of surprise. "Oh, Georgiana, I didn't realize you had company. One of the local farmers?"

"My grandfather, Fig. You met him before. He stayed at Castle Rannoch once, remember?"

Fig now peered at him as if he was an interesting specimen in the natural history museum. "Oh yes. Your grandfather. Of course." She held out a stiff hand in regal manner. "How do you do? So nice to meet you again."

"Pleasure's all mine, ducks," said my grandfather, giving her hand a generous pumping.

When he got me alone later he said, "I think I should go home after all, love. That woman gives me the willies. Did you see how she looked at me? As if I was something the dog brought in."

I put my hands on his shoulders. "Granddad, you are my guest. I want to have you here. I'd rather have you than Fig, so don't let her get to you. She tries it with me too. Come to think of it, she finds fault with everyone. It's her major hobby. Besides, in a few days we'll be gone and you'll have a lovely Christmas with the best food ever, I promise you."

"Well," he said, "I suppose I can give it a try."

I let Queenie know that Mrs. McPherson would need to be shown around the kitchen and then gradually take over the cooking. That gentle old lady was tactful enough to make it seem as if Queenie was the teacher and she the pupil and they got along beautifully.

"That old woman's just shown me how to make éclairs," Queenie said when I complimented her on her tea. "And you'll never guess what we're having for dinner tonight.

Cocky vain. Something the Frogs do with chicken and wine, apparently."

Now all that remained was to have everything packed and ready to go. I popped into Haywards Heath and splurged a little on chocolate liqueurs in case we had to exchange gifts with other guests. I wondered what to give Darcy's aunt and was tempted to buy her a rather nice painting of a stag I saw in an antiques shop window. Instead I decided to give her a carved African giraffe we had brought back from Kenya. We had seen them at a stall in the market in Nakuru and had bought a lot of them, since they only cost pennies. I decided Podge and Addy might like the smallest ones to make a zoo or Noah's ark. I realized I'd have to give Binky and Fig a gift too and asked Darcy what he suggested.

"Get Binky a bottle of Scotch," he said. "You can't go wrong with that."

"Expensive," I replied. "But you're right. It will be appreciated and I think he gets very few creature comforts. But what about Fig?"

Darcy grinned.

"It's all right. I won't get her what I'm thinking. Slippers or a scarf. It's always cold at Castle Rannoch."

So that just left Darcy. It was so hard to

buy him presents with my limited funds. That's when I remembered my idea of the puppy. Perfect!

By December the twenty-second all was arranged. Darcy and I would drive the Bentley, laden with our various hampers of food plus all the luggage. Binky, Fig, children and nanny would be driven in a hired car and would return to London later by train. The servants would go by train and be met by a local hired car. I was amazed how smoothly everything was falling into place.

On the twenty-first we all went out into the estate and cut down a small spruce tree, then I let the children help decorate it while the footmen helped Darcy and Binky hang holly and ivy over windows and mantelpieces. Then Darcy put on the Father Christmas suit and we held a little party in the village hall. The food, luckily, was prepared by the Churchwomen's Guild so all we had to do was have Darcy appear at the right moment and be suitably jolly as he handed out presents. I was rather amazed and humbled at how delighted the village children were to get such small gifts. We took far too much for granted.

That evening we hosted the dreaded mince pies and hot toddy party for the upper-class neighbors. It went surprisingly well. Nobody found a button in a mince pie. Everyone was delightedly jolly and brought us gifts from homemade wine to a couple of pheasants. I began to feel the tension slip away. We had managed two events with no mishaps. I was going to a place where someone else was in charge of the holiday celebrations.

On the twenty-second we packed and supervised as the servants loaded up the motorcar in preparation for the next morning. When we sat down to dinner that night I was finally feeling excited. A big Christmas house party — exactly what I had wanted, except that it wasn't in my own house.

Queenie, with guidance from Mrs. McPherson, produced wonderful pheasant.

"Really, Georgiana, you have the most marvelous cook these days," Fig said. "I suppose she came with the house? Lucky old you. Of course pheasant is something we have with monotonous regularity at home. The estate is teeming with them and Binky seems to find the time to go out shooting all winter. Surprisingly enough he manages to hit one occasionally."

"But this pheasant is jolly tasty, Fig," Binky said, giving me an encouraging smile. "Delicious wine gravy. We don't normally have wine in our gravy, do we?"

"Good gracious no. Not with the price of French wines these days. We only dare to treat ourselves on special occasions. But then I suppose you can help yourselves to Sir Hubert's wine cellar, Georgiana."

"Absolutely," I said, giving her a sweet smile.

The main course was just being cleared away when Hamilton, who had taken over the role of butler for the time being since we didn't have one of our own, appeared in the dining room in that miraculously silent way butlers have. "I'm sorry to trouble you, my lady," he said, "but you have an unexpected visitor. I have shown her into the drawing room."

"A visitor?" I said. "At this time of night? Who on earth is it?"

"Shown me into the drawing room. I ask you. Bloody cheek." A small blond person, draped in a long dark mink, swept past him into the room. "I hope there's some food left because I'm absolutely starving. I've been traveling since dawn."

"Mummy!" I exclaimed. "What are you doing here?"

CHAPTER 6

December 22
Eynsleigh, Sussex

This Christmas is turning into one surprise
after another! What could possibly happen next?

I had risen to my feet, my napkin falling to
the floor. Darcy and Binky, like all well-
trained males, had also stood up. My mother
looked from one surprised face to the next.
"Well, I must say, that's a warm welcome.
How about 'How lovely to see you!' "

"But you just wrote to say you couldn't
join us," I said. I pushed back my chair and
went over to hug her. "Of course we're glad
to see you, but what a surprise. Where is
Max?"

"Lying dead at the bottom of the River
Spree as far as I'm concerned," she said,

those fabulous blue eyes absolutely spitting venom.

"Oh dear, what happened?"

"His mother. That's what happened. I told you he always spends Christmas Eve with her, didn't I? That much I was prepared to go along with. Well, now she insisted she wanted him there on Christmas Day too. All alone and grieving her poor, departed husband and the only thing she has in the world is her adored son. So Max had the nerve to suggest I go to stay with the Goebbels and he'd join me later."

She did a dramatic sweep of the room as only an accomplished actress can. "Can you imagine it! Me, spending Christmas with a bunch of Nazis? I said absolutely not and if he chose his mother over me, I'd go where I was wanted and appreciated."

"Quite right," Binky said. He had always been very fond of my mother, who became his stepmother when he was a small boy.

"Well, I'm glad you came. It's lovely to have you here," I said. I looked up at Hamilton, who was still hovering in the doorway. "Could you please have one of the maids set another place at table? And I suspect the pheasant may need to be heated up again. Perhaps a bowl of the leek and potato soup first for Her Grace?" (I know she was no longer officially Duchess of Rannoch, but Hamilton had been her butler and knew her as such. I don't think he had ever been too fond of her, since she came from a humble background and could be rather bossy.)

"Certainly, my lady. May I take Your Grace's coat?"

My mother let it slide from her shoulders in an elegant gesture. "Thank you, Hamilton," she said, bestowing her dazzling smile on him. "How lovely to see you here. I hadn't known that Binky and Fig were to join us."

Hamilton gave a noncommittal nod as he took her mink, bowed and left the room. Mummy looked around, deciding which was the best place at the table. "Oh hello, Daddy. What a lovely surprise to find you here too," she said, going over to kiss the top of his bald head. "So the gang is all assembled." She pulled out a chair next to Darcy, graced Fig with a smile and sat. Darcy motioned to the footman standing behind the table and a glass of wine was poured for her. She took a generous gulp. "What a journey," she said, putting the glass down again. "I thought I'd take an aeroplane because it was quicker. Well, my darlings, don't ever take an aeroplane in the winter. Utter torture. It was supposed to take off at ten. Then it was delayed for high winds. Then finally we took off and bounced around and everyone was sick. Then it had to put down in Amsterdam with engine trouble and we sat in a freezing waiting room until the motor was fixed and we bounced all the way across the Channel and everyone was sick again. Luckily I was in the front seat. I would have personally strangled anyone who dared to throw up on my new mink."

"It is a lovely coat," Fig said enviously.

"Max bought it for me as an early Christmas present," she said. "I've a good mind to return it to him. Or perhaps not. I intend to make him pay in more ways than one."

We looked up as our parlormaid came hurrying in and set a place for my mother, followed by Queenie who bore a bowl of hot soup. I held my breath until the soup was deposited on the table without Queenie tipping it into my mother's lap.

"Get that down you and you'll feel better," Queenie said cheerfully, making Fig raise her eyebrows in horror.

Queenie then whisked the platter of pheasant and potatoes out of the room to reheat.

Mummy took a mouthful and nodded. "Good soup," she said. "Don't tell me that girl has finally improved?"

"We have Mrs. McPherson with us," I said. "It was probably her recipe."

"Mrs. McPherson." Mummy sighed. "How often I have dreamed of her cooking. You must never let her retire, Binky."

"She is rather good, isn't she?" Binky beamed as if she had complimented him.

"Queenie's not bad, but I'm afraid her experience is limited to the foods she knows. However, she is already learning from an expert. Too bad they can't be together for a longer time."

"Why is that?" Mummy asked between mouthfuls.

"You're lucky to find us at home," I said. "We're leaving tomorrow."

"Leaving?"

"That's right," I said. "We received an invitation from Darcy's aunt to go to her house in Norfolk. So we're all off in the morning."

"Why on earth do you want to go to Darcy's aunt? I thought you were looking forward to Christmas here at Eynsleigh."

"I was," I admitted. "But Darcy's aunt is a close chum of the queen, so it seems. And you know they are at Sandringham right now, and the aunt's house is at the edge of the estate. The letter rather read like an indirect summons from the queen, so it was hard to say no."

"Oh God. Not a royal Christmas!" Mummy gave a dramatic sigh. "You know how utterly tedious the king can be. Every year identical to the one before. He'll give his speech on the radio and we'll all have to sit around and listen. And no drinks before six and no good wine . . ."

"Oh, I don't think we are expected to be part of the royal festivities," Darcy said hastily. "My aunt is having her own house party. It was just that my aunt mentioned how much the queen would like to see Georgie again. And knowing that the king is unwell, we decided it would be churlish to refuse."

"Is it a big house? Lots of people invited?" Mummy perked up.

"We've no idea," Darcy said. "I didn't even know she had left Yorkshire."

"Yorkshire?" Mummy's expression immediately changed. "Not that aunt? The Earl of Aysgarth's widow? Irmgard, wasn't it?"

"Ermintrude," Darcy said.

"But, my darlings, she's quite batty, isn't she? And he was a little too friendly, if I remember correctly. I remember the wandering hands and being pinned against a wall in a dark corridor. She didn't even appear to notice — up in her tower painting all the time. We stayed with them once at that dreadful bleak house on the moors."

"I'll agree she is . . . eccentric," Darcy said cautiously. "But I'm afraid it's all arranged now. We leave in the morning and you're most welcome to come with us. We can squeeze you into the Bentley. I don't suppose one extra will make any difference to a big party. She did offer us six bedrooms, after all."

"How frightfully jolly," Mummy said. I noted she always reverted to public school language when Binky and Fig were around. "Much better than those awful Nazi types, clinking beer steins and singing patriotic songs."

She lapsed into silence as she devoured an amazing amount of food and wine for such a small person. As I watched her I found myself wondering, not for the first time, how such a woman could have been my mother — so petite, so lovely, so completely self-centered, and with an incredible effect on the male sex. I noticed that even Binky and Darcy were jolly attentive all evening. I hoped her presence wouldn't cause problems with Aunt Ermintrude.

But later that evening, when I was showing Mummy her room and the bathroom nearby she slipped her arms around my neck. "To tell you the truth, darling, I wanted to be here with you all along. The way things are going in Germany I just don't feel that I belong. I only stay because Max is so adoring and devoted."

"And so rich," I reminded her.

"That too," she agreed. "But if he's not going to be so devoted anymore — well, one must scope out other options. You haven't heard from Hubert recently, have you? He's not likely to be home?"

Ah, so that was it. Not the desire to be with her only child. She was scoping out her other options. Typical Mummy.

"You didn't bring your maid?" I asked.

"I decided not to," she said. "She hates travel and of course she'd have had to come by train, which would have taken forever. I expect I can borrow yours, can't I?"

"If you want to take the risk," I said.

She looked puzzled. "I thought you had a sweet new little maid. A local girl."

"I do," I said, "but she has refused to come with me over Christmas, claiming her mother is at death's door. So I'm afraid it's going to have to be Queenie for both of us."

Mummy looked aghast. "Queenie's going to be your maid? Darling, I can put up with a lot of things, but I'm not letting Queenie within a mile of my lovely clothes. Hasn't she ruined everything of yours she has touched?"

"Almost everything," I agreed.

"And didn't she forget to pack one of your wedding shoes so you had to jam your feet into a pair of mine?"

"She did."

"Then I think I'll just have to go maid-less," she said. "I am already getting visions of her trying to iron my mink."

"Fig has brought her maid with her. I expect you can borrow her if needed," I said.

"I never thought I'd be grateful to Fig." She gave me a little squeeze. "But I am so glad to be with my only child for Christmas. And I'm waiting for grandchildren, you know."

"Me too," I said.

"Any signs yet?"

"Not yet."

"Ah, but it's the trying that's the fun part, isn't it?" She gave me a wicked wink and went into her room.

CHAPTER 7

December 23
En route

Off to Norfolk and strange Aunt Ermintrude, together with my brother, Fig, the
children, Queenie and now my mother.
What next? I don't think I'd raise an
eyebrow if King Kong showed up on the
doorstep and asked to come with us.

We set off at first light. The hired car had
arrived early and had driven the servants to
the station first before loading up with
Binky and family. I suggested that Mummy
might like to ride with them, as they should
have more room in their car. She rolled her
eyes. "God forbid, Georgie. 'Tis the season
to be jolly. Fa-la-la-la-la and all that. Anything less jolly than five or six hours with
Fig I cannot imagine. It's a wonder her
mother didn't take one look and drown her

81

at birth."

I tried not to chuckle. "Her mother is even more awful," I whispered. "Lady Wormwood. Haven't you met her?"

"Never. One of the reasons I escaped from your father was that we had to keep meeting people like that. But Binky kindly agreed to take my little suitcase in his car so I'm sure there's a teeny corner of yours where I can fit in."

Her little suitcase turned out to be two very large ones, a hatbox, and a train case. We agreed to take half her luggage and try to fit the smaller items into Binky's car. I saw Fig go to say something as Binky nobly attempted to pile them around the children and nanny in the backseat. Mummy, of course, was oblivious to the fact that a six-year-old had to ride all the way to Norfolk jammed between a hatbox and a train case. She was busy rearranging everything on our backseat so that she had plenty of room.

"Careful, Mummy. That's the champagne," I warned. This made her move more cautiously. She was fond of champagne.

"A crate of champagne? Where did that come from?"

"Princess Zamanska. Zou Zou, you know. She couldn't join us but she brought us a jolly nice hamper and the champagne. I'm leaving most of the hamper for the staff at Eynsleigh but I thought the champagne would be a nice contribution to the festivities. And a giant turkey too."

Granddad came out to say goodbye. I hugged him. "I'm sorry we won't be with you on Christmas Day," I said. "I've left your present under the tree." (I'd bought him a cashmere scarf.)

I felt guilty as I watched him waving to us as the car pulled away. But then I had to admit that he couldn't have come with us. We wouldn't have known where to put him and he'd have hated every minute of it. At least now he was going to have a good time with Mrs. Holbrook. And hopefully he'd enjoy playing draughts with Hamilton, now I'd had a little chat with my former butler. Once again I found myself thinking how stupid the English class system is.

We set off with Darcy driving. We had decided to leave the chauffeur behind so that he could enjoy Christmas with his own family nearby. The countryside was swathed in mist. Trees loomed like ghostly shapes in fields. Cows and sheep looked sorry for themselves. I tucked the rug more firmly around my legs.

"Thank God I brought the mink," Mummy said. "Can't you turn up the heat in this vehicle, Darcy?"

"It takes a while to warm up," he said. "But Mrs. McPherson has given us a thermos with broth in it."

"Isn't she a treasure," Mummy said. "You know, she was almost worth staying with Bertie at Castle Rannoch for." She paused. "Almost."

Darcy gave me a fleeting glance and I tried not to smile.

"I hope the aunt has a good cook," Mummy said, "I'm trying to remember what the food was like at Aysgarth. Quite good, I think. The one redeeming feature of that stay. I wonder if she has brought all her old staff with her. I must say I don't blame her for fleeing from that ghastly place. Perhaps she's become more normal now."

"I think that's highly unlikely," Darcy said, "judging by the painting she gave us as a wedding present."

Mummy chuckled, then let out a little gasp. "Oh God, I wonder if I have brought warm enough clothes. I remember that castle was absolutely freezing, wasn't it, Darcy? It made Castle Rannoch feel like the Riviera. And gloomy? And if this place is anything like it, we'll need to leave a trail of bread crumbs to find our way back to our rooms. The most convoluted and confusing place I ever saw."

I wished she would shut up. I had been a little nervous about going to start with and now Mummy was painting a house of horrors with a crazy aunt. We picked up the main road and headed toward London, passing through pleasant leafy suburbs with new semidetached houses until we came to Kingston-upon-Thames, then through Clapham and we were in the city sprawl. The mist from the countryside was now the smoke of the city. Darcy had to crawl along, peering through the windshield to see where he was going. We crossed the Thames by Westminster Bridge, then Darcy avoided the worst of the crowded streets of the West End by driving up to Paddington, along Marylebone, to the less salubrious areas of Camden Town, Tottenham, Edmonton and finally out again into the leafy suburbs of Essex.

"I'm glad that part is over," Darcy said, giving a sigh of relief. "I could hardly see a thing. How do people live like that? I wonder. It must do awful things to their lungs."

"Look at Granddad," I said. "His lungs are bad from living all his life in the East End. If you hadn't bought him that house in Essex, Mummy, he would be dead by now."

"One does what one can," Mummy said graciously. "And I thought you navigated beautifully, Darcy. I should have been hopelessly lost in five minutes." She glanced at her watch. "Should we not be stopping for a bite to eat soon? It is almost lunchtime."

"I think we should press on," Darcy said, "in case the mist gets worse as the day progresses."

"Mrs. McPherson has packed a picnic for us," I said. "Do you want me to hand you things while you drive, Darcy?"

"That's probably a good idea," he said.

We found the picnic basket and I poured everyone a cup of broth. It was most welcome but it was really too cold to enjoy ham sandwiches or sausage rolls.

"Let's hope we're not too late for luncheon when we get there," Mummy said. For a tiny slim person she had an enormous appetite. "You would expect they might have saved us a morsel or two."

A morsel for my mother was probably a five-course meal. I was actually feeling a little carsick and was glad to have found the digestive biscuits. Mummy promptly fell asleep as we passed through rolling countryside, with one pretty village of thatched cottages following another. The landscape became flatter and more open. And bleaker.

Hints of snow now lay in the fields and among the trees. Then the sun emerged and suddenly everything looked nicer. I found some chocolate biscuits and perked up. I was going to have a jolly time and was not responsible for organizing anything!

We drove through the market town of King's Lynn, where everyone was out in force, stocking up on supplies for Christmas, staggering home under the weight of a goose or a small spruce tree. Groups of carol singers were standing on corners. "Good King Wenceslas looked out" floated toward us. It was all very festive and I felt a surge of excitement that one always experienced as a child, wondering what Father Christmas would bring.

"You have the map, Georgie. You're in charge of getting us there from now on," Darcy said. "I have no idea about this part of the world."

I swallowed hard but didn't say "golly." "So we're heading to Hunstanton?" I asked, peering as we passed a signpost.

"That's right. But we come off quite soon. Find Sandringham and see where we turn."

I stared at the map, tracing the line with my finger, hoping I was not leading us astray.

"Damn," Darcy muttered. "Just as I

thought. Blasted mist is coming down again."

And the landscape around us became indistinct, making sign-posts hard to read. We had one close call when we came around a bend to find a tractor going very slowly ahead of us, but otherwise there was nothing on the narrow lanes. There were now trees all around us, sending out a canopy of bare branches and dripping moisture onto the roof of the car.

"We turn right here," I said, seeing the sign to Sandringham when we came to a crossroads.

"No left," Darcy corrected.

"Look, it says Sandringham right."

Darcy studied the signpost harder. "And left." He laughed. "Both ways. Still, I suppose that means we can't miss it if we go either way."

He glanced at my face and chuckled. "Cheer up. It's going to be fun."

"I'm just feeling a bit carsick, staring at that map," I said. "I'll be fine when I've had a cup of tea."

Luckily there was a police guard on the road leading to Sandringham House itself and he was able to direct us around the estate to Wymondham Hall. I don't think we would have found it alone. The royal residence was surrounded by lawns with two lovely lakes, but the estate was ringed by thick woodland. We found the narrow track between trees, so narrow, in fact, that bushes brushed against both sides of the motor.

"I knew she'd live somewhere gloomy," Darcy said. "It will be like Hansel and Gretel's house, you'll see."

"I wouldn't be surprised if she didn't bake children in her oven," Mummy chimed in. "We'd better watch Podge and Addy like hawks."

Then the trees ended. We came out to a broad forecourt and there was the house ahead of us. I'd been bracing myself for a smaller version of Castle Rannoch — a fortified ruin of a place with turrets and tiny windows but what was ahead of me was a substantial brick house with white trim at the windows, rather like Sandringham House itself. It wasn't very grand — more the sort of house a prosperous farmer would own rather than a lord, but it looked pleasant enough. I gave a sigh of relief.

Mummy stirred in the backseat. "Oh, have we arrived?" she asked.

"We have."

"And this is it?"

"It seems to be."

"Oh. Not bad at all." She gave a little snort of approval. "Better than the Goebbels' country monstrosity, anyway. And what's more, we're arrived ahead of Binky and Fig. That is satisfying. I do hope they didn't get lost."

That made us laugh and we were in good spirits as Darcy came around to open the car doors for Mummy and me. I was ahead of the others when the front door opened. Dogs rushed out, barking and wagging tails.

"Quiet, you brutes. Come here now!" said an imperious voice. The tall, gaunt woman standing framed in the doorway was dressed in a severe gray dress, her hair in an old-fashioned bun, her face expressionless. My mind immediately went back to the terrifying housekeeper Belinda and I had encountered earlier in the year. That had not ended well.

"Lady Aysgarth is expecting us," I said. "Lady Georgiana and the Honorable Mr. O'Mara, as well as —"

I thought I saw a flicker of amusement in the woman's eyes as Darcy hurried up behind me. "Good God, Aunt Ermintrude, what on earth are you doing opening your own front door?" he said.

I had been just about to ask, "Are you the housekeeper?" Talk about a narrow escape.

CHAPTER 8

December 23
Wymondham Hall, Norfolk

I'm pleasantly surprised. The batty aunt
seems completely normal. The house is
nice, warm and comfortable. I think we'll
enjoy ourselves.

"I don't make a habit of opening my own
front door," Darcy's aunt Ermintrude said,
"but I was looking out of the window and
since Heslop has become so confoundedly
deaf recently I thought you might be standing on the doorstep knocking for half the
afternoon. Freezing your toes off. Do come
in."
We stepped into the foyer, surrounded by
several very friendly dogs. I had pictured
Darcy's aunt Ermintrude quite differently.
She had been described as batty and she
painted exceedingly strange and awful

pictures, so I had been expecting someone with crazy eyes; wild, untamed hair; dressed in flowing garish robes and trailing scarves. This woman looked like someone who would be Queen Mary's friend. Her only adornment was a row of good pearls at her neck.

"How are you, Darcy?" she said in a deep, cultured voice. "Such a long time since I've seen you that I thought you might not recognize me. Since I wasn't invited to your recent nuptials."

"Sorry about that, Aunt," he said, stepping over the threshold to plant a kiss on her cheek. "We were limited in our number of guests by the size of Georgie's brother's drawing room and since the king and queen were there, we couldn't make it too crowded. Besides, we thought you were still in Yorkshire."

"Luckily I escaped a couple of years ago," she said.

"Oh dear," I exclaimed. "We sent the thank-you letter for the lovely painting to Aysgarth Abbey. You must have thought us rude."

The gaze that was now directed to me was quite warm. "My letters have been forwarded to me, so I did receive your kind note," she replied. "How are you, my dear?

We meet at last." And she held out a hand to me. Thank heavens I wasn't expected to kiss her cheek. She looked out past me. "Is this all your party? You have others following, I hope?"

"My brother and his wife and children are in a second motorcar," I replied, "and we have brought . . ."

I didn't have a chance to finish the sentence before Mummy, swathed in mink, appeared beside us. "I don't know if you remember me, Lady Aysgarth, but I stayed at your place once when I was still married to —"

Aunt Ermintrude reached out her hands to Mummy. "Your Grace. What an honor. I had no idea." For a moment I thought she was going to curtsy. Mummy did too.

"No longer 'Your Grace,' I'm afraid," Mummy said, "but I suppose I can claim the title of dowager duchess now that my stepson is the duke. How are you, Lady Aysgarth?"

"I am quite well, thank you," she said. "Are you unaccompanied?"

"Except for my family," Mummy said.

"Splendid."

I thought for one moment she was going to hitch Mummy up with someone — a mad cousin, maybe. But she went on, "That makes the numbers even and I do hate uneven numbers, don't you?"

"Oh definitely," Mummy said. "So untidy."

"Anyway, you are most welcome," Lady Aysgarth continued. "And I was sorry to hear of the death of your husband."

"Which one?" Mummy asked.

"The duke, of course."

"Ah yes. Poor Bertie. He was a good sort in many ways," Mummy said. "He just happened to live in an awful Scottish castle. Which reminds me, I was sorry to learn of the death of Lord Aysgarth."

Again I saw that flicker of amusement in Aunt Ermintrude's eyes. "But, like you, I was not sorry to escape from the castle on the moors. But don't let's stand here letting the cold air in. Let's show you to your rooms." She rang a little bell that was on a hall table. "James. Annie. Guests have arrived. Bags to be brought in." There was the sound of running feet. "The O'Maras have the big room on the left-hand side at the front. The dowager duchess should have the room next to theirs. And a family will be arriving with children. The Duke of Rannoch and his family, mind you." She wagged a finger at them. "Make sure everything is ready in the nursery."

Two servants had appeared, and behind them an elderly man, rather stooped and with wisps of gray hair on an almost bald head. "I'm so sorry, my lady," he said. "I was polishing silver in the pantry and did not hear the doorbell."

"That's all right, Heslop," she said kindly. "Luckily I was looking out of the window and saw them pull up.

"Get rid of these confounded nuisances, Jimmy," Darcy's aunt continued, while actually petting the dogs. "They are bothering the guests."

"Oh no, we love dogs," I said, but the footman and maid were already dragging them away by their collars. Mummy looked relieved — they had shown too much interest in the mink.

"Peace finally reigns. They are friendly enough but they can be a trifle overwhelming." Darcy's aunt turned her attention to us. "Have you had a meal?"

"Not really," Darcy said. "A sandwich in the car."

"Well, we must arrange for some luncheon," she said. "Heslop, tell Cook the guests want to eat. And maybe a little brandy first. I'm sure they are cold." She put a hand on Mummy's arm. "But I'm sure you would like to freshen up first." She looked around, then yelled, "Shortie!" in the sort of voice a sergeant major would use on parade.

There was the patter of running feet and a small, round woman came scurrying in.

"Come on, Shortie. Buck up," Lady Aysgarth said impatiently.

"Oh, have the guests arrived, Lady A.? I didn't hear the doorbell."

"That's because I spotted them from the window and opened the door myself," she said. "Perhaps you'd be good enough to show them their rooms."

"Happy to," the woman said. She gave us a shy smile.

I had thought Lady Aysgarth rather rude to call a servant by a cruel nickname until the woman said, "How do you do. I'm Jemina Short, Lady Aysgarth's companion."

Oh dear. Another person with an unfortunate name. Still I suppose it was better than being called short when you were long and skinny like me.

We went up the stairs and were ushered into a large bedroom. It wasn't what you would call elegant or even fancy. Rather rundown, I think describes it. Furniture that has seen better days, a couple of faded rugs on the floor. But it was clean and warm enough. I found myself wondering whether she was just renting this place furnished and had left all her nice things in Yorkshire.

"Do let us know if there is anything you need," Miss Short said. "Towels are on the chair by the basin. Bathrooms at the end of the hall." And she scurried away again, like the resident mouse.

Darcy and I exchanged a questioning smile. "Not what I expected," he said. Then his gaze froze. "Oh God. I see we've been graced with one of her paintings on the wall. I thought everything was far too normal to be true."

I looked across to the wall behind the bed and there was a large, utterly horrendous painting. It showed, as far as I could make out, a giant toad devouring a house. Or maybe it was a normal-sized toad devouring a small doll's house. Hard to tell, as it was splashed across with orange and red splatters.

"I'm glad it's over the bed so we don't actually have to look at it," I whispered, not sure whether Miss Short might be lingering outside.

"It will probably fall in the night and hit us over the head if we're not careful," he replied.

"Then you'll have to behave yourself and not shake the bed around, won't you?" I gave him a challenging grin.

"Spoilsport," he replied.

We were just removing coats and brushing hair when there was a rap on our door. "Are you two ready yet?" she called. "I'm starving, children."

I opened the door. Mummy was standing there, tapping a tiny foot impatiently.

"How is it you are always hungry but you never put on weight?" I asked.

"It must be my metabolism," she said. "Plus, I usually expend so much energy at sex."

I wished I hadn't asked.

"How is your room?" Darcy rapidly changed the subject as we went along the hall.

"I've seen better and I've seen worse," she said tactfully. "The bed has enough covers on it and that's all I really care about."

The aged butler was waiting with a tray of brandy glasses and led us into a big dining room with a blazing fire. It was a pleasant room with oak-paneled walls and a couple of nondescript paintings hanging — the sort of thing one finds in English country houses: two children beside a hay wagon, a stag in the highlands. Quite different from Aunt Ermintrude's own art style and much less conducive to indigestion.

We took our places at a long oak table. A maid came in with a tureen of hearty soup. It was good and I gave a sigh of relief that Queenie was going to be serving under a competent cook, who would give her orders and not let her make mistakes. The soup was followed by meat pie and cauliflower cheese and then by a steamed pudding with custard. All basic foods but most satisfying. Lady Aysgarth came in to join us as coffee was served.

"Bedrooms all right?" she asked. "I'm afraid we only have the basics here. I had to leave the best of the furniture behind. You heard I was thrown out on my ear, did you?"

"No, what happened?" Darcy asked.

"After Roddy died the lawyers had a long search for an heir, as we were childless. They found a third or even fourth cousin. Common little man named Harold. Nasty little fat toady person. Can you imagine an earl named Harold?" She shuddered. "Anyway, Harold arrived with his wife and three sniveling brats and promptly ordered me out of the house. Oh, he offered me the lodge, which was a place you wouldn't keep your favorite spaniel." She paused and I saw her fighting to control emotion.

"How awful," I said. "What did you do?"

"Frankly I was at a bit of a loss," she said.

"I certainly wasn't going to stay in the lodge and watch Harold destroying our legacy and reputation. Then dear Queen Mary sensed my plight. She suggested that this house on the estate had been vacant for some time so why didn't I move in and be close to her when they were visiting? Naturally I jumped at the chance. But I'm afraid I find myself in rather reduced circumstances. The only furniture I have is what dear Harold didn't want, and some pieces that the queen could find for me. I'm pleased to say that my butler and cook chose to come with me, even though I expect Harold would have paid them more. But then they are both elderly and he probably would have sacked them anyway. I've hired a couple of new maids and a footman and manage to get by."

"We've brought an assistant cook for you and some good additions to the food supply," Darcy said, "but why plan a big house party in such circumstances?"

"Because I was fed up," she said. "Most of the year, when the royals are not here, it can be very isolated, you know. Quite boring. So I thought to hell with it. Why not have a splendid Christmas for once, and sent out an invitation to all and sundry."

"And are all and sundry coming?"

Mummy asked.

"Enough people to make it pleasant, I hope. But a mixed bag. You'll meet them at dinner. And we have one guest arriving late." She gave an enigmatic smile, then turned at the crunch of tires on gravel. "Ah, I think the rest of your party is coming now."

And sure enough Binky and Fig emerged from the motorcar, followed by the children and a rather carsick-looking nanny.

"Absolutely ghastly drive," Fig complained as they were ushered in. "First Addy felt sick and we had to stop. Then nanny felt sick and we had to stop. Then the driver got lost. Useless man. Awful driver. Swayed around all over the place. If we'd known, we would have brought our chauffeur from Scotland."

"You didn't want to bring him, Fig, remember?" Binky said. "Saving money, you said."

She shot him a glare but said nothing more as they were introduced to our hostess. While they were at lunch Darcy and I went for a walk on the grounds and Mummy had a rest. She had slept most of the way in the car but it's what she always did when she was bored.

"Well this is a rum do, isn't it?" Darcy said. "She's clearly as poor as a church mouse but she's hosting what seems to be a big house party. Like I always said, 'batty.' "

"Perhaps she's sold some of her paintings," I suggested, making him chuckle.

We walked through the leafless woodland, hoping for a glimpse of Sandringham House, but gave up after the ground became rather too soggy and arrived back in time to see the motorcar drawing up, bringing the servants from the station.

"You took a long time," Darcy said as the driver opened the rear door for them. "I thought the train would have been quicker than motoring."

"We were doing fine, Your Grace, until we lost Queenie," Binky's valet said to him, shooting her a distasteful glance.

"Queenie?" She was just emerging from the car as large as life. "I see you found her again."

"Yes, but only after we missed our train," the valet said.

"What happened, Queenie?" I asked.

She was giving me a rather belligerent stare. "I was faint from the want of nourishment, that's what. And they wouldn't let me go to the buffet on King's Cross Station. So I was getting myself a chocolate bar from the machine and it wouldn't take my penny. It got stuck. Well, I'd already put two pennies in and I wasn't going to give up and let it take my money, so I started giving the machine a good whack, and a ticket taker saw me and came over and said I was a hooligan and he was going to call the police."

"And by the time we rescued her the train had left," the valet said, nodding to Fig's lady's maid for confirmation.

"Oh, Queenie, how could you?" I said. "You're lucky the hired car waited for you at the station."

"I didn't do nothing wrong," she said. "It was that machine that stole my pennies. And I still ain't had nothing to eat."

"Go on in. Change into your uniform and then report to Cook," I said. "No doubt she can find you something to keep you going until your next meal. And make sure you show her that you are willing to learn. She's a good cook."

"Bob's yer uncle," she said and went off, happily enough.

"That girl will drive us all to drink." Darcy shook his head.

CHAPTER 9

December 23
Wymondham Hall (pronounced Wyndham, I
gather), Norfolk

> I think it's going to be quite pleasant after
> all, apart from a couple of small compli-
> cations. Well, actually one small compli-
> cation . . .

I thought it wise not to ask Queenie to help
me dress for dinner. Darcy was able to help
me with hooks and eyes and to fasten the
clasp of my ruby necklace. A brief glance at
myself in the mirror confirmed that I didn't
look at all bad. Quite civilized in fact. A
married woman with a handsome husband.
I gave myself a little smile.

There was conversation coming from the
reception room on the other side of the hall
as we came down the stairs. We went in to
find Binky and Fig already there, talking

with another couple. Lady Aysgarth was over by the fire with yet another couple — the man tall, powerful looking with gray hair that curled, rather long for a man, and the woman rail thin, with a made-up face so it was hard to tell how old she was.

"Ah, here is my sister now," Binky said. "Georgie, come and meet Major and Mrs. Legge-Horne. The major helps arrange for the king's shooting parties."

"Enchanted, dear lady." We shook hands. His fingers brushed my palm, although I thought this might be accidental. Then I noticed his eyes traveled up and down my person appraisingly. His wife, as was often the case with flamboyant men, was a colorless person with brownish hair, a brownish dress and an expressionless face. When we shook hands it was like touching a fish.

"Although this year it's questionable whether the king will be able to participate in any kind of outdoor activity." The major had that sort of hearty, fruity voice that some men develop. Maybe it comes from yelling orders on parade grounds. "His health is sadly deteriorating."

"Oh dear," I said. "I hoped that fresh air at Sandringham might have bucked him up again."

"The queen is quite worried about him,"

Lady Aysgarth said, "as I'm sure she'll tell you when you pay her a visit tomorrow, Georgiana."

"Tomorrow?"

"Yes, when I was having tea with her the other day she suggested you call round before the festivities start with the family. She's most anxious to see you again."

Fig shot me a look of pure spite. The queen had never expressed interest in seeing her.

"Certainly," I said. "Did she mention what time?"

"Around eleven would be convenient," she said. "Oh, and do remember that they keep their clocks half an hour fast at Sandringham, won't you?"

"Oh, yes," I said. "I'm glad you reminded me. The king is obsessed with people being late, isn't he? I'll leave in good time."

"Darcy can drive you over. It's quite a walk, as I now know, not having a car at my disposal any longer."

"How impressive that this young lady is on visiting terms with the Queen of England," the big man said and I realized why he looked different somehow. He spoke with the slow drawl of the American South. He stepped forward, extending his hand to me. "How do you do, ma'am. I'm Colonel

106

Huntley from South Carolina and this is Mrs. Huntley."

"Georgiana O'Mara," I said, "and my husband, Darcy."

"Georgiana is related to the king," Lady Aysgarth said as we shook hands all around. "Her father was Queen Victoria's grandson."

"Did you hear that, Dolly?" the big man said. "You're in the presence of royalty. Fancy that. That will be something to tell them when you're playing bridge at the country club back home."

"Colonel and Mrs. Huntley are actually part of the reason for this little gathering," Aunt Ermintrude said. "I was told that they were alone in England at this joyous time and would welcome the chance to participate in the festivities. So I put together this little party at the last minute."

"Mighty decent of you. We appreciate it. Don't we, Dolly?"

"Sherry, everyone?" Aunt Ermintrude asked, nodding to Miss Short, who was lurking in the corner by the drinks tray.

"Do you happen to have bourbon?" the colonel asked.

"I'm afraid I don't even know what it is," Aunt Ermintrude said. "I do believe we have a bottle of whiskey if that would suit you."

"That's what bourbon is — whiskey," he said, laughing.

"Lady Aysgarth is talking about Scotch," the major said in withering tones. "The real whiskey."

There was a moment's uncomfortable silence, then the major turned to me. "Do you shoot, Lady Georgiana? I'm sure your husband does."

"Oh God, Archie, not more talk about killing things," his wife said. "All day long it's boasting about how many things you've killed."

Another uncomfortable silence was broken by the arrival of Mummy, looking absolutely stunning in a gold evening gown that accented her perfect golden hair (thanks to a hairdresser's bottle, I had come to suspect). Everyone turned to look as she framed herself in the doorway and said in that honeyed voice of hers, "Oh, am I late? I do hope I haven't kept you waiting."

I noticed that all the men were now staring openmouthed. Thank heavens I didn't have that effect on men.

"Do come in, my dear duchess," Lady Aysgarth said, now hinting at a much warmer relationship than she ever had with Mummy. "This is Her Grace, the Dowager Duchess of Rannoch."

Fig opened her mouth to say that Mummy, being divorced, could no longer count as a dowager duchess, but Binky dug an elbow into her side and shook his head. Every man in the room, Darcy included, went to get her a glass of sherry.

"You'll have to excuse us, Duchess," the colonel said, "if we haven't yet gotten the hang of these royal titles. Your Grace and Your Highness and God knows what else."

"Don't worry about it," Mummy said, giving him a dazzling smile. "My name is Claire and since we're to be in this jolly party together for a few days, I say we revert to first names."

"Decent of you. Real friendly," the colonel said. "We'd heard that the Brits were stuffy and aloof but that hasn't proved to be the case, has it, Dolly?"

"Not so far," Dolly said. "Most welcoming."

"Well, you are among the right sort of people," Major Legge-Horne said in his hearty voice and added a chuckle.

I took a sip of sherry and looked around the room. It was an unremarkable room, with an inglenook fireplace at its center and a variety of sofas and chairs dotted around. Again none of Aunt Ermintrude's paintings graced these walls, just a couple of harmless and undisturbing landscapes. In spite of the fire the room felt cold, as if something was missing. Then it dawned on me that the whole place was remarkably un-Christmassy. No decorations and no tree. Aunt Ermintrude must have noticed my discouragement because she said, "We all have a task tomorrow and that is to decorate the house properly. A magnificent tree has been delivered from the Sandringham Estate. It's up to us to gather winter greenery."

"Jolly good fun," the major said.

"Let's just hope it all goes smoothly and there isn't a repeat of last year," Mrs. Legge-Horne said, giving Lady Aysgarth a knowing look.

"What happened last year?" Mummy asked.

"I expect she's talking about the accident during the Boxing Day hunt. A poor man fell off his horse and broke his neck. Quite tragic." Aunt Ermintrude shook her head. "One of the royal retainers. A secretary or something, wasn't it?"

"From what I heard, the man wasn't much of a rider," Major Legge-Horne retorted. "Shouldn't have attempted to join the hunt over such difficult terrain. Couldn't handle one of the fences."

"Is there to be a hunt on Boxing Day?"

Darcy asked. "Damn, I should have brought my hunting pink."

"It's never a proper hunt, rather a paper chase, you know," the major said, "just to give the young people some good sport while the king holds his shoot."

"Neither are going to take place this year, I'm afraid, as the king is in such delicate health," Darcy's aunt replied. "We are going to try for a small shoot sometime, if he's up to it. He does love his shooting."

"What exactly is a paper chase?" Dolly Huntley asked.

"A rider goes ahead, leaving a trail of paper and the others try to catch him. All good fun," Darcy's aunt said. Then her face broke into a smile. "Do you remember that the Mitfords used to hunt their children?"

"Hunt children?" Dolly asked in a horrified voice. "You're not serious?"

Aunt Ermintrude was still smiling. "Oh, indeed. The children loved it, apparently."

Fig glared at Binky. "We are never going to hunt our children, Binky. Positively barbaric."

Heslop appeared in the doorway and rang a small gong. "Dinner is served, my lady," he said.

"Shall we go in?" Lady Aysgarth asked. "Duke and Duchess, do lead the way, followed by the Dowager Duchess and Lady Georgiana."

I stepped into line behind Binky, with Darcy holding my arm on one side and my mother's on the other, feeling as always that this was a very silly custom — to process in to dinner in order of rank. It always resulted in bad feelings. As was the case now. Major Legge-Horne fell into line behind me, only to have Colonel Huntley say, in his smooth southern voice, "I believe a colonel outranks a major, old man."

Major Legge-Horne turned bright pink. He went to say something. His wife put a restraining hand on his arm. "Of course. Go ahead," he snapped.

As we broke ranks to find our places at table he muttered, audible to those around him, "I was in the damned Coldstream Guards, for God's sake. Not some namby-pamby American regiment."

I was seated between the major and Dolly Huntley and across from the colonel. He gave me an encouraging smile as we took our places.

"We seem to have extra places," Mummy said, noticing the empty seat to the right of Lady Aysgarth. "Are we expecting more guests?"

"I hope so. But they are coming from

abroad, so who knows if they will be delayed. We were told not to wait for them."

"Oh no," Miss Short suddenly exclaimed, making us all look at her.

"What's wrong, Shortie?" Lady Aysgarth asked.

"Thirteen at table. So unlucky. There is always a death when there are thirteen at table."

"Nonsense," the major said. "Old women's superstitions."

I remembered Lady Aysgarth saying to my mother that the numbers were now even. Obviously she hadn't thought Miss Short to be worth counting!

The footman appeared with a tureen of clear soup with croutons. Wine was poured.

"I understand that you were kind enough to bring a crate of champagne, Darcy," his aunt said.

"A gift from our friend Princess Zamanska," Darcy replied.

"Much appreciated, I can assure you. We shall certainly eat well during the festivities. When I think of that distant cousin, the new earl, living on the bounty of my late husband's estate, it makes my blood boil."

"You should have invited him here and killed him off during the hunt," Mummy said.

Everyone laughed.

Lady Aysgarth only shook her head. "Then they would have found a fifth or sixth cousin. I'm a mere woman and not a member of the family by birth. I'd be turned out by whoever inherited."

"Jolly unfair, I say," Binky said heartily and got a frown from Fig.

"I'd say you were much better off here than on that bleak and dreary moor miles from anywhere," Mummy said.

"You're right," Lady Aysgarth said. "One can contribute to society much better here."

Filet of turbot with a parsley sauce followed and then an impressive piece of roast beef, surrounded by crispy roast potatoes, parsnips and a Yorkshire pudding.

"Do we have a gentleman who is an expert carver?" Darcy's aunt looked around the table expectantly.

"Count me out," the colonel said. "The help does that sort of thing where I come from."

I glanced at Darcy, who shook his head. "I defer to the more experienced gentlemen."

"I'll have a go if you like," Major Legge-Horne said.

"Oh, Reggie, you'll butcher it," his wife replied.

"Why don't you do the honors, Your Grace, as senior male present?" Lady Aysgarth indicated that the platter should be put in front of Binky. He tried to protest but got to work, doing an amazingly good job. I had come recently to realize that I underestimated my brother.

While we waited for the meat to be carved I felt something brush up against my leg. I thought it might be a cat and looked down. It wasn't a cat. The major had stretched out his leg so that his knee was against mine. I gave him a haughty stare and moved away. What was the matter with these men that they thought they could play kneesies? At least it wasn't a hand, as had happened to me in the past. That gentleman got a fork stuck in him!

We had just started on the meat course when we heard voices in the front hall and Heslop appeared, looking pink and flustered. "Your ladyship, the Prince of Wales is here."

Lady Aysgarth rose to her feet. "Oh, good. So they did manage to catch the boat train."

She broke off as my cousin the Prince of Wales came into the room. "Here we are, Trudy old thing," he said. "Sorry we're a bit late. Terrible drive up from London. Anyway, I hope you've kept us a morsel or two because we're starving."

He looked around the table. Everyone had now also risen.

"What ho, Binky. Georgie. Splendid. Faces I know. I do hate eating with strangers. One always feels that they are watching one with the fascination of watching animals in a zoo."

"You're not alone, sir?" Lady Aysgarth said cautiously.

"Good heavens, no," he said. "Wallis has gone up to powder her nose or whatever women do. She'll be down in a moment."

That was when I realized that the other member of the party was to be Mrs. Simpson.

CHAPTER 10

December 23
Wymondham Hall, Norfolk

When I had wondered who might join us, it had never occurred to me that it could be Mrs. Simpson. Oh crikey. A whole Christmas with her. Still, Mummy will enjoy sparring with her, which is always amusing.

The prince refused to take his place until Mrs. Simpson arrived.

"Do carry on," he said. "Don't let it get cold." But we felt obliged not to eat anything until he sat down. The colonel started to cut a slice of meat but was warned with a glance from his wife and put his fork down again. When the food was well and truly cold Mrs. Simpson came in. She was wearing a black lace gown — the very gown that Princess Zou Zou had once worn at the same dinner party, causing much displeasure. The gown was simple but Mrs. Simpson sparkled with diamonds — diamond necklace, earrings, bracelet. She positively glittered.

"So sorry to keep everyone waiting," she said in that slight transatlantic drawl that had now been refined by years among the prince's friends. "It took some time because my maid got held up in Switzerland. I told her not to bother to come here because we won't be staying long, so to go straight to the London house instead."

"You're sitting here, darling," the prince said. I heard an intake of breath from those who hadn't known the extent of their relationship. He personally pulled out a chair for her to sit, then took his own place.

"So if one of you ladies would be kind enough to share a maid with me for the next couple of days?" She looked around the table.

Mummy and I exchanged a glance. "Go on. I dare you to offer Queenie" the glance was saying. It was tempting. Darcy also picked up on this and gave me a warning frown. I had a great desire to laugh and put my napkin to my mouth in case a giggle burst out. Luckily Darcy's aunt stepped in first, saying, "My girl will be happy to oblige. She's only a local Yorkshire lass, not trained in Paris or anything, but I've no doubt she can do up hooks and eyes and brush hair to your satisfaction."

"Most kind," Mrs. Simpson said.

Wine was poured for them. The prince took a sip and nodded appreciation. "Is this the wine we had sent over for you?" he asked. "It's jolly good, isn't it?"

"It is, Your Highness, and I'm most grateful."

"You've just come from abroad, sir?" Binky asked. I should point out that even though the Prince of Wales was a cousin — a first cousin once removed — one always addressed him as "sir." It was the done thing.

"We've been skiing in Switzerland, old man," the prince said as a bowl of soup was filled in front of him. I was praying that Queenie would never be asked to serve at table. I could just picture soup in Mrs. Simpson's lap. "Wonderful time. Perfect powder, eh, Wallis?"

"Apart from those confounded newspaper reporters hounding us everywhere we went." She rolled her eyes. "We'd come down a slope and there at the bottom were all these horrid little men with cameras, shouting questions at us. So annoying." As she spoke she looked around the table. "Oh, Homer, Dolly, you made it. I'm so glad."

"You're looking mighty good, Wallis," Colonel Huntley said.

"One tries," she said, her gaze sweeping on until she saw me. "Georgiana. I didn't expect to see you here. How are you, honey? Last time we met it was in Africa, wasn't it?"

"It was," I said. "An upsetting time."

"Well, if a stupid man got himself killed, it wasn't going to spoil my holiday," she said. "It wasn't as if we knew him, and I gather he was quite unpleasant. And then unfortunately the king commanded David to get on with his royal duties elsewhere, so it wasn't much of a holiday anyway."

"But jolly good polo," the prince said.

"Polo! All you men think about: shooting and polo. So boring." Then she finally spotted Mummy. "Well if it isn't the actress," she said.

"The dowager duchess, actually," Mummy replied. "How are you, Wallis?"

"What happened to the Nazi friend?" Wallis asked.

"I left him at home, being a good Nazi," Mummy replied smoothly. "And you'll never guess who I just bumped into in

Berlin. Your pal Ribbentropp. He sends his love."

Mrs. Simpson's smile didn't falter but I saw daggers shoot from her eyes. Score one for Mummy, I thought. It had been rumored that the German ambassador was more than a pal of Mrs. Simpson's. I had seen Mummy's exchanges with Wallis Simpson in the past and had come to the conclusion that she held her own beautifully.

Our cold beef was now carried away. We waited until the prince and Mrs. Simpson had eaten their main course before the dessert was brought in.

"Well this looks interesting," Colonel Huntley said, prodding at it. "What do you call this? A local specialty?"

"I'm not sure," Lady Aysgarth said. "I thought we were to have a soufflé with brandied cherries."

I knew immediately what it was but wasn't going to say until the prince blurted out, "My God, it's roly-poly pudding. I haven't had jam roly-poly since I was in the nursery."

It had become all too clear to me. Queenie had somehow had a hand in the production of the soufflé and ruined it. The cook had had hysterics and Queenie had made roly-poly pudding to provide a dessert. I opened my mouth to say "I'm afraid . . ." when the colonel said, "Very tasty. Good and hearty. Exactly what you want in this sort of weather."

Others nodded agreement.

"I haven't had this in years," Binky said. "Why don't we have it more, Fig?"

Darcy caught my eye and winked.

We ladies left the men to their cigars and brandy — all except Mrs. Simpson, who stayed with the prince, much to the disgust of the major. Then the men joined us and plans were made to gather greenery to decorate the house.

"Shall you be joining us, sir?" Lady Aysgarth asked.

"I'll certainly try," the prince said. "I should probably head for the big house now and pay my respects before the old fellow goes to bed — since we had to give up our skiing trip and were summoned back on account of his health."

"How bad is it, do you think?" Fig asked.

"It doesn't look too good," the prince said. "He hasn't been right since that nasty turn a few years ago. His lungs are failing, I suspect. I pray to God he can hold on for a few more years. The last thing in the world I want is to find myself king right now." And he squeezed Wallis's hand.

"No Mr. Simpson in tow this time?" Mummy asked sweetly.

"Mr. Simpson is no more," Wallis replied.

"He died?"

"Dead to me," Wallis replied with a little smile. "Actually we are still good pals. However, divorce proceedings have been initiated. Let's hope they don't take too long. If David finds himself king before everything is settled . . ."

"I must go." The prince stood up, kissed Lady Aysgarth's hand, waved to the rest of us and headed for the door. Wallis followed him. As soon as she was out of the room Miss Short whispered to Lady Aysgarth, "She surely can't intend to marry him, can she? That would be unthinkable."

"That is exactly what she intends," Lady Aysgarth whispered back.

Soon after that the party broke up.

"Now I understand the whole reason for this charade," Darcy said. "Don't you?"

"An excuse to host Mrs. Simpson close to Sandringham, you mean?"

"Exactly." He shook his head. "You can bet that the prince sent over a generous check so that Aunt E. could host and feed Mrs. S. and her American friends."

"The king and queen would have a fit if they found out she was nearby," I admitted.

123

"Are you coming up to bed?" Darcy saw me lingering in the foyer.

"I really wanted a word with Queenie."

"About the pudding?"

"Exactly."

He smiled. "It's probably better that we don't know. Come on." He took my hand and led me upstairs.

I changed into my nightclothes and then went down the hall in search of the loo. When I emerged the lights had been dimmed so that only one bulb at the end of the hall was still sending an anemic glow. A man was standing, waiting. I nodded politely (as one does when emerging from the lavatory) and went to pass him, but he didn't move. The dim light revealed him to be the major, in a most unappealing striped red and white dressing gown, making him look like a red version of a marmalade pot.

"Excuse me," I said, stepping to one side.

He stepped to the same side, effectively blocking my path.

"You're a damned attractive young filly," he said in a low voice. "I don't suppose you'd fancy a spot of fun — make a change, what?"

As he talked he moved closer. He had an unpleasant leer on his face. "A quickie in the spare bedroom down the hall, eh?"

I gave him a cold stare. "Major, your idea of fun and mine are clearly not the same, and if I mention this to my young and very fit husband, I think you may be sitting down to Christmas dinner with a black eye at the very least."

"Loosen up, old thing," he said. "Just joking, you know. A little bit of fun, eh?"

"Not my idea of fun," I replied, trying to sound starchy and disapproving when really I was feeling definitely uneasy. I knew he couldn't do anything to me in a house full of people, with my own husband down the hall, but just the way he was looking at me made me feel threatened.

He backed off by a few inches and to my horror and annoyance he reached out a hand to touch the cord of my dressing gown. "Your royal cousins certainly aren't prudish. They all seem to enjoy a little nighttime sport, don't they?" He yanked the cord of my dressing gown, making it fall open to reveal, thankfully, a long winter nightie. I gave a silent prayer of thanks that I had abandoned the negligees of my honeymoon.

"How my cousins behave is their own business." I stepped back, hastily retying my gown, and gave a nervous laugh. "I am extremely happily married, but if ever I decided to bed-hop it would not be with an unattractive middle-aged man like you. Now, are you going to stand aside or do I scream loudly enough to wake the entire household?"

"Spoilsport," he muttered. "You must be a throwback to Queen Victoria."

"Oh, I do hope so." I gave him a dazzling smile, then pushed past and stalked to my room. I decided not to mention this to Darcy. I didn't rate the major's chances too highly by the time Darcy was done with him.

CHAPTER 11

December 24
Wymondham Hall and after at Sandringham
House, Norfolk

This morning I have to pay my respects to
the queen. Oh gosh, I do hate visiting
the royal relatives. I'm always terrified I'll
knock over a priceless antique or spill
coffee. I wonder why the queen is so
anxious to see me. You'd think she'd
have enough to do with the whole royal
family in residence.

The next morning we awoke to that strange
yellow light that indicates snow. A dusting
of white now lay on the ground and soft
flakes were falling.

"It's going to be a white Christmas," I said
as I pulled back the curtains.

Darcy sat up. "I wonder if that means the
expedition to gather greenery is off?"

"Oh golly. I've got to visit the queen. I'd much rather be gathering greens. I wonder why she wants to talk to me so desperately."

"Why do you think it's desperate?" Darcy fished around for his slippers, then got out of bed.

"If she just wanted me to pay a courtesy call, wouldn't she wait until after Christmas? Wouldn't she just say I'd enjoy a visit from Georgiana while she is staying here?"

Darcy nodded.

"Oh gol— oh heavens," I corrected myself. "You don't suppose she has an assignment for me, do you?"

"Like what?"

"Retrieving antiques, spying on people?"

"I'd say the latter is likely. She's heard that Mrs. S. is staying with us and she wants you to keep an eye on things. No secret weddings or plans for elopements."

"Yes, that could be it," I agreed. We washed, dressed and went down to breakfast. Darcy was wearing heavy tweed trousers and a fisherman's jersey. I, on the other hand, had to look right for the queen. I put on a pleated skirt, white silk blouse and cashmere cardigan and a string of pearls (wedding present from the king and queen) for good measure. The image in the mirror looked quite suitable. I nodded. I no longer looked like the unpolished young girl. Being married to a gorgeous bloke is good for one's self-esteem.

On the way down I was tempted to go into the kitchen but Darcy took my arm. "Leave it," he said. "They all enjoyed her pudding, after all."

"It was quite tasty," I agreed. "But she has to understand that she can't go making the sort of food she serves to us."

We found that the colonel and Dolly were already in the dining room, standing with puzzled expressions in front of the row of covered dishes on the sideboard.

"Can I help you?" I asked.

"There doesn't seem to be anybody to wait on us," he said.

"Oh no. At breakfast one serves oneself."

He lifted the lid of one of the dishes. "What exactly do people eat for breakfast here?"

"There seems to be a good range," I said.

"And this brown mess is?"

"Kidneys," I said.

"Kidneys? Offal, you mean?" Dolly sounded horrified. "That is the sort of thing we feed to the help."

"They are jolly tasty," I replied.

"And this?" the colonel asked.

"Kedgeree. It's kippers cooked with rice

and things. An old Indian dish from the colonies."

"Don't you have any regular food like sausages and bacon and pancakes?"

"I'm sure you'll find scrambled eggs, boiled eggs, bacon, sausages," I said. "Just no pancakes. We have those for pudding."

They shook their heads sadly. At that moment Queenie appeared, carrying a bowl of boiled eggs.

"Wotcher, miss — I mean, my lady," she said, giving an embarrassed little grin.

She lowered the bowl of eggs into the warm water of the food warmer. I followed her as she made her exit. "Queenie, about last night's dinner . . ." I began.

"Yeah? Pretty good, wasn't it?"

"Except the pudding, Queenie. Were you anything to do with the soufflé disaster?"

She stuck out her chin defiantly. "I certainly ruddy well was," she said. "If she hadn't had me there, she'd have been in a right old mess."

This threw me off guard. "What happened?"

"Well, she took the soufflés out too soon, didn't she? I told her but she said she knew her stove better than me. And what happened? They went flat. So she said, 'I can't serve them like this.' She got quite upset.

'Think of something to do,' she said. So I said I'd make something instead. Well, we already had the cherry compote for the soufflés so I whipped up a batch of jam roly-poly and shoved it in the oven. Made some custard and bob's yer uncle. She was ever so grateful."

I tried not to smile as I shook my head. "Queenie, I don't think I will ever cease to be surprised by you, in both good and bad ways," I said.

"So I can't be your maid and cook the food," Queenie said. "I ain't leaving that kitchen before dinner or she won't half get shirty with me. But I can come up after dinner to help you undress if you like."

"That's kind of you, Queenie," I said. "I expect Mr. Darcy and I can manage."

"It's no problem," she said. "I used to like putting away your jewels and brushing your hair. It was like having a big doll, what I never had when I was a kid. I only had a rag doll that my mum made and it wasn't half ugly."

"Well, if you can find the time, you can come up and brush my hair," I said. I smiled, almost fondly, as I watched her depart.

At ten o'clock I prepared for Darcy to drive

me over to Sandringham House. The others had yet to embark on their foliage-gathering expedition, waiting for the snow to stop. It seemed there wasn't a high level of enthusiasm. Mrs. Simpson had naturally declared that there was no way she was trudging through snow to find a few bits of holly and ivy. Dolly agreed that's what one had servants for and they were definitely going to stay and keep Wallis company. Besides, the colonel had a weak chest and shouldn't be exposed to the cold. The major said that he and his missus would be happy to join in the fun, but first he had to go over to the house and see whether the king was up for a small shoot that day. That left Binky and Fig, Miss Short and Lady Aysgarth, plus the children, who were itching to be allowed to play in the snow. Mummy had remained conspicuous by her absence. She had probably had breakfast in bed.

"You'll join us when you've dropped off Georgiana?" Lady Aysgarth asked her nephew.

"Happy to," Darcy replied.

"I can give the young lady a lift over to Sandringham House," the major said.

Oh crikey, I did not want to find myself alone in a motorcar with him. I glanced across at Darcy. "Thank you, Major, but I left my gloves in our motorcar, so why don't I drive myself? I'm quite capable, you know."

"If you're quite sure," he said. "Snowy road, snowdrifts and all that."

I grinned. "I did grow up in Scotland where we actually have blizzards. I'm quite used to driving through snow."

This, in fact, was a lie. In winter Castle Rannoch could be snowed in for days and nobody went out unless they had to. And it was always our chauffeur who drove us.

"You'll be all right?" Darcy asked, coming into the hall with me as I retrieved my coat and hat. "You're sure you don't want me to drive you?"

"Actually I can't lose face in front of the major now," I said. "I'll be fine."

We exchanged a kiss. I retrieved the motor from the stables, now serving as garages, and off I went. It was a pretty Christmas card scene ahead of me with snow decorating bare branches and lying on the fir trees. I couldn't enjoy it as fully as I would have liked because I had to concentrate on keeping to what I hoped was the road. Fortunately the snow was not yet deep and the drive only took a few minutes. I felt that apprehension I always feel about visiting my royal relatives as I pulled up in the forecourt. As I approached the house I heard squeals of laughter. I turned to see the two little princesses on the lawn, having a snowball fight while their governess looked on. They recognized me right away. Elizabeth waved. Margaret called out, "Come and join us, Georgie. We want to build a snowman."

"There isn't enough snow to do that yet, Mummy said," Elizabeth replied, "but you could join our snowball fight, Georgie. Then it could be two on two."

"I'm afraid I've been summoned to meet your grandmother," I replied. "It doesn't do to be late."

"Absolutely not here." Elizabeth managed a little smile. "Grandpapa is a stickler about time, isn't he?"

I nodded.

"You know all the clocks at Sandringham are kept half an hour fast, don't you?"

"Oh yes," I said. "I'm well aware of that. But I must rush. Enjoy your snowballs."

CHAPTER 12

December 24
Sandringham House, Norfolk

About to face the queen. Trying not to look too nervous. Oh dear. I hope my hand doesn't shake if I have to drink coffee. I wonder what she wants.

As I went up the steps a footman came out to greet me. "Her Majesty is expecting you," he said and I was escorted inside. I was always a bit confused with the layout of Sandringham, which was a big sprawl of a house. I had only been a couple of times before and was about to turn in the wrong direction.

"Her Majesty is actually in the king's morning room," the footman corrected me.

"With the king?" I had no wish to be interrogated by King George, who terrified me, although I suspected he liked me. He always referred to me as "young Georgie" and had a twinkle in those bright blue eyes when he said it.

"No, my lady. The king is going shooting, I am led to believe. The queen is not pleased about it."

I glanced into the main drawing room as we walked past. Sandringham might be a family home, as opposed to a palace, as it was owned by the king and not the country, but it is still jolly grand. Lots of wood paneling; huge portraits and paintings; as well as gilt, painted ceilings; giant fireplaces. But the room into which I was shown was small by royal standards and quite cozy. Paneled walls, a tiger-skin rug in front of the fire — clearly a man's room; and the queen, perched in one of the oversized leather armchairs, looked tiny and out of place, but she gave me a lovely smile and held out her hand to me. I managed to take it, curtsy and then kiss her cheek, all without mishap. See, I was growing up at last.

"How lovely to see you, my dear. And looking so well too. Married life obviously suits you. I can remember how happy I felt after I married dear George. And look at Bertie and Elizabeth. So well suited. So happy. What a blessing that boy found her. He'd have been lost without her. Do sit

136

down." And she waved to a seat on the other side of the fire.

"I came in here because it's the warmest room and one of the servants could not get the fire going in the main morning room. Wrong sort of wood, one gathers. It smoked horribly, so I retreated. Besides, the king has gone out to shoot. Did you ever hear of anything so silly? With his chest on a snowy day." She shuddered. "I begged him not to and do you know what he said. 'What if it's my last chance, eh, May?' he said. 'What if this is my last Christmas? Would you begrudge me a final pleasure?'

"I told him not to talk that way. That he'd get well again and live on for many years. 'You have to,' I said. 'Until that silly boy is tired of the American woman.'

" 'Or she gets tired of him,' was the king's response."

I began to wonder if, after all, this was just a friendly courtesy call and not an important tête-à-tête.

"You'll take coffee?" she asked.

"Yes, please, ma'am." I sat cautiously, feeling myself being swallowed into the giant armchair. "So was there a shoot arranged for today?"

"Not an official one," she said. "The king has gone out with the man who arranges these things, Major something or other, and the Prince of Wales. David seemed reluctant, but I told him it was his duty to humor his father at this time. He wanted to be with *her,* of course." She gave me a look of pure disgust.

When I tried not to seem surprised, she gave me a sad smile. "Oh yes. I know all about it. This is a small community. Nothing much escapes our attention. So my son persuaded my old friend to host his mistress so that he could be near her." She gave an exasperated sigh. "You know the Simpson woman well, Georgiana, don't you?"

"I've met her on several occasions, ma'am. I couldn't say that I know her well. I rather feel with Mrs. Simpson that you only know the façade she presents to you."

"Very wise," she said. "Yes, she always resembles a brittle shell to me. If you broke her she'd smash into pieces and there would be nothing inside." She paused. "But the thing that worries me, Georgiana, is that David fully intends to marry her once the divorce is final, and do you know what? The woman actually imagines she'll be queen someday."

"Parliament would never allow it, ma'am," I said.

"I agree, but my son is so besotted that he

believes he can wave away laws once he becomes king." She sighed again. "Why, oh why, couldn't Bertie be the oldest? I agree he has problems with speaking in public and he's not of the strongest constitution but he's a good chap, solid through and through. And his wife is a tower of strength. You know how that Simpson woman makes fun of her?"

"I've seen it, I'm afraid, ma'am."

The queen leaned across to me. "She underestimates her adversary. Elizabeth may look soft and gentle but she has a will of iron and a similar sense of duty. That woman had better beware." She looked me right in the eye. She had the most piercing clear blue eyes like many of the royal family. "You'll keep an eye on things at Wymondham, won't you, Georgie. And if that woman tries —" She broke off as a tray of coffee and biscuits was wheeled in and two cups were poured.

"So did you know Lady Aysgarth before this visit?" the queen asked while there was still a maid in the room.

"I'd never met her," I said, "but she's Darcy's aunt."

"A good woman. Not had the most pleasant of lives until now. He was a bounder, you know. Roddy Aysgarth. They married her off to him when she was far too young to know what she wanted. He was handsome, of course. And dashing. The sort of chap to turn a young girl's head. But she soon found out he couldn't keep his hands off anything in skirts."

"So she is better off without him?"

"In some ways, I suppose," the queen admitted. "She's virtually penniless now that the new earl has turned her out. Which is why I offered her this grace-and-favor house. And it's comforting to have her nearby. We were good friends when she was my lady-in-waiting. It was around the time we lost my son John. Distressing for all of us. She was a comfort. And of course she liked being at court as it meant she was away from her husband."

I took a few more sips of coffee, nibbled at a biscuit and wondered if the interview was over. I noticed that the queen seemed on edge. She fidgeted, when she normally sat ramrod straight and still. I know it was not done to initiate a conversation with royalty. They always have to ask the questions. I sat forward, with some difficulty in that big chair. "Perhaps I should go and help the others with their gathering greenery for decorating," I said, "if there is nothing more you need me for, ma'am."

"Oh yes, yes of course. If you must go," the queen said.

I dared to do the forbidden. "Is something wrong, ma'am? I hope I'm not being impertinent but you seem — unsettled."

She put down her coffee cup firmly on the side table and folded her hands in her lap. "I may be imagining things, Georgiana. It is perhaps just worry about the king that has distorted my sensibilities, but I just feel that something is wrong."

" 'Wrong'? In what way?"

She leaned closer to me. "You heard what happened last Christmas, did you? One of the participants was thrown from his horse on the Boxing Day hunt and broke his neck."

"I was told about this," I said. "Jolly bad luck."

"It wasn't bad luck," she said. "I have come to the conclusion that it was intentional."

I looked up, startled. "But surely, ma'am, I was told that the man was a novice rider who should never have attempted to jump fences."

She shook her head impatiently. "I'm not talking about that poor boy. Of course he should never have attempted to join a hunt with only minimal riding skills. No, I'm

141

talking about poor Jeremy. Jeremy Hastings. My son's equerry."

"Two men died during the same hunt?" I was horrified.

"I know. Shocking, absolutely shocking. That first one was unlucky, I suppose. He fell and was trampled, but Jeremy — he was a splendid horseman, a great polo player. He would never have fallen off during a hunt. I have come to the conclusion that something or someone knocked him off in a place where he would have landed on rock."

"Do you have any proof of this? Somebody saw something?"

She shook her head. "Pure instinct, but I pride myself on my heightened senses." She reached out now and covered my hand with her own. "Georgiana, do you believe in evil?"

"Well, yes, I suppose I do," I stammered. I thought about this for a moment. I had come across murderers. Some were undoubtedly evil, with no regard for human life. But others were not evil, rather tragic figures, pushed beyond endurance into corners from which murder was the only way out.

"I sense evil around us at the moment," the queen said, looking around to make sure nobody else was in hearing range. "I can't explain it except that a few little things have occurred to make me believe that something terrible may happen again."

"What sort of things?" I asked.

"Again silly little accidents — someone falling into the lake when the path gave way. Someone tripping down a flight of stone steps. All easily explained, but . . ."

"But your sense of danger tells you they were not accidents?"

"Precisely. That is why I'm glad you are here, because my concern is that my son David —"

She broke off as someone came into the room. It was the Prince of Wales himself, dressed in plus fours and tweed hunting jacket. He stormed over to his mother.

"David, you can't just barge in like this," his mother said, looking up angrily. "Can't you see that I have a guest?"

"What? Oh yes, sorry." He seemed to notice me for the first time. "Hello, Georgie. Didn't mean to interrupt."

"What are you doing back so quickly?" the queen said. "It's not your father, is it? He hasn't been taken ill? He's all right?"

"Oh, Father's fine," he said. "Never been better. Enjoyed every moment. So did I until some idiot mistook me for a pheasant."

"What on earth do you mean?" the queen asked.

"Only I heard the sound of a shotgun firing behind me, thought it was my father and then something whizzed past my ear, something gave my shoulder a glancing blow and another pellet lodged in the brim of my hat."

"David! That's terrible. Who was it?"

"That's the darndest thing. Father and the major were both standing in a line with me. The keepers and beaters were behind them but not in a position to hit me if they'd tried. Besides, those with a gun were fully occupied in reloading for my father and the major."

"You weren't shooting with them?"

"I was," David replied, "but I got a bit bored. Damned pheasants were falling from the sky like snowflakes. All too easy. So I thought I might slip away for a while and that was when this happened. In quite a thick little coppice. Rhododendron bushes, you know. I rushed back. We all searched but found nobody."

"Footprints in the snow?" I asked.

Again he looked at me as if he had forgotten I was there.

"Good point, Georgie. The trouble was that we'd approached the shoot from that direction, so the ground was a mass of footprints from us and the dogs."

"So what do you think? Someone was actually taking a shot at you?" I could see the fear on the queen's face.

"Hardly likely, Mother. Our private grounds are fenced and there were certainly enough staff around. Besides, if you wanted to bump me off, why not wait until I'm at Fort Belvedere? I'm often out alone in the grounds there. An easy target."

"So what do you think, then?" she asked.

"I think someone was out poaching on the wrong day. Wanted to bag himself a pheasant for Christmas, maybe. And he hadn't realized the power of the gun."

"Is your father still out there?" Queen Mary stood up. Naturally I did too.

"No. The major thought that given the circumstances we should bring him back to the house. Just in case, you know. His police watchdogs are combing the area, but I don't think they'll find anyone. Too easy to get lost."

"I must go to your father," the queen said. "He'll be most distressed."

"Don't fool yourself, Mother," David said. "He'd be only too happy if someone dispatched me and my brother became the heir. In fact he might have arranged for the incident himself."

He laughed. Queen Mary glared at him. "What a despicable thing to say, David. I think you should go up and change while I attend to your father." She turned back to me. "Georgiana. I'm so sorry I have to abandon you. Do you need a lift back to Wymondham?"

"No, thank you, ma'am. I brought my own motorcar," I said. "I'm very sorry for what happened, sir."

"Accidents will happen," he said.

The queen gave me a knowing look before she left the room ahead of me.

CHAPTER 13

December 24
On the way back from Sandringham House,
Norfolk

Oh dear. Now the hostess is missing. I
hope it's not going to be one of those
Christmases.

A footman was waiting to escort me to the
front entrance. As it was still snowing, he
held an umbrella over me as I made my way
to my motorcar and opened the door for
me.

"Merry Christmas, my lady, if I may be so
bold," he said.

I smiled at him. "Of course you may. And
I hope it's a merry Christmas for you too."

"I'll be working too hard to notice," he
confessed. "It's always a bit chaotic with the
whole family here and the king's speech and
all, but I will be able to go home and see

my people on Boxing Day. They only live in King's Lynn, so that's good."

I was relieved when the motor started, as it had been out in the cold for a while, and I drove off. More snow had fallen and was falling harder now. There was no sign of the princesses and their governess, but at least they would be able to build their snowman later in the day if the snow stopped. The falling snow had partially obliterated my tracks from earlier and it was hard to see where the road lay. Also snow was now building up on my windshield as the wipers pushed it down. I was peering forward, concentrating hard, so that I didn't see the figure who stepped out from between the trees. It was swathed in a woolly hat and scarves and I couldn't see the face.

I gasped, slammed on the brakes and felt the motor skid on the snow. I fought to right the steering wheel while the person jumped out of the way. We bumped over uneven ground and came to rest inches from a tree trunk. I was breathing hard as I wound down the window. "I'm most awfully sorry," I said. "I didn't expect to meet anybody. Are you all right?"

"I'm fine," the person said. "Although you did give me a bit of a fright." She pulled down the woolen scarf that covered her face and I saw that it was Miss Short. "I hope you haven't gone off the road into a ditch," she said.

"I hope so too. Shall I try and back up?"

I put the car into reverse, and to my relief we bumped and slithered until I felt the smoother surface of the track beneath the wheels. "That's a relief," I said. "Do you need a lift back to the house? Or are you in the middle of finding greenery?"

I presumed she had been part of the greens-gathering expedition, but she wasn't carrying anything in her hands.

"I was," she said, "but I've been looking for Lady Aysgarth. You haven't seen her, have you?"

"I've just come from the queen at Sandringham," I replied. "And I've seen no sign of anybody on the way back."

"Oh dear, I hope she's all right," Miss Short replied. "We couldn't find her and she didn't answer when we shouted."

"What about the dogs?" I asked. "Weren't they with you?"

She shook her head. "We left them behind. Lady Aysgarth thought it wise if there was going to be shooting going on in the vicinity. We couldn't risk them running into the line of fire, or flushing out birds when they weren't supposed to. Oh dear. If only we'd brought them, they'd have stayed with her. They adore her, you know. Very protective of her."

"I expect she's fine," I said, although Queen Mary's words echoed in my head. "Why don't we drive back to the house and see if she's come back by now," I said. "If not, we can bring the dogs out to help look for her."

"Perhaps that would be the wisest thing." She opened the passenger door and got in. "We were doing quite well and had several trugs of holly and ivy and someone even found some mistletoe, then we realized the snow was getting worse and it was jolly cold, so we started back. That was when we couldn't see Lady Aysgarth. So we split up and started looking for her."

I put the car into first gear and we eased forward along the track.

"Have you been her companion for long?" I asked after we had driven for a while in silence and I watched her scanning the countryside intently.

"Oh yes. For donkey's years," she said. "I was there when the earl was killed."

"He was killed?" I asked. "He didn't die of a heart attack or Spanish flu?"

"Oh no. He was out on the moors when a boulder fell on him," she replied. "It was a terrible shock for Lady A."

"Not a relief?" I asked. "I gather he was a bit of a ladies' man."

"That's as may be," she replied rather tartly. "I can't say he treated her well, but she was fond of him in her way. And of course it meant that she had to leave her home, all the things she had come to love there. That brute who inherited didn't even let her bring her favorite pieces of furniture. The stuff she has now came from the lodge or was found in local secondhand shops. It's been a great trial for her, but she has borne it bravely. She's a true trouper."

I sneaked a quick glance at her. I got the impression that Lady Aysgarth didn't treat Miss Short too well, but here she was giving her glowing praise. I wondered how old she was. The face was ageless, the bobbed hair tinged with a hint of gray.

"What did you do before you came to Lady Aysgarth?"

"I had a little tea shop," she said and her face was quite transformed. "Such a pretty little place. I put the money my father left me into setting it up. In Harrowgate, you know. Such a nice, refined town. And for a while it was doing well. But then came the time of the general strike, of people out of work and I could no longer make a go of it.

I got behind on the rent and I had to close. Such a blow. And I had lived in a little flat above it, so I had nowhere to go. When I saw the advert for a lady's companion it seemed like an answer to a prayer. Of course it's not an ideal life — rather lonely, except when we have guests. I don't have a chance to make many friends and I sort of fall between, if you know what I mean."

I could imagine. "Not a servant and yet not Lady Aysgarth's class either?"

"Exactly. When we have guests and I'd like to join in the conversation I have to remind myself that nobody is interested in what I have to say. But when we're alone Lady A. and I play canasta and do the crossword and get on splendidly."

I didn't know what else to say. I too had been a hanger-on, an unwanted extra person at my brother's place. I had not enjoyed the feeling.

The house appeared through the trees in front of us. I saw that there were people standing in the forecourt and recognized Darcy among them.

"Have you found her yet?" I asked, getting out of the car.

He came over to me. "Not yet. I don't know where she can have got to. We'd all wandered off in different directions and then the children got cold and it started snowing harder and someone said they had had enough and let's go back. It was then that Miss Short asked where my aunt was. And nobody could recall seeing her for some time. So we searched and called, then we came back here. I can't think where she could have got to."

"I hope she hasn't fallen or put her foot into a rabbit hole or something," I said.

"But then she would have heard us shouting and responded, wouldn't she?"

"I suppose so. What's going to happen now?"

"Binky and I thought we'd go out looking again. Fig and the major's wife say they are too cold. So are the children."

"I'd like to help search." Miss Short came around the Bentley to join us. "Count me in."

"Should we bring a couple of dogs with us?" Binky asked. "They'd find her quickly enough."

"I was worried that dogs might run into the line of fire, with the shooting going on," Miss Short said, looking around nervously.

"It's over now, I think," I said. "I know the king came home." A worrying thought had now occurred to me. "It's not possible that she wandered into the area of the shoot, is it?"

"That would be dashed stupid," Miss Short said. "She knows her way around here better than most. She would have known where they were shooting."

"Perhaps one becomes disoriented in the snow," I suggested.

"Oh God. I hope nothing's happened to her." Miss Short gave a distressed wail.

"Let's take the motorcar," I said. "We can cover more ground that way."

Darcy and Binky got into the front seat with Miss Short and me in the back. We drove until we came to the place where Miss Short had startled me, appearing suddenly from the trees. We left the car and followed her tracks back into the woodland; at least I let the others go ahead while I stayed close to the motorcar. My feet were already cold and wet enough. After half an hour of tramping around we realized it was hopeless. Many tracks crisscrossed and now a new layer of snow was falling. What we didn't find was any sign of a person. We made our way back to the car.

"We should drive to Sandringham and ask if their beaters and dogs can be spared to look for her," Binky said. "I'm sure they know this ground like the back of their hands."

"Won't they still be at the shoot?" Darcy asked.

"I said the shoot is probably over. The king came home," I said, not wanting to tell them that somebody had taken aim at the Prince of Wales.

"Then that would be a good idea," Darcy said. We drove toward the estate.

I found I was shivering, partly from the cold, since I was wearing my smart clothes and court shoes rather than tweed trews and wellies, but also partly from nerves. If they had to bring out the dogs, who knew what they would find? I tried to shut the image of a bloodstained body lying in the snow from my mind. Memories of that Christmas in Devonshire kept creeping back — that awful Christmas when so many people were found dead and I might well have joined them. Why, oh why, did we agree to come here? We could have been enjoying a quiet Christmas at home with Binky's children, and Mummy and Granddad. Instead I was now involved in another royal intrigue and in less than one day we had a missing hostess. Hardly ingredients for a jolly holiday.

"Why don't you go and ask them, Georgie," Darcy said. "You're the one who is on pally terms with them all."

Oh gosh, I thought but managed not to

say. This was not a good time to intrude. But perhaps I'd only have to see the estate manager and he'd set things going. As I got out of the car someone was coming around the side of the house, carrying a hamper. I looked across and to my surprise it was Lady Aysgarth.

"Hello, you lot," she called. "What perfect timing. I was about to ask the gamekeeper to run me home in the shooting brake. So I can squeeze in with you."

Miss Short wound down her window. "What in God's name are you doing here?" she called angrily. "You gave us the fright of our lives. We've all been searching the woods in the freezing weather for you."

"Oh dear. I am so sorry," Darcy's aunt replied. "It never occurred to me that you would worry. I was trying to find a good patch of holly I'd noticed once before but I must have walked past it somehow when suddenly a pheasant fell from the sky right in front of me. I waited, but no dogs appeared, so I thought it shouldn't go to waste. I picked it up and headed for where the shots were coming from." She opened the back door, making Miss Short scoot into the middle, while she took her place, with the basket on her knees. "Didn't the major tell you where I was? I know he saw me."

"The major hadn't returned home when we started out," Darcy said.

Lady Aysgarth frowned. "That's strange. I was sure he had left. The shoot was called off some time ago. After a little incident, in fact."

"What kind of incident?" Darcy asked, his voice suddenly sharp.

"Well, my dears" — Lady Aysgarth leaned forward, thrusting her face between Binky and Darcy — "I arrived to find everything in turmoil. It seems the Prince of Wales had a lucky escape. Someone fired at him."

"Someone took a potshot at the Prince of Wales?" Darcy asked sharply. "Was he hurt?"

"He didn't seem to be."

"Did they find out who did it?" Darcy's tone was still sharp.

Lady Aysgarth shrugged. "It didn't seem to be anybody in the shooting party, or at least nobody would own up to it. Poachers were suggested. My own inclination would be the king."

"The king? Shooting at his own son?" Binky asked in horror.

"Oh, not deliberately, of course. But his hands have become shaky recently and he does have these bouts of weakness. Maybe his arms could have fallen just as he pulled

157

the trigger. Anyway, he was the most shaken up of any of them. So naturally I went along to accompany him back to the house. Men are useless on such occasions, aren't they? They never know the right things to say. Present company excepted, of course. And I made sure he was safely delivered to the care of his wife." She looked around for confirmation of this good deed. "Well, they were all terribly grateful and I've come away with a basket of pheasant to add to our festivities. How about that?"

"How about it, indeed?" Darcy said. "Really, Aunt Ermintrude — why is it that things seem to happen to you?"

"It runs in the family, dear boy. Haven't you noticed? We are the sort of family that things happen to."

That was when I remembered that Lady Hawse-Gorzley, my hostess at that other disastrous Christmas, was also Darcy's aunt. And the words rattled around inside my head. Darcy was a member of the family that things happened to.

The moment we pulled up outside Wymondham Hall and the others had gone into the house, Binky now carrying the basket of pheasants, Darcy grabbed my arm and pulled me close to him. "Did you hear anything about that — someone shooting the Prince of Wales?"

"I was there when it happened," I said. "David burst in on the queen and me. He was livid, but the queen was clearly upset and worried. He just thought it was a stupid carelessness on someone's behalf, but she wasn't so sure. She's rather worried, Darcy."

Darcy's face was grim. "It was shotgun pellets, not a bullet, then?"

"It was. One brushed against his shoulder and another got the brim of his hat. Luckily he was wearing stout clothing or it could have been worse."

Darcy hesitated, looking past me, out to the bare branches of the woodland. "I suppose we have to take it as an accident, then, or a silly prank. If someone really intended him harm, they would have used something more powerful." He paused again, staring out, thinking. "Look," he said, "I think I had better go and have a word with the prince's equerry — maybe make a couple of telephone calls. If I'm late for lunch, please present my apologies."

"What should I tell them?"

"That I was looking for a last-minute Christmas gift for my wife?" He gave me that disarming grin, kissed me and got into the motorcar.

CHAPTER 14

December 24
Wymondham Hall, Norfolk

Finally I hope it will feel a little more like
Christmas. No more drama, please. I
want to be able to enjoy myself.

I felt cold and miserable as I changed out
of my silky blouse and and into a warm
jumper, and put on a pair of dry stockings
and house shoes. I certainly hadn't been
dressed properly for tramping through snow
for hours and the added worry had made
me feel quite sick. I had had enough of
drama in my life. I wanted things to run
smoothly. Surely the episode with the Prince
of Wales had been an unlucky accident,
nothing more. But I had to remind myself
there were people in the world who would
make it their mission to kill the heir to the
British throne — Irish republicans, Russian

communists, anarchists. Darcy was obviously thinking along these lines. But then, as Darcy pointed out, they would have used a bullet to do the job properly, not bird shot. If you wanted to kill someone with a shotgun, it would have to be at very close range. After a few yards the shot disperses enough to make killing someone unreliable. No, the shooting had to have come from one of that group and had to have been accidental. I thought the explanation of the king suddenly being too weak to hold up the gun was the best one. And naturally nobody was going to admit to that truth.

I brushed my hair, put on a little lipstick and a dab of rouge, as I thought I looked rather pale, and went down, hoping that luncheon would be served soon. I was jolly hungry, even though I had enjoyed a hearty breakfast. Maybe it was the shock of the morning. I came out of my bedroom to find the major coming along the hall toward me. Remembering his behavior the night before I was about to dart in again but he entered his room without appearing to notice me. I continued down the stairs. Lady Aysgarth was sitting by the fire in the drawing room with the dogs around her feet. They greeted me, wagging tails as I came in, then surrounded me when I took a seat. I found myself with three furry heads on my lap.

"If they are bothering you, just push them away," Lady Aysgarth said.

"Oh no, I love dogs," I said. "I grew up with them. I've missed having one for some time now. I'm hoping to get one now that we've a home of our own."

"My yellow Lab bitch, Tilly, has just had pups," she said. "If you want one, it's yours."

"Golly, how lovely." I looked up from stroking the two golden retrievers and the black Lab. "I was planning to give Darcy a dog as a Christmas present but I thought I'd have to wait until we returned home. Now I can surprise him on the actual day."

"They are in the gardener's cottage if you want to take a look. The gardener's wife is taking care of them, away from the hustle and bustle. Sweet little things. I believe she had eight, so you've a good choice."

"Do you mind if I go and see them right away?" I asked.

"Feel free. Luncheon won't be for at least another half an hour."

I got up again. The dogs looked hopeful, but I shook my head. "You have to stay home. You'd only bother the new mother."

I put on my coat and scarf and this time I changed into my wellies before walking around the house to a small cottage at the edge of a field. Smoke was curling up from the chimney and the cottage had a picture-book feel to it. I knocked, and was greeted by the gardener's wife, who led me into a small kitchen–living room already decorated with a tiny Christmas tree and strung with paper chains. The room was full of the scent of baking. The gardener's wife wished me the compliments of the season and offered me a cup of tea and a slice of gingerbread, fresh from the oven. I accepted the former because it would be rude to refuse but told her I was about to eat lunch. She seemed thrilled that I was going to take one of the puppies. "Dear little things they are too. And their mum — you've never met a more good-natured beast in your life." She took me through to a scullery and there was the mother lying on an old blanket with her puppies around her. They were all adorable — still tiny and lying side by side as they nursed. Three of them were black and the rest light gold. I knelt down beside them, stroking the mother's head.

"They won't be ready to go home for a week or so yet," the gardener's wife said, "but if you're staying until New Year's, I reckon you can take one with you then. Do you have a favorite?"

"It's hard to tell at the moment," I said.

"They look like a row of little sausages, don't they?"

"They do indeed, my lady." The gardener's wife laughed heartily.

"Do you think I could bring one over to the house tomorrow to show my husband?" I asked. "I'd like it to be his Christmas present."

"I don't see why not, if you keep it nice and warm inside your coat. Do you want a boy or a girl?"

"I don't really mind."

"Better get a boy if you don't want to worry about puppies all the time and have all the dogs in the neighborhood bothering her."

"Oh right. Good idea." We exchanged a smile.

"Do you have children of your own who will be thrilled about a dog?" she asked.

"Not yet. I'm newly married," I said, "but I'm hoping soon." I hoped my voice didn't betray that I had started to worry about this.

"Enjoy the peace and quiet while you can. I've had four boys." She took down one of the best cups from the dresser and poured me tea. It was stronger than I like but we sat at her kitchen table while I drank it. She told me her husband had gone to get the goose for tomorrow and her grown-up boys would be joining them with their wives. As I left again I was struck how country folk seem to enjoy their simple lives and how much importance we attach to unnecessary things like status.

As I returned to the house Darcy was just pulling up in the Bentley. "So I made it back in time for lunch after all. Where have you been?" he asked.

"Oh, just for a little walk around outside. Fresh air, you know."

"I thought you'd had enough fresh air looking for my batty aunt," Darcy said. "You said you were freezing."

"I was until I put on warmer clothes," I replied. I hated lying to him, but I wanted the dog to be a surprise. "Now I'm starving." I walked beside him toward the front door. "Did you learn anything?"

"Not much. If they know who accidentally discharged a firearm, they are not letting on. But I tell you one thing. They are a bit jumpy. It seemed there were a couple of palace retainers killed this time last year. One stableboy spoke of a curse on the estate."

"That's cheerful," I said. "Does Wymondham Hall count as part of the estate?"

"I'm rather afraid it does." He grinned. "So did the major finally show up?"

"He did. I encountered him on the up-stairs corridor. He didn't seem to notice me and dashed into his room."

"That's interesting," Darcy said "According to the chaps at Sandringham he bowed out hours ago. Left them to clean up. They weren't pleased." He hesitated, then smiled. "Probably nipped to the nearest pub for a quick one."

"Or to see the barmaid," I added.

"What makes you say that?"

"I get the feeling he's a ladies' man," I replied, not wanting to disclose his advances from the night before. "And his wife has that long-suffering look."

"You'll probably develop that before too long." He laughed, put his arm around me and steered me back into the building.

The company was now gathered in the drawing room. Sherry had been poured. I helped myself to a glass. There were also hot sausage rolls and cheese straws. Most satisfactory. I wondered if Queenie had been responsible for making either. Pastry was her forte. Major Legge-Horne came to join us and received a cold look from his wife. He seemed almost too jolly, as if he was trying to put on an act and didn't mention the prince's accident, if it was an accident. I found myself observing him. Was it possible that he had anything to do with that? But then what reason could he have for wanting the Prince of Wales out of the way?

At that moment Mrs. Simpson came into the room. She paused, looking around with a disgruntled frown on her face. "Sherry?" Lady Aysgarth pointed to the tray. "Sausage roll?"

Mrs. Simpson gave an audible sigh. "You English and your eternal sherry," she said. "All that sugar. No wonder you have bad teeth."

"I'm sure we could find you a Scotch and soda if you'd prefer," Darcy's aunt said amiably enough.

Mrs. Simpson shook her head. "I'll wait for wine with the meal. I know David sent over some decent bottles." She went to the fireplace and sank into one of the armchairs. "What a dreary place this is. No civilization for miles. And to think we left Saint Moritz for this. If I'd known he'd be spending every moment with Mummy and Daddy, I think I'd have stayed in Switzerland."

It was extremely rude to say this in front of the hostess, but Lady Aysgarth took it in her stride. "Buck up," she said. "After luncheon we're going to be decorating the house and the tree. And I believe some of the farm children will be coming by to sing

Christmas carols."

"Goody, goody," Mrs. Simpson said flatly. For the hundredth time I wondered what he could see in her. "I could have stayed at the Dorchester if I'd known he wouldn't be allowed to escape."

"There's still time," Mummy said sweetly. "I'm sure there are trains from King's Lynn."

Mrs. Simpson shot her a dagger's look.

I realized, of course, that Mrs. Simpson had not been told about David's brush with death.

"You have to realize that the prince's first duty is to his family at Christmastime," Binky said. "Especially with the king being so ill."

"So ill that he could go out shooting things," she said. "How poor David must be suffering. Stuck with that dreary family all telling him what a monster I am and how they'd like him to marry a twenty-year-old virgin princess. And that awful Cookie muttering lies about me."

" 'Cookie'?" Lady Aysgarth asked.

Mrs. Simpson gave a patronizing smirk. "You know, the chubby little duchess of York, Bertie's wife. You've never seen anyone look so disapproving any time I enter the room. And of course Shirley Temple, who can do no wrong in their eyes."

" 'Shirley Temple'?" Fig asked. "You mean the film star?"

"I mean the older princess," Mrs. Simpson said. "Shirley Temple is what David calls her. Because she's so perfect and the king thinks the sun shines out of her head. Ghastly child. We much prefer the younger one. At least she's got spirit, even if she is terribly naughty."

There was a sort of embarrassed silence in the room, as if everyone was thinking that an American outsider had no right to criticize our royal family. We were heartily glad when Heslop appeared to announce "Luncheon is served."

"Let's be quite informal this time and sit anywhere we choose," Lady Aysgarth said. I knew exactly what she was thinking. She wanted no unpleasantness about where to put Mrs. Simpson in the procession into the meal. Certainly not at the head.

CHAPTER 15

Christmas Eve
Wymondham Hall, Norfolk

It's been a lovely afternoon. Just how I
imagined it would be. Now we can put
all that ghastly worry behind us.

Luncheon was a simple affair — a hearty
game soup followed by baked apples. Just
right after a morning in the cold air. When
we had finished our coffee, Lady Aysgarth
stood up. "Now, who is ready for an afternoon of decorating? Darcy, would you take
the duke, find James and bring in the
Christmas tree? It's standing ready outside
the scullery door."

"Of course." The two men left the room
ahead of the rest of us. "And you go and
get the tree decorations, Shortie," Lady Aysgarth said. "They are in the attic, right
beside the stairs. Be careful how you pull

down that staircase, won't you? It does surprise one sometimes."

"It's surprised me more than once," Miss Short said, "but I've learned how to stand out of the way now."

"Do you want some help?" I asked, being the youngest woman present.

"That's awfully kind of you, your ladyship," Miss Short said. "I'm sure I can manage alone."

"I don't mind at all," I said. "You'll need someone to hand the boxes down to."

"You're right. And you are so tall. You'll be able to reach up better than I." She gave me a grateful smile. I followed her up the first flight of stairs and then a second, humbler one with stained wood instead of carpet on the treads. Along the hallway I heard young voices. That would be Podge and Addy in their nursery. I decided to bring them down to help decorate. I had fond memories of decorating the tree at home.

The hall in the other direction was bathed in darkness. Miss Short paused in the middle and looked up. "Ah yes. Here it is," she said and took a pole with a hook on it from where it had been leaning against the wall. "I'm glad you came along, my lady," she said. "It's such a stretch for me to catch the little loop."

She handed me the pole and pointed up to the ceiling, where there was a wooden panel with a rope loop on it. I reached up and managed to snag the loop.

"Careful," she warned. "You'd better let me pull it. I know how it works. I suggest you stand out of the way."

She took the pole and gave a sharp tug. The stairs tumbled open with a clatter.

"See," she said. "You wouldn't want to be standing in the wrong spot when they fell down."

She went ahead of me cautiously, one step at a time, into the blackness of the attic. I followed a couple of steps behind.

"So much interesting stuff up here," she called down. "An absolute treasure trove. Vases, statues, lamps, mirrors. Of course we are only renting, so they don't belong to us unfortunately. Ah, here is the box labeled *Christmas Ornaments.* It's quite heavy. Can I pass it down to you?"

I took the box from her and rested it on the top step as I made my way down. Miss Short descended, then lifted the steps until a spring took them up and she pushed the trapdoor shut with the pole.

"Well, that's that, then." She insisted on taking the box from me and went ahead down the stairs, while I hurried along the hall to rescue my nephew and niece from their nursery. They were excited when I told them what we were about to do and Addy skipped all the way to the stairs.

"Make sure you behave well and don't touch anything you're not supposed to," I whispered as we went down the stairs to the drawing room, where the men had now set up the big Christmas tree in the corner.

"Here they are now!" Lady Aysgarth clapped her hands and sounded quite excited. "Come and see what we are doing, children." They came forward shyly, as children always do when thrust into a room full of strange adults. Darcy's aunt was kneeling beside the table, unwrapping one item after another. She looked up like a child who has been given a special present. "At least I brought my favorite Christmas ornaments from my old home. That rascally Harold will have to make do with his own. And some of mine are quite lovely. I believe my parents bought them in Germany when they used to tour Europe in the good old days before the Great War."

Items were placed one by one on a low table. They were indeed lovely — tiny hand-blown musical instruments that really sounded clear notes, carved wooden angels and candleholders that clipped to branches. A miniature crib set and funny little German people in national costume: a chimney sweep, a man carrying a Christmas tree, a woman carrying a loaf of bread.

"We should put the star on top first, don't you think, Darcy?" she said, handing him a lovely glass star. Darcy obliged by standing on a stepladder and fixing it to the top branch.

"Then the lights," Darcy's aunt instructed. "We won't be using those lovely old candleholders. Too much risk of fire and the lights do a perfectly good job, even though real candles are lovely."

Binky passed one end of the strand up to Darcy and between them they wound lights around the tree.

"Now it's all hands on deck," Lady Aysgarth said.

I encouraged the children to go forward and helped them put some of the funny little people onto lower branches as well as some of the smaller glass balls. The finishing touch was a draping of tinsel; and when the lights were plugged in, there was a collective "Ah!" from all assembled. Addy jumped up and down, clapping her hands.

"And who is going to come tonight, if you are good?" Lady Aysgarth asked.

"Father Christmas!" the children chimed in together.

Seeing her face with them I thought it was such a shame that she hadn't had children of her own. Some people are made to be mothers; others, like Fig, could not have been less interested. I knew I was dying to be a mother. The thought flashed through my head — what if I couldn't have children, like Darcy's aunt? It's only been a few months, I told myself.

"Now, on to decorating the house," Lady Aysgarth said. "James — the greenery is waiting out in the scullery. And bring some twine."

"Very good, my lady." The footman went out.

While we waited I looked around to see that we were not all assembled after all. Mrs. Simpson was not present. Neither was Mummy. Both women had a knack of vanishing when there might be any kind of work. The basket of greenery was brought in, and we spent another hour trailing ivy up the banister, decorating the mantelpieces, the portraits and door lintels with holly and other shiny green leaves. Candles were placed on windowsills and tables. Finally a sprig of mistletoe was hung from the chandelier in the entrance hall.

"Lovely. Lovely. Good job, everyone," Lady Aysgarth said. "I think we all deserve some tea, don't you?" She rang the bell and a trolley was wheeled in, containing tea things as well as plates of shortbread and small cakes. With her unerring sense of timing my mother appeared.

"Doesn't the room look lovely," she said. "You have done a good job. Full marks all around." And she helped herself to a generous plate of cakes.

The children were allowed to stay down for tea and came to sit beside me in one of the big chairs.

"Auntie Georgie, do you think Father Christmas knows we're not at home?" Podge asked, a worried look on his little face.

Fig gave Binky an exasperated sigh. "Isn't it about time that child learned the truth?" she said in a low voice that I could overhear. "He'll be the laughingstock if he goes to school still believing in silly fairy stories."

Binky shook his head. "Fig, you are sometimes an absolutely wet blanket," he said. "Let them make the most of their childhood, for heaven's sake. It goes by fast enough as it is."

I thought back to my own childhood. Castle Rannoch had been remote and lonely most of the time. No other children to play with, except Binky, ten years older, who came home from school for holidays. Luckily my nanny had been the kindest of souls and let me believe in Father Christmas for as long as I wanted. I think I secretly knew the truth long before I admitted it, but I didn't want to spoil it for her!

We were still enjoying our tea when the butler appeared at the door with a discreet cough. "The Prince of Wales, my lady," he said. And my cousin David came into the room.

"My, my. What a jolly scene," he said. "So much nicer than that dreary place I've just come from." He looked around. "Where is Wallis?"

"Taking a nap, I believe," Lady Aysgarth said. "Would you like me to send someone to wake her for you?"

"No need. I'll go and wake her myself," he said. "Don't worry. I know the way."

And we heard him bounding up the stairs, calling, "Wallis. Wake up. Your prince has come for you."

Glances were exchanged around the room but nothing was said. The heir to the throne rushing up to a lady's bedroom might have happened many times before in our history but never so obviously. Major and Mrs.

Legge-Horne shook their heads and rolled their eyes.

The prince came down a few minutes later. "She'll be down in a while," he said. "She's got one of her headaches."

"Oh, I'm so sorry," Lady Aysgarth said. "Should we send up a cup of tea?"

"No, thanks. Let her be. Much better." He grinned. "In truth I think she's having a little sulk because I didn't come to visit this morning. But the old man wanted us to go out and shoot so I had to go along."

"And you bagged some fine pheasants, sir," Lady Aysgarth said.

"Oh yes. Jolly fine." He didn't mention that he had also almost been bagged. In fact when Podge and Addy had been beckoned to join their father, the prince slid onto the arm of my chair. "Don't mention what happened this morning, if you don't mind," he muttered to me. "I'd rather keep things like that from Wallis. She does tend to worry."

"Of course, sir."

He patted my shoulder. "You're a good egg, little cousin. And you've chosen a good chap too. You don't know how much I envy you your quiet settled life. I already know there will be hell to pay if I try to marry Wallis." Then one of those charming grins he was so famous for. "Of course, if we wait until I'm king, I can do anything I bloody well like, can't I?"

Mrs. Simpson finally made an appearance, looking pale and long-suffering. I offered her my chair. David perched on the arm beside her.

"David. Get me a cigarette, honey," she said.

Again there was a discernible gasp from those who hadn't seen her behave this way before. Not only bossing him around but calling him by his first name instead of "sir." The heir to the biggest empire the world has ever known jumped up and went to find her cigarettes.

"Should we not think about changing for dinner?" Major Legge-Horne asked. But at that moment there was a knock at the front door and then children's voices could be heard singing "Away in a Manger."

"Bring them in. Bring them in," Lady Aysgarth called; and the group of children, their cheeks red from the cold, came in, looking extremely shy and nervous. "All right. Off you go. Let's hear some carols from you," Lady Aysgarth said.

They shuffled their feet and looked at one another before the bravest began "O Little Town of Bethlehem." Only they called it

"Beflehem." It was very sweet and I think we were all touched. Then they launched into "Good King Wenceslas" and finally "We Wish You a Merry Christmas." Lady A. nodded to the servants, who brought out mince pies and sugar mice. One for each child. They seemed too overawed to eat and they retreated faster than they had come in.

"So sweet," Lady Aysgarth said. "They do this every year. It puts one into the spirit of Christmas, doesn't it?"

"It certainly does, doesn't it, Fig?" Binky said heartily.

"I hope none of those children were infectious," Fig said. "Did you notice that boy on the end with the runny nose?"

"They've just come in from the cold, old thing," Binky said. "Anybody's nose would run."

Darcy caught my eye and winked.

"I thought they were absolutely charming," Mrs. Legge-Horne said. "Makes one nostalgic."

"Do you have children?" Dolly Huntley asked.

"Two boys. Now quite grown up and in the army themselves," Mrs. Legge-Horne replied, looking more animated than I had seen her. "I felt I never saw enough of them — up in the nursery and then off to boarding school at seven. We moved around a lot in those days, of course, and it would not have been healthy to take them to India."

"I can't see this English custom of shipping your kids off to school at a young age," Colonel Huntley said.

"But then we didn't have children, did we, Homer?" Dolly asked sweetly. "You might well have wanted to ship them off."

"Homer — what an interesting name," the prince said. "Were your parents classicists?"

"Were they what?" Colonel Huntley looked confused.

"Students of the classics. *The Iliad,* don't you know?"

Suddenly Colonel Huntley understood. "Oh Homer. I get it. No, my dad was a baseball fan. I'm named after home runs." And he burst out laughing. We all joined in and that seemed to put the company into a good mood as we went up to change. The prince had taken his leave shortly after the carolers had departed.

"I'm afraid I have to trot along now, Trudy, old girl," he said to Darcy's aunt. "Duty calls and all that. I am required to join the family for Christmas Eve celebrations, including the lighting of the candles on the tree — passed down from our great-grandparents Prince Albert and Queen Victoria." I found myself picturing that scene. "My family," I whispered to myself. My great-grandmother and -father. Sometimes it didn't seem real, especially when I had been struggling to survive alone on tea and toast. How I would have loved to meet them, even though I'd have been scared stiff of her.

"And tomorrow?" Mrs. Simpson asked coldly.

The prince went red. "Ah, well, tomorrow is absolutely set in stone. Tradition, don't you know. Church. Lunch. The old boy's speech. Family games. Two little nieces being adorable and being fawned over. No escape, I'm afraid. I am required to play the dutiful son. Mama was heavy-handed with the guilt — it might be my father's last Christmas and since he enjoyed it so much, it was up to us to bring him every ounce of happiness."

He gave Mrs. Simpson an appealing look, begging her to understand.

"So I might as well have stayed in Switzerland," she said angrily. "I expect I could have found plenty of attractive men who'd want to ski with me."

"Don't be like that, Wallis. Not much longer now, you know." He touched her shoulder, then went over to Aunt Ermintrude and shook her hand. "Take good care of her, won't you?" he asked.

"So there is not to be your usual hunt on Boxing Day?" Darcy's aunt asked the prince.

"Afraid not. My mother wants minimal excitement and few outsiders. We may go out to shoot if His Majesty feels up to it in the coming days. But as for Boxing Day, I plan to go out riding early. Maybe follow the general route the hunt would have taken." Suddenly he spun around to address me. "So what about it, Georgie? And Darcy? Are you up for a morning gallop?"

I said, "I'd love to," at the same time as Darcy said, "I'm sorry, but I didn't bring any riding gear."

"Oh, in that case," I began, but Darcy put a hand on my arm.

"You go and enjoy it. How long is it since you've had a decent ride? There are enough horses, I take it, sir?"

"Oh yes. A good selection of splendid mounts. Anyone else?"

"I'm not sure . . ." Binky began.

Fig cut him off. "The children will expect you to be here. It is Boxing Day, after all. How often do they have a chance to play with you?"

Binky went pink and said no more.

"I might join you," the major said.

"Oh, Reggie, how long since you've ridden? Properly ridden, I mean, not a trot down a bridle path. You're not as fit as you used to be," his wife said.

"Nonsense. Fit as a fiddle. I did join the hunt last year, remember."

"Then don't blame me if you fall off like that poor chap last year," she said. "I don't want to have to arrange for your funeral."

On that happy note the prince left and we went up to change.

As we came down to dinner Darcy's aunt did not look happy. "That woman," she muttered to Darcy and me. "I lent her my maid and she hasn't returned her. I had to try and fasten my own dress. I had to call in Miss Short."

Mrs. Simpson appeared, looking terribly haute couture but clearly displeased at having been abandoned by her beau.

"Perhaps you'd care to accompany Mrs. Simpson into dinner, Your Grace," Lady Aysgarth said to Mummy, who was also looking perfect and glamorous, in spite of having no maid.

I held my breath, waiting for the answer. I had expected to hear she would rather accompany a hungry alligator, but Mummy smiled sweetly. "Anything to avoid a scene," she said. "Come, Wallis. We can be two abandoned women together."

If looks could kill, Mummy would have been lying on the floor at that moment, but Mrs. Simpson fell into line behind Binky and Fig. We took up our places behind them and we processed through to the dining room. We had already strung greenery around the walls; but since we saw it last the room had been transformed with sparkling chandeliers on the tables and candles on the windowsills, sideboard and mantelpiece. The well-worn furniture had suddenly become magical and I felt a twinge of excitement that this was indeed Christmas Eve.

The dinner was another simple one, a leek and potato soup followed by pheasant in a red wine reduction, and a puree of potato and swede, baked in the oven until the top was crisp. Simple but satisfying! As was the apple and blackberry crumble that followed with cream. And the port and cheeses after that. Even Mrs. Simpson didn't complain.

"I should probably give you the rundown for tomorrow," Lady Aysgarth said after we had repaired to the drawing room for coffee. The Christmas tree lights had been switched on, candles on the windowsills and mantelpiece had been lit and the room looked quite different with the sparkle and firelight. The sweet smell of fresh pine hung in the air. "Breakfast as usual, but let's make it snappy so that we have time to open presents. We have to be at Saint Mary Magdalene Church on the estate for the morning service that the royal family attends. We must leave by ten o'clock at the latest."

"What time is the service?" Fig asked.

"Eleven."

"Surely it won't take us an hour to get across the estate?" Fig insisted. "The children will want to have time to enjoy their presents."

Lady Aysgarth frowned. "Don't forget that it will be on Sandringham time. Half an hour early."

"There is a separate time zone for the royal family?" Dolly asked.

Lady Aysgarth smiled. "No, it's just a royal custom to keep all the clocks half an hour fast at Sandringham. Therefore the church service will really be at half past ten."

"Perhaps we should put off opening presents until we return after the service," Fig suggested.

"That will be cutting it fine for luncheon at one o'clock," Darcy's aunt said.

"Lunch at one? Isn't that a tad early?"

Colonel Huntley asked. "We normally have our Christmas feast at two or three."

"Ah, but we have to be done with the meal and ready to listen to the king's speech at three," Lady Aysgarth said.

"We have to go over to the big house with the royals?" Dolly asked, sounding both excited and nervous.

Darcy's aunt shook her head. "He broadcasts to the empire from Sandringham at three o'clock and we listen on the wireless."

"So it doesn't really matter if we listen or not," Mrs. Simpson said with a smirk.

"Not listen to the king's speech?" Miss Short almost squeaked out the words. She had been sitting quietly on the window seat, and frankly we had all forgotten about her.

Mrs. Simpson was still giving that patronizing smile she reserved for people who crossed her. "It's not like he will ever know."

"But I would know," Lady Aysgarth said coldly. "I know this is not your country, but we are bound by our traditions and woe betide anyone who tries to break them." She made it quite clear whom she was talking about. So clear that Mrs. Simpson announced that her headache had returned and if we'd excuse her, she'd be going up to bed. And not to be surprised if she didn't join us for church in the morning. There would be photographers.

"It sounds like a day in the army," Mrs. Legge-Horne said after Mrs. Simpson had made her exit. "Talk about regimented. Breakfast at oh six hundred hours. Walk to church at oh seven hundred and a half . . ."

Everyone laughed except the major.

"How many times do I have to tell you, Mildred? I've explained military time terminology to you. Please try to get it right."

"As if it matters," Mrs. Legge-Horne said. "It's not as if you're in the army now."

"I think maybe you are right," Fig said, looking at Binky for confirmation. "We should all try to get up early and open gifts before church."

"Won't the children be opening their stockings in the nursery?" I asked. "That's half the fun, sitting up in bed and finding what's in the stocking."

"The stockings are only for small gifts," Fig said. "We have a couple of bigger ones that wouldn't fit. They can have those around the tree in the drawing room with everyone else."

The party broke up soon afterward with another reminder from Darcy's aunt to be up bright and early. I handed Binky and Fig the presents to be put in their children's stockings and Binky said he was going to creep in with a white beard on so that if they woke up they would think it was Father Christmas in person.

"My brother is a nice person," I whispered to Darcy as we went up the stairs.

"It runs in the family." He slipped his arm around my waist and was about to lead me upstairs when he looked up, then suddenly grabbed me.

"What is it?" I asked, alarmed.

"One should always take advantage of mistletoe, don't you think?" he said and kissed me.

When we reached our bedroom there was no sign of Queenie so I asked Darcy to unhook my dress. I was just about to pull the frock over my head when I heard a terrible noise. A scream, a shout, a cry of pain. We rushed out of the room, Darcy ahead of me. It was coming from the other side of the landing at the far end of the hall. Other doors were opening as we ran past.

"What's up? What's happening?" people called.

Darcy flung open the door at the far end of the hall and was met with an extraordinary sight. A headless person was blundering around, waving arms in panic, while Queenie stood beside it, a look of horror on her face.

"I didn't mean it," she said quickly. "She asked me to unzip her dress and lift it over her head. But it's stuck somehow."

By now I had recognized the Paris couture of Mrs. Simpson and rather a lot of her legs, including an unflattering glimpse of a suspender. Darcy and I came to the rescue, trying to lift off the dress, which made her scream even louder. From under the layers we heard, "That idiot girl. She's got my hair caught in the zipper."

With difficulty we lowered the dress back to its original position until her red and angry face appeared, her makeup smudged in an unappealing manner and a large chunk of her hair caught in a now closed zip, effectively yanking her head back. It took a while and rather choice language before she was finally free.

"What were you doing, anyway, Queenie?" I asked.

"She asked me," Queenie said, sticking her chin out in a stubborn manner. "I was coming up to see if you needed help, like we said, and she came up and said, 'You, girl. Are you a maid?' and I said I was and she said, 'Good. You can help me undress.' So I did. But that frock wasn't like anything I'd seen before. Zips here and zips there. I didn't realize there was a second zip fastener under the arm and I tried to open it as it went over her head and then her hair got stuck in it and the more I pulled the more she yelled."

"I think you'd better apologize to the lady and go," I said.

"Bob's yer uncle," she said, not looking too remorseful. "Sorry if I took your dress off wrong, missus. I ain't never seen anything like it. If you ask me, you should get yourself a new dressmaker. Someone who knows what they are doing."

Mrs. Simpson's eyes were flashing dangerously. "A new dressmaker. My dear girl, this is a Schiaparelli." The glare turned to me and she pointed in dramatic fashion. "Get her out of my sight and don't let her ever come near me again, do you hear?"

As Darcy and I walked back to our room he whispered to me, "I don't think you could have done that any better if you'd orchestrated the whole thing, could you?"

I smiled.

CHAPTER 16

Christmas Day
Wymondham Hall, Norfolk

I woke at first light, and for a moment I wondered where I was. Then I remembered. It was Christmas Day. All the memories of childhood — waking to see a stocking or pillowcase beside the bed, full of gifts, and to know that Father Christmas had been. I even raised my head and looked around, stupidly hoping that a stocking had been left for me. Of course it hadn't. As Podge had worried yesterday, Father Christmas wouldn't know where to find me. I smiled at that silly thought, then turned to look at Darcy. As if sensing my gaze he opened his eyes, focused on me and smiled. "Happy Christmas," he said.

I bent to kiss him. His arms came around me. The kiss turned a little more intense and for a while there were no more words spoken.

"Was that my Christmas present?" he asked, laughing.

"We'll have to see if you've been good or not," I teased. "I might have a lump of coal for you. And as to your present, I don't have it right now, but I know what it will be."

"Same here," Darcy said. "I know what I want to give you, but I haven't brought it with me."

"I understand. That's all right," I said, although I did have an absurd feeling of disappointment that I wouldn't have a gift to open. Never mind. It was going to be a fun day and the best part was that I wasn't in charge of arranging any of it. I debated what I should wear, then decided that Christmas should be duly celebrated. So I opted for the family tartan kilt, with a frilly white blouse and my long gray cashmere cardigan over it. Darcy had changed yesterday's tweeds for a formal suit.

"I think we'll do, don't you?" I said. "Frankly I was surprised when I met your aunt. She looked — well, the sort of person who would have been Queen Mary's lady-in-waiting. I had expected her to look like an artist with flowing robes and turbans."

"Funny, but that is exactly how I remember her," he said. "Bright colors and scarves and things. Definitely bohemian. She has obviously become more subdued as she has aged."

We came downstairs to find we were the first ones up and placed our gifts under the Christmas tree. I gave a small sigh of relief that I had brought enough boxes of chocolate liqueurs for everyone except Miss Short. But I had also brought a box of embroidered hankies, just in case, so I wrote her name on that package.

"The problem with not bringing a maid is no cup of tea in bed," I said. "I really miss it. But I couldn't expect Queenie to bring me tea when she's obviously busy cooking breakfast. That pheasant was jolly good last night, wasn't it? It was the same recipe that Mrs. McPherson cooked for us, so Queenie is a quick learner when she wants to be."

Darcy chuckled, then sighed. "Unfortunately Queenie is always one step away from disaster, like last night. One just never knows."

"Ah, but it makes life interesting, doesn't it?"

"My life is already interesting enough," Darcy said, "without wondering if one of my servants is going to poison me or burn down the house." He saw my expression. "But I know you are fond of her in a strange way, so we have to keep her on. And I do admit she's becoming quite a decent cook."

We went through to the dining room and saw that coffee was already in the carafe and hot water had been poured into the dish warmers on the sideboard, anticipating the arrival of the breakfast dishes.

"Oh good. Breakfast any moment now. I'm starving," I said. "It must be the Norfolk air but I've been ravenous since I got here."

"You must take after your mother," Darcy said. "I've never seen a small person like her put away so much food."

I nodded, went to say something but stopped as I heard footsteps coming toward us. It was Lady Aysgarth, today wearing a grand burgundy dress with a bright patterned silk scarf at her neck.

"Happy Christmas, dear children," she said, giving us both a kiss on the cheek this time. "I see breakfast is about to be served. I asked for it early today, as we have to leave the house sharply at ten." She went over to the fire, which was blazing merrily, and warmed her hands. "Nice clothes always tend to be so cold, don't they?" She looked to me for confirmation. "Unless you have a lovely tartan like yours. Alas I have no Scottish claim on our side of the family. These days I feel I should dress appropriately in case I'm ever surprised by a visit from the queen. She doesn't approve of self-expression."

"Speaking of self-expression, I don't see any of your paintings on the walls," I said.

"I put them away for now, knowing that the Prince of Wales would be in and out of the house. I don't want him reporting my taste in art back to his mother. Not everybody appreciates modern art, you know. Simply can't understand it. But I love it. When I was at Aysgarth it was my one escape, my one means of expression." She gave a little sigh. "Darcy will remember that I hung my pictures all over the house. Then do you know what that wretched little man did? He took one look and said he hoped I'd have that rubbish removed before he came to live there. He had no desire to keep any of them."

We nodded understanding. "Clearly not educated in the way we would behave," she said. "So I packed the lot up and brought them with me. But since I've come here I don't seem to have the desire to paint like I used to."

"I'd love to see your paintings sometime," I said. I had meant it to be kind, thinking how horrible it must be to be turned out of your house and only coming away with a few bits and pieces. But then I realized I did have a genuine desire to see her art. One learns a lot about a person from their artwork, and Aunt Ermintrude was an enigma to me — a free spirit, creative woman who nevertheless dressed to conform with what the queen expected.

She looked absurdly pleased. "Would you? Would you really? How jolly nice of you. I'd be happy to show them to you when all this merrymaking has quietened down. I've stacked them in the library for now."

The maid and footman came in, bearing platters of kidneys and bacon, sausage, scrambled eggs, smoked haddock.

"I do hope everyone will be ready on time," Darcy's aunt said. "You know what the king is like about anyone being late. We have to be in our pews before the royal family arrives. That is, of course, if he is well enough to walk over to the church."

"Is it a long walk?"

"Not far for them. The church is close to Sandringham House. A longer way for us, of course, although I do walk it in more clement weather. We should cram into motorcars if we can." She glanced back at us. "I hope the others realize what a great honor it is to be part of the congregation with the royal family. The public is not admitted, only those who live on the estate."

"Well, Georgie counts as family," Darcy said. "So does Binky. The rest of us slink in on their coattails. Of course I only married her for her connections." And he grinned at me.

We started to help ourselves to plates of food. I reminded myself that there would be an enormous luncheon at one, so I'd better eat sparingly. Besides, the sausage and bacon looked rather greasy and the kidneys also unappealing. I settled for a piece of smoked haddock, which I adored, with some scrambled egg. Before we had finished we were joined by the major and his wife, then Binky and Fig.

"I'm already quite exhausted," Fig complained as Binky poured her a cup of tea. "We've been with the children opening their presents. Now they are completely overexcited, of course. I'm not sure about opening any more gifts or especially taking them to church. We can't risk Addy having a tantrum when the royal family is present."

"She'll be fine, Fig," Binky said. "Of course the child is excited, having both parents watch her while she opens gifts — it's enough to go to any child's head. Once she's had her breakfast and Nanny has dressed her for the outing, she'll be good as gold."

I wasn't quite so sure about this. Podge had always been an adorable little boy, but Addy, like many second children, had been born with a will of her own. The American couple joined us and then Mummy, who had, surprisingly, been given breakfast in bed. I don't know how she managed that, but she looked radiant in peach silk and cashmere with enough hint of diamonds to remind Mrs. Simpson she wasn't the only one who was showered with gifts. We went through to the drawing room, where the fire was now giving off a good heat and the lights were twinkling on the Christmas tree. Mrs. Simpson came in to join us, putting little packages under the tree. Oh golly — I hope she wasn't giving expensive gifts when she was only getting a box of chocolates.

"Merry Christmas, children," she said to us, giving a friendly smile for once. "Although I get the feeling it won't be incredibly merry. But better for us than poor dear David, stuck with those dreary relatives all day." She turned to Mummy, who had conveniently hogged the best chair by the fire. "So you didn't fancy Christmas in Germany? I gather it's a wonderful celebration there. Much better than here."

"I didn't fancy Christmas with the Goebbels," Mummy said. "And that was Max's plan."

"Oh, but the Goebbels — I found them charming in a slightly Germanic way. And Herr Hitler himself might have come to join you. You know how close he is to that family. What an honor that would have been."

"Do you admire him?" I blurted out before I realized I should have kept quiet.

"Oh, most certainly," she said. "So does David. The way he has brought that country back to its feet and established law and order and given Germans something to be proud of. So much more efficient than the way this country is run. Even the trains now run on time!"

More might have been said but we were now joined by the others as well as Binky's two children, each holding one of Nanny's hands.

"Now remember, children, best behavior or you'll be taken straight back to the nursery," she said to them in her calm Scottish voice.

"Darcy, will you be Father Christmas for us?" his aunt asked.

"Father Christmas has already gone," Podge said, frowning. "He's now delivering presents somewhere else in the world."

"But I'll only be pretending to be him," Darcy said and Podge nodded agreement.

Darcy squatted beside the tree and looked over the gifts. "There is a big parcel here," he said. "I can't think what it is. Probably brushes to scrub floors, I expect. It says, 'To Podge, from Mummy and Daddy.'"

"For me?" He jumped up and ran to take the package. The paper was ripped off in seconds. "It's a train set!" he shouted and jumped for joy before going to hug his parents. Fig looked embarrassed as her son flung his arms around her. "A little more decorum, if you please, Podge," she said.

"We'll put it together properly when we get home," Binky said. "Maybe we can add the rails from my old train set and have it going all over the room."

"Which room?" Fig demanded. "I don't want to find myself tripping over trains."

"We'll find a room," Binky replied. "We do have twenty-four bedrooms, you know."

"Where's my pwesent?" Addy demanded, coming up to Darcy. "Do you have one for me?"

"Let me see." Darcy pretended to be searching around, then handed her a big wrapped object. She needed help removing the paper, then was thrilled to find a doll's pram.

"You can give your new dolly a ride," Binky said. "What a lucky little girl you are."

Darcy now turned to the adults. Our chocolate liqueurs were appreciated. Darcy's aunt loved her carved African giraffe. Miss Short was grateful for her handkerchiefs and touched that I had included her. Then Mrs. Simpson's gifts were distributed. We all opened them with anticipation. It was a framed photograph of herself and the prince.

"Oh, how thoughtful," Mummy said. "And a tortoiseshell frame too. How clever. It doesn't detract from the photograph the way silver would."

Mrs. Simpson smiled.

"I must apologize," Mummy said, "for not bringing gifts. I thought I'd be spending Christmas just with my family and didn't find out we were coming here until it was too late to shop. I do have a present for Georgie and Darcy, however." And she handed me an envelope.

It was a pretty German Christmas card and inside was a check for a hundred pounds.

"Mummy, you shouldn't," I gasped.

"Thank Max," she said with a wicked smile. "He's very fond of you, you know."

Major and Mrs. Legge-Horne had brought

jars of her homemade chutney, but the colonel and Dolly also apologized for not having gifts for everyone.

"We didn't realize it was to be a big gathering, you see. Wallis just invited us to keep her company. We had no idea. . . ."

"You sent that lovely hamper from Harrods," Lady Aysgarth said. "We shall all share in the bounty therein."

Then her gifts were handed out. One of her smaller paintings to each couple. These weren't quite as outlandish as the one on our wall or the one she had given us for a wedding present, but were still rather — unique, shall we say? Their expressions as they unwrapped them were such fun to behold. Trying to hide horror and disgust, to appear delighted and grateful. Some succeeded more than others. Most realized instantly that the paintings had been done by the hostess, but Colonel Huntley exclaimed, "What on God's earth?" before his wife quickly patted his knee. "An original painting by our hostess, Homer. We are so honored."

I was waiting for our painting, but instead she handed a small leather box to me. I opened it and my jaw fell. It was a gold brooch in the shape of a lizard, its back studded with emeralds.

"Oh gosh," I said. "I don't know what to say. It's so lovely."

She smiled at my confusion. "It belonged to my mother and I have no children to leave it to," she said. "I'm sure my sister, Darcy's dear departed mother, would want it to be passed to the next generation."

Then Darcy was given a long, slim package.

"Is it a sword?" he asked. "The family sword that went to the crusades?"

He opened it and it was an ebony walking stick, its silver head in the shape of a hare.

"It belonged to your grandfather, whom you never met," his aunt said. "I'm sure he'd like you to have it."

I could tell that Darcy was moved as well. "What a really kind thought, Aunt Ermintrude."

"We should think about getting ready for church." Aunt Ermintrude got to her feet. "Let's assemble in the front hall in fifteen minutes."

The colonel wasn't sure that they should go, since they were Baptists and this was Church of England, but Dolly wasn't going to miss a chance to see the royals at close range.

And so we set out for the church in the motorcars. Binky's family crammed in with us, the children on our knees, Lady A., Miss Short and the Americans squeezed in with Major and Mrs. Legge-Horne. Only Mummy and Mrs. Simpson declined to come. I wondered what they would talk about and whether we'd return to find they had killed each other.

The morning mist had cleared and snow sparkled on the ground as we drove through the woods toward Sandringham House. Smoke curled up from an estate worker's cottage chimney and the pleasant smell of wood smoke drifted into the motorcar. It was a perfect English country scene. All it needed was a few deer and a robin!

We arrived in good time and were ushered to the pews at the back of the church. Addy, carrying her new doll, wanted to sit beside me, so we positioned her between me and Darcy. While we waited I had time to look around. It was a dark little church with lots of carved wood paneling and choir stalls at the front. The light came through an ancient stained glass window, mainly in shades of green, so the effect was a little like being in an aquarium. But it had that lovely old-church smell — one that can never be replicated anywhere — a mixture of polish, old hymn books, candles and a touch of damp.

The organ struck up, playing "O Come, All Ye Faithful." The choir in their white surplices processed in and took up their places in those lovely carved choir stalls. We were instructed to stand. In came the royal family, King George and Queen Mary at its head. He was walking proudly, head erect, as if there was nothing wrong with him. But I noticed she kept a firm grip on him. The Prince of Wales was right behind, accompanied by his sister, the Princess Royal. Both kept a close eye on their father. Behind them were the Duke and Duchess of York. She spotted me and gave me a lovely smile. So did the princesses. Margaret waved. Addy waved back. The Dukes of Gloucester and Kent followed but no Princess Marina, with whom I had become friendly. I thought she must have been at home with her new baby. Last of all came the vicar with his attendants.

The service began. Luckily it was peppered with plenty of carols and we all sang along. Addy started to fidget during the sermon, in which the vicar talked about peace and goodwill to all men being so important at this unsettled time. But I fished in my coat pocket and found a peppermint that I gave her to suck. So all was well. The service ended with the organ blaring out "Hark! The Herald Angels Sing" and the royal family processed out. As the king and queen passed us he recognized me and smiled. "Why, it's young Georgie," he said. "You didn't tell me she was staying."

"Nearby, dear," the queen replied. "With Lady Aysgarth." And she reached out her hand to her old friend.

"Happy Christmas, sir, ma'am," I said.

"Let us hope so," the queen replied as they moved on.

The Duchess of York reached out a hand to me as she passed and recognized Addy, who of course was a neighbor when they were in Scotland. "Hello, sweet girl," she said. "Weren't you good in church. Daddy will be proud."

Her husband the duke looked preoccupied and worried and merely nodded to us.

"I got presents," Margaret said. "Lots and lots of presents and Lilibet got another stuffed horse for her stables."

Elizabeth frowned at Margaret's outspokenness. "Now I have twelve," she said. "You should see them. They are lovely."

"I'd like to," I replied.

After they had departed we were allowed to leave. I heard Dolly whisper to her husband, "Did you see that, Homer? They all spoke to young Georgiana. They were all real friendly. I can't wait to tell the ladies at the bridge club."

CHAPTER 17

Christmas Day
Wymondham Hall, Norfolk

What a perfect day. Now I'm really glad I
came. This is the Christmas I'd always
dreamed of.

We arrived home to find hot mulled wine
and mince pies waiting for us. Then, at one
o'clock, the gong was sounded and we
processed in to the Christmas feast. The
table looked magnificent, decorated with
candles in their silver candelabras, holly and
ivy. Shafts of sunlight came in through the
tall windows, making the crystals on the
chandeliers sparkle. There were Christmas
crackers beside each place setting. We took
our assigned seats. This time I was seated
with my brother on one side and Mrs. Simpson on the other. For once the children were
allowed to join us and Podge sat next to his

mother, across from us, while Addy sat with Nanny at the far end of the table — closest to the door should Addy decide not to behave well.

The first order of business was to pull the crackers. There was laughter as the crackers exploded with a bang, and really good crackers they were too. They all contained a paper hat and a riddle but some had indoor fireworks in them, or tiny whistles, clever puzzles and even a small kaleidoscope. Darcy gave that to Podge, who was thrilled. Then, wearing our silly paper hats, we said grace and the butler poured champagne as the first course was carried in. It was a shrimp bisque — absolutely yummy and not too heavy. While plates were cleared away we started reading the riddles — always so silly and so much fun: "Where do you find the Andes? On the end of the wristies!"

Then came the main event. One platter contained the turkey, another a goose, both brown and glistening with crispy skin. There were roast potatoes, roast parsnips, brussels sprouts, chestnut stuffing, oyster stuffing and gravy. Binky was asked again to carve the turkey while the major attacked the goose. I thought Binky did the better job but nobody was about to complain as plates were piled high and silence reigned. I noticed Mrs. Simpson had taken very sparingly.

"So many calories," she muttered to me. "I have to think of my figure."

I glanced across to my mother, whose plate was piled as high as any. I hoped I had inherited her metabolism so I never had to worry about my figure in future. But then, the Duchess of York was becoming a little chubby and she didn't seem to mind. When nobody felt they could eat another morsel, the plates were cleared away, a bell was rung and Heslop the butler appeared carrying the flaming Christmas pudding. I wondered if it was the one we had brought with us.

"It's got fire on it!" Addy exclaimed and was told that the fire was on purpose. The maid cut the pudding and the footman handed around slices.

"Remember the custom of putting silver charms in the pudding," Lady Aysgarth warned. "I believe you might find some in your slice, so chew carefully."

We took generous helpings of brandy butter and started to eat. Colonel Huntley got a boot. "That means travel," Mrs. Legge-Horne said, "which is appropriate, as you'll be going back to the States soon."

Fig got the pig, which meant she was a glutton, which was absolutely untrue as she was rail thin. She was not amused. Podge got the silver button.

"The bachelor button, Podge. You're not going to get married this year," Binky said and we all laughed.

Then Mrs. Simpson exclaimed, "What on earth . . . ?" And she was looking at the bone button from Queenie's uniform now residing on her fork.

"Oh, you've got the bone button!" I exclaimed.

"How quaint," she replied. "What does it mean?"

"Mean?"

I was trying desperately to remember what explanation Darcy had come up with.

"It's an old custom in our part of Sussex, made from the bone of a stag killed on Christmas Day," I managed to say.

"Yes, but why put it in the pudding? What on earth is it there for? Highly dangerous, if you ask me. I could have swallowed it."

Now my mind went blank.

"It means opportunity," my mother said smoothly. "The person who finds the bone button has a new door open for them during the year."

"Well, fancy that," Mrs. Simpson said, clearly pleased at this good fortune. "Lucky I didn't break my tooth on it."

Mummy caught my eye and we exchanged a grin.

"Oh, look at the time!" Darcy's aunt jumped up. "I fear we must head to the sitting room immediately. Come on, chaps."

"What on earth is the matter?" Colonel Huntley asked.

"The king's speech. Three o'clock. We have to make sure the radio is working and we're all seated. Come on, you lot."

She shepherded us through like a sheepdog and we all found somewhere to sit, while she turned on the radio. A cheerful brass band playing Christmas carols was just coming to an end. "We now go to Sandringham House for the Christmas address to the Empire by His Majesty the King," said the solemn announcer's voice. The national anthem was struck up. We all stood.

Mrs. Simpson gave an audible sigh as we took our places again.

"On this most joyous of family celebrations I am speaking to you from my home at Sandringham, surrounded by my own family," came the king's voice, strong and resilient. Nobody would have known that he was ill. I tried to picture how it would sound when David had to make a similar speech. Would he be light and flippant or would he rise to the occasion and deliver an address to his people around the world that would make them feel proud to belong to our great community of nations? I glanced across at Mrs. Simpson, who was sitting with her eyes closed as if it pained her to listen.

"Well, that was very nice. Very appropriate," Major Legge-Horne said when the speech finished.

"I thought he did jolly well," Binky added. "That gentleman who was speaking was your king, children."

"I know," Podge said. "He's your cousin too, right, Papa?"

"He is, and therefore your cousin as well. One day you'll be the duke and maybe your cousin Elizabeth will be a queen."

Mummy glanced across at Mrs. Simpson, went to say something then thought better of it. Instead she declared that she was going to take a rest to sleep off that meal.

"I think I might go for a walk, to walk off all that food," Darcy said. "Do you want to come with me?"

"I think I'll join the others for a rest," I said, having my own plan in mind.

"All right. See you later," Darcy said.

I waited until he was out of sight then I slipped on my coat and wellies then headed over to the gardener's cottage. From inside came loud voices and laughter. "I'm sorry to disturb your celebration," I said when the door was opened by a burly young man, wearing a paper hat. "But I wondered if I could borrow the puppy I'm going to have. I want to show it to my husband as his Christmas present."

"Oh, right you are," he said, with a strange smirk. "You'd better come through and see for yourself."

I passed through their living room where they were all crammed around a table with the remains of the meal still on it. I was wished the compliments of the season by everyone and invited to have a glass of port, but I politely declined, saying I had to get back before my husband returned. They chuckled at this, which I found strange, until I went through to the scullery and there, squatting with a black puppy in his arms, was Darcy. He looked up in utter shock.

"You followed me!" he accused. "I wanted this to be a surprise for you."

I put my hand to my mouth. "Oh no! I was going to surprise you with a puppy! I had already arranged to give you him for your Christmas present."

"Him?" Darcy asked. "I'd already chosen this little girl."

"And I'd chosen a yellow male," I said. I reached down and picked up the pretty blond puppy I had chosen before.

"Shall we get them both? We have plenty of room and they'll be companions growing up." We looked at each other, each snuggling a puppy, and leaned forward to exchange a kiss.

The gardener's wife came in, was delighted to hear we planned to adopt two of them and immediately tied a bow around each of the dogs we'd selected.

"You come and visit whenever you've a mind to," she said, "and I reckon you can take them home with you in a week or so."

As we came out, reluctantly leaving our new family members in the care of their watchful mother, I turned to Darcy. "I should have brought them something — chocolates or wine."

Darcy gave me a smug smile. "I took them over a bottle of champagne. It went down well."

"I've told you before that you are a nice man," I said.

"Well, you do have good taste." He put his arm around me as we walked back to the house, debating over names. I suggested my golden boy should be called something noble, maybe from mythology or history.

Hercules, Ajax. "How about Castor and Pollux. They are twins after all."

"Castor and Pollux? That's sounds like a disgusting patent medicine," Darcy said laughing. "How about Bubble and Squeak. Or Muffin and Crumpet."

We were laughing as we entered the foyer and heard voices. Some members of the party had roused themselves from slumber. Podge's train set had been assembled on the far side of the room and the train was running around a circle of track.

"I think it's almost time for tea, don't you?" Lady Aysgarth asked.

I couldn't imagine how anybody could eat another crumb, but a cup of tea seemed like a good idea. Others apparently had the same feeling.

"More food?" Mrs. Simpson asked. "All you people do is eat."

"Well, it will be a simple supper tonight," Lady Aysgarth said. "We won't even change. It will be cold, so that the staff can have their Christmas celebration."

"Jolly good idea," Binky said. "That's what we always do at home, isn't it, Fig?"

"I don't see how anybody would want to eat more anyway," Fig said. "Podge, do stop that infernal train from rattling round and round. You are giving Mummy a headache."

"Let's go and see if the cake has been set out yet, shall we?" Lady Aysgarth stood up. The word "cake" had a magical effect on Podge, who followed her willingly into the dining room.

There on the table was a magnificent cake. It was covered in royal icing to resemble a snow scene and on top of it were all kinds of delightful china figures — children skating and sledding, a snowman, woodland animals. . . .

Podge gave a little exclamation of joy.

"It seems a shame to cut it," Mrs. Legge-Horne said.

But the cake was cut and we all managed a small slice. It was extremely rich, having been doused in rum at least a month earlier. After tea we went back into the drawing room. Binky demonstrated the indoor fireworks for the children, lighting them on the hearth. One was a strip of paper that, when a match was touched to one end, made the paper twist and turn and end up in the shape of a dragon or snake. Another made lines of fire rush across the paper to end with a little pop. They are always such fun and unexpected. Darkness had fallen and the tree and candles were lit, giving the room a cozy feel.

"I think we should play some party games,

don't you?" Lady Aysgarth said, "before the children go to bed." She looked around for enthusiasm. "What about sardines? It's quite a good house for sardines."

"I don't like sardines," Podge said. "They are too fishy."

"Not the ones in a tin." Binky laughed. "This is a game where someone goes to hide and if you find them, you hide with them until everybody is squashed in one place."

"Right," said Lady Aysgarth. "How about you and your daddy start, Podge. You go and hide and we'll find you."

Off they went and we heard whispers and giggling as they crept up the stairs. Then we set off to find them. In spite of the fact that I was now a grown woman I still got a thrill out of discovering the hiders and creeping in with them, holding our breaths as others went past our door and then laughing as there were finally too many people to creep into the cupboard. After several rounds we had had enough and collapsed onto chairs again as the butler offered more mulled wine and mince pies.

Mummy was the one who looked around and asked, "Where is Mrs. Simpson?"

"I haven't seen her since we started playing," Lady Aysgarth said. "Perhaps she had another of her headaches and went for a rest."

"Or sneaked out to meet the prince?" Mummy suggested.

"She couldn't do that. She doesn't have a motorcar here."

"Perhaps he came here and spirited her away for a bit," Mummy said.

"I think we would have noticed a motorcar. And someone would have had to answer the front door."

She rang a bell and Heslop appeared. "Heslop, did Mrs. Simpson go out?"

"No, my lady. Nobody has been out since teatime."

"Perhaps you'd send the maid up to tap on her door and see if she needs anything," Lady Aysgarth said.

"Very good, my lady." He gave a little bow and departed, only to return a short time later. "Annie says the lady is not in her room."

"How strange."

Lady Aysgarth had only just uttered the words when we heard a scream coming from high above. I immediately thought of Queenie's disaster of the night before, but surely Mrs. Simpson wouldn't have been stupid enough to ask for Queenie's help twice. If I recalled correctly she had made it clear that she never wanted to see Queenie again. Darcy and Binky sprinted up the stairs first, while I followed in hot pursuit. The screams were coming from the floor above, up the second flight where the nursery and maids' rooms were situated. We arrived into a dark and narrow corridor. A female figure rushed toward us, sobbing hysterically.

"I found her there. I nearly tripped over her," she said.

Darcy looked around for a light switch, found one and an anemic bulb threw some light onto the form of Mrs. Simpson, lying unmoving on the floor.

CHAPTER 18

Christmas Evening
Wymondham Hall, Norfolk

Oh dear, why is it that when everything seems to be going swimmingly something terrible happens? I had hoped this Christmas would be one of peace and goodwill to all men and that nothing would spoil it. Now it seems I was wrong.

It was clear immediately what had happened: the collapsible staircase up to the attic had come unfolded and hit the unfortunate Mrs. Simpson on the head at the moment she was going past. Darcy was already kneeling on the floor beside her, taking her pulse.

"Is she . . . ?" Binky stammered the words but didn't dare to finish the sentence. I found I was holding my breath.

"Knocked unconscious." Darcy looked up.

"Pulse is okay. She'll have a bad headache when she wakes up."

"I was in my room and I heard the noise," the woman said. From her black maid's uniform I guessed she was Lady Aysgarth's personal maid. "A sort of clatter and a cry, and I came out and nearly tripped over her. It's the American lady I helped last night." She didn't look too devastated and I suspected Mrs. S. had not been too gentle with her either.

"Would you go and find your mistress, please?" Darcy said sharply as she showed no signs of moving.

But there was no need. Lady Aysgarth had arrived beside us, breathing a little heavily.

"That dratted staircase again," she said. "I thought we'd fixed it. Oh no — don't tell me it hit somebody?"

"Not only somebody but the very person you wouldn't want it to hit," Darcy replied with a grim smile. "It's Mrs. Simpson."

"Oh God! She's not dead, is she?"

"I think she's coming round," Darcy said. As he uttered the words Mrs. Simpson stirred, opened her eyes and tried to sit up.

"Where the hell am I?" she asked. "What happened?"

I knelt beside her. "The folding steps to the attic fell and hit you," I said. "Don't try and get up yet. You were knocked out."

"What were you doing up here?" Lady Aysgarth demanded. "Surely you weren't playing sardines with us?"

" 'Sardines'?" Mrs. Simpson frowned as if trying to think what little fish had to do with her lying on the floor. "I wasn't playing anything. I'm not a fan of these stupid English party games you all seem to enjoy. If you want to know, I was going in search of your maid. My dress needed pressing and I wasn't going to let that creature from yesterday anywhere near me."

"Miss Short can't have secured the latch properly when we came up to get the Christmas ornaments," I said.

"That latch has a habit of coming loose at times," Lady Aysgarth said. "I take full blame for this. Edith, go down and see if we have ice for an ice pack. Then perhaps one of these gentlemen will be kind enough to take Mrs. Simpson to the nearest hospital. I suppose that is King's Lynn."

Mrs. Simpson did try to sit up now. "I'm not going to any local hospital in this godforsaken corner of the planet," she said. "Can you imagine what a field day the newspapers would have when they found out who I was?"

"I don't think the average person in

England has any idea who you are," Darcy said. "Lord Beaverbrook has kept a tight rein on any gossip about you and the prince."

"Dear man. Bless him," Mrs. Simpson said.

"But you should be seen by a doctor," Lady Aysgarth said. "Should we not go and fetch the local quack?"

"It's Christmas night. He won't thank you for calling him out. And what could he do besides telling me to keep quiet and rest and take aspirin for my headache?"

This was probably true.

"So do you want us to help you to your room and have some brandy and milk sent up?" Lady Aysgarth asked. She looked worried.

"A large Scotch over ice would be more to the point," Mrs. Simpson said.

"But I really do think you should be checked out by a doctor in the morning," Lady Aysgarth insisted.

Mrs. Simpson shook her head. "Don't worry, I'll be out of here first thing in the morning. I'll go straight back to my London house and see my personal physician down there. If David can't be bothered to visit me on Christmas Day, he can come and find me in London. Can someone drive over to

Sandringham and arrange for a car?"

Darcy and Binky assisted her to her feet and I went ahead to open the door of her room and turn back her bed. I stayed with her until an ice bag and hot water bottles were brought, while Darcy returned with a large Scotch. "I'm not sure if this is good for her after she's had a nasty bang on the head, but at least it will help her sleep."

"I'll have Lady Aysgarth's maid help you get undressed," I said and went to find her. She was standing outside the kitchen door and whispering with the housemaid Annie.

"It's the curse, that's what it is," Annie was saying. "See, didn't I tell you that this place was cursed?"

"It was that staircase, Annie. It just fell open," Edith, the lady's maid, said. "It could have happened at any time."

"But why then did it fall at the very moment she was walking under it? You tell me that?" Annie demanded.

They broke off when they saw me coming.

"Edith, would you go and help Mrs. Simpson to get undressed, and be very careful about it."

"Very good, my lady," she muttered and hurried off, leaving me with Annie.

"What's all this about a curse?" I asked.

"That's what they say around here, your ladyship," she said. "The servants who work at the big house and on the estate. They've all been saying there's a curse. When Queen Victoria's son, the then Prince of Wales, bought the property the royals drove out those who were living hereabouts and had their cottages pulled down. And one of them was a witch, they say, and she cursed them. And she said bad things would happen for a hundred years. Well — it wasn't long after that Prince Albert died, was it? And then the king's oldest brother? He died of influenza. And the king's youngest, Prince John — he was born with something wrong with him and only lived to thirteen."

"I'm afraid there are examples of untimely death in any family," I said.

"But it's not just the royal family themselves, your ladyship. It's them what's associated with the royals. All these accidents happening of late: those two men who fell off their horses and died last Christmas, and the year before that two of the guests were skating on the lake and went through the ice and drowned. It seems every year, about this time, something evil is going to happen. Leastways, that's what they've been saying."

"Well, luckily with Mrs. Simpson there's

no real harm done. She seems all right and her own doctor in London will check her out tomorrow."

"Well, she would be all right, wouldn't she?" Annie said. "It's not like she's got royal blood or anything. The curse wouldn't really apply."

"It's only country superstition, Annie," I said gently. "Please don't worry about it anymore. I'm sure everything will be fine."

But as I returned to the group in the sitting room I found myself thinking that Binky and I had royal blood. So did the children. Only a country superstition, I told myself. But I couldn't shake off the unease.

The atmosphere in the sitting room was subdued when I returned.

"Is she going to be all right?" Dolly asked.

"I think so. She was knocked out for a while, which is concerning," I replied.

"I should go up to her," Dolly said. "No, Homer, you stay put. The last thing a lady wants when she feels bad is a man hovering about, not knowing what to say."

"This might be a good time for some supper," Darcy's aunt suggested. "It's all laid out on the dining table. We help ourselves."

I don't think anybody actually felt like food but we welcomed the chance to have something to do, so we followed her into the dining room and found the table laden with cold turkey, ham, pork pie, cold sage and onion stuffing and pickles. There was chilled champagne in a bucket, fruit and more mince pies. It all looked good but I found that I couldn't eat a thing. In fact I felt rather sick and shaky. I kept thinking of that Christmas, not too long ago, when one terrible thing had followed another. I wished Annie had not mentioned the curse. And Queen Mary had hinted at the same thing. She had said that she sensed evil.

"Come on, old girl. Buck up," Binky said, handing me a plate. "It all looks good, doesn't it? Actually I prefer cold turkey to hot."

"Thanks, but I'm not hungry. I'm still upset over what has just happened."

"No real harm done," he said. "She'll no doubt have a nasty headache in the morning, but apart from that —" He gave me a reassuring grin. "Just a silly accident. I gather that Short woman hadn't secured the catch properly. Just extreme bad luck that Mrs. Simpson happened to be passing."

With that he started to pile his own plate high. I took a slice of ham, a pickled onion, a slice of bread and butter and poured myself champagne. That's all it was, I told myself. A nasty accident. But it seemed too coincidental that a nasty accident had happened to the Prince of Wales only a day ago and now another accident had struck the woman he wanted to marry. I paused, causing the person in line behind me to bump into me. Did that mean that someone in this house was actively working against the royal family?

I kept these thoughts to myself until Darcy and I were snuggled up in bed. A fierce wind had sprung up that rattled the windows, and when I had peered out into the darkness beyond, I could see bare tree branches dancing wildly.

"I still think Mrs. Simpson should have gone to hospital, or at least been checked out by a doctor," Darcy said. "Head injuries are something not to be taken lightly."

"Speaking of taken lightly," I ventured, "don't you think it suspicious that someone takes a potshot at the Prince of Wales and the next day a folding staircase falls on his ladylove?"

"As a matter of fact that did cross my mind," he said. "I had a word with Dickie Altrungham yesterday — he's the prince's equerry, you know, and between ourselves he's been assigned by Scotland Yard to keep an eye on the prince. He was at the shoot and he couldn't understand how a shotgun was fired in the wrong direction like that. He said he'd looked around the whole area afterward and didn't find any trace of intruders. It certainly rattled the prince, I gather. It's not the first time that something happened to him at Sandringham. Last year a vase fell off a high shelf when he was walking through a corridor. Apparently he had slammed a door behind him and that had made it wobble. Perfectly reasonable explanation, I suppose, and long forgotten until now."

"But Mrs. Simpson, just now," I said, thinking as I spoke. "I mean, we were all together in the sitting room, weren't we? Who could have known that she'd visit your aunt's maid? And been on hand to let the staircase fall at that moment?"

"One of the servants, I suppose," he said. "But I think my aunt brought them with her when she left Yorkshire, apart from Annie and James, and they are young locals. Devoted retainers, one would have thought."

"Anyway, the good thing is Mrs. Simpson will be on a train to London first thing in the morning," I said. "I expect she'll be as glad to see the last of us as we will be to see her go."

Darcy nodded. "This has all been a ridiculous charade, hasn't it? Your cousin wants his mistress beside him, so he bribes my aunt to create a house party so that she has somewhere to stay." He slid an arm behind my neck and pulled me toward him. "At least you got the house party you wanted and plenty of excitement at Christmas!"

"A little too much excitement," I said. "Now I wish we'd stayed home for a quiet Christmas with Granddad."

"Some people are never satisfied," Darcy murmured, nuzzling into my hair.

CHAPTER 19

December 26, Boxing Day
Wymondham Hall, Norfolk

> Mrs. Simpson has gone. I saw the motor-
> car coming for her just as it was getting
> light. Now perhaps we can all breathe
> more easily.

I had pulled back the curtains to see a misty
morning — quite expected in such a low-
lying area near the sea. The headlights of
the car that had been summoned for Mrs.
Simpson cut eerie beams of light through
the thick mist. I didn't see her actually getting into the car, but I heard words exchanged, the car door slamming shut and
then the front door closing below us. At
least she was well enough to walk to the
motorcar, I thought. That was good.

Darcy was still sleeping. I was going to
crawl back into bed beside him, as the room

had an icy chill, then I remembered I had promised the Prince of Wales to go riding with him. He had said he would send someone to pick me up but hadn't specified a time, so I put on my riding togs and went down to find a cup of tea before I set out. There was no sign of breakfast in the dining room. I'm just not good at doing things without something in my stomach. The fire had been lit but nobody seemed to be around. I was about to ring a bell when I remembered it was Boxing Day — when all the unessential servants can visit their own families. Meals would therefore be simple and we'd have to fend for ourselves. So I went in the direction of the kitchen and found a harassed-looking cook at the stove. There was no sign of Queenie. The cook jumped when she saw me come in.

"May I help you, your ladyship?" she asked.

"I just wondered if there was any tea yet," I said. "I have to go out riding and I'm not very good on an empty stomach."

She scurried over to the teapot, sitting under a quilted cozy in the shape of a rooster. "Of course, my lady. Coming right up."

"Are you all alone?" I asked. "What happened to my girl?"

"That's what I'd like to know," she said. "She was supposed to take over most of the work today so that I could have a bit of a rest, after yesterday, you know. But we had a good meal ourselves last night — duck and all the trimmings, and the wine to go with it, so I'm thinking she might have overslept today."

"Send one of the servants up to wake her and tell them Lady Georgiana says to get going or there will be trouble."

The cook grinned.

"Other than that, how has she been doing?"

"I can't complain, your ladyship," she said. "She does tend to be a bit clumsy, shall we say, but she's a good enough little cook and a dab hand with any kind of pastry." She gave me a shy little smile. "She certainly enjoys her food, though, doesn't she? My, but that girl can eat."

At that moment Annie the housemaid came into the kitchen.

"Annie, would you go upstairs and make sure Queenie is up?" I said.

A look of pure terror crossed her face. "I ain't going down that hallway again. Not for all the tea in China. Edith reckons it might be haunted. She thought she saw a ghost last night, right before the steps fell on that poor lady. All in black it was, with a veil over its face. And then it just disappeared."

"I think Edith has a good imagination," I said, "and of course she did have a shock, almost falling over Mrs. Simpson in the dark."

"Buck up, girl. It's daylight now," the cook said. "Do what her ladyship asks you, and the longer you hang around, the longer before you can go home to your family for the day."

She went upstairs, then came straight down, her face white. "She's not in her room, your ladyship."

Now I was worried. All the silly nonsense about curses and ghosts suddenly didn't seem so far-fetched. Queenie was not the type to go out for a brisk walk. What could have happened to her?

"I'll go myself." I tried not to break into a run as I came out into the entrance hall and ascended the stairs. Queenie's room was indeed vacant. Her uniform had been thrown over a chair. Her brush and comb were on top of the dresser. And her shoes were on the floor. So she definitely hadn't gone out, then.

I stood in the dark and narrow hallway, looking around desperately. The folding steps had been returned to their normal position. A wild idea crossed my mind of someone, a crazy relative, maybe, living up in the attic and coming down to claim Queenie.

"Queenie?" I called, my voice echoing louder than I intended. "Are you here?"

Edith's door opened, so did Fig's maid's door at the other end of the hall.

"What's wrong, my lady?" Fig's maid asked.

"We can't seem to find my assistant cook. Have you seen her?"

Two heads were shaken. Just then there was the sound of a toilet being flushed. A door opened and Queenie came out. She was in her nightdress and her hair stuck out wildly in all directions.

"Queenie, what on earth's the matter? Are you sick?" I asked.

She seemed to notice me for the first time. "Oh, wotcher, miss!" she said.

"Were you in the lavatory all this time?" I asked. "You're not well?"

"Well, I'm not feeling too chipper after that big blowout last night," she said, "but to tell you to the truth I was sitting on the lav and I must have fallen back asleep again. I was that tired when I woke up this morning. My old dad said I'd fall asleep in the bath and drown meself one day. Although that wouldn't have happened in our house cos we only had the tin bath in front of the fire and I only just fit into it."

I looked at her, not knowing whether to laugh or be angry. "Well, cook is waiting for you so you'd better get a move on," was all I could think of and stomped down the stairs.

I was just finishing my cup of tea when Darcy's aunt came to find me. She was wearing a woolen dressing gown and still looked sleepy but a little flustered. "A motorcar has just pulled up with presumably the Prince of Wales. You'd better get going," she said.

I put down the cup and hurried to grab my bowler and crop. Darcy's aunt opened the front door ahead of me. "Oh, hello, Captain Altrungham," she said. "I suppose the prince sent you for Lady Georgiana. You're going riding with them, are you?"

"Absolutely. Have to keep an eye on the prince, you know," he said.

"And who keeps an eye on you?" she asked.

He chuckled. The man who was standing outside the door was strikingly good-looking, with a military bearing and the sort of rugged chin one sees on advertisements for men's cologne. He flashed a winning smile at me. He was also dressed in a Harris tweed hacking jacket and riding breeches.

"Good morning," he said as I came to the front door. "I'm Dickie Altrungham, the prince's equerry." He took in my riding togs. "You must be Lady Georgiana."

"That's right."

"Delighted to meet you, my lady," he said, extending a hand to me. "And may I say that you look absolutely spiffing in that outfit. Ready for a good ride, then?"

"Oh, absolutely," I said.

"Is it just you?" He looked around the hall. The way he said it made it sound as if this might be an added bonus — two of us sneaking off together. I decided that he looked not unlike the prince, although taller. And with a naughty twinkle in his eye.

"At the moment. I thought Major Legge-Horne said he might want to join us," I replied, "but I haven't seen him this morning. I expect he slept in. We did consume a lot of food and alcohol yesterday."

"Didn't we all?" He chuckled. "Although when one is with the royals and we are facing the king's speech, restraint is called for." He glanced back at the motorcar. "Right.

We shouldn't keep His Royal Highness waiting."

I saw then that the prince was just getting out of the motor.

"Good morning, young Georgie. Ready for a good gallop, then?"

"Oh rather, sir," I said, smiling because this was what the equerry had said.

He noticed Aunt Ermintrude, standing in the doorway. "Hello, Trudy, old thing. Too bad you're not coming with us."

"My wild riding days are long past, Your Royal Highness," she said. "You forget I'm almost as old as your mother. But it's good of you to come for Georgiana in person."

"Ah well" — he turned to glance back at Captain Altrungham — "I had to keep an eye on my young cousin. After all, Dickie is certified NSIT."

"What?" Aunt Ermintrude asked, looking askance.

"Not safe in taxis, Aunt Ermintrude," I explained. "It's shorthand we used to give each other when we were debs."

"I resent that," Dickie Altrungham said. "I'm a happily married man. Child number two on the way."

"Of course you are, old chap," the prince said smoothly. "Come on, then, let's get going. They should have the horses saddled

240

and ready by the time we get there," he said. But he lingered, not heading back to the car and peering at the upstairs windows. "I suppose it's a bit early to imagine Wallis is awake? Yes, of course it is. I'm very tempted to creep up and wake her — like the prince in Sleeping Beauty, you know."

He too gave me a wicked smile, then shook his head. "But she'd probably be furious with me. She doesn't like anyone seeing her without her makeup and hair in place. But I'm jolly well going to pick up some pebbles to throw at her window when we pass this place on the way home. Which window is hers?" He laughed like a naughty schoolboy. I found myself thinking that the schoolboy image was a good one. He might be over forty but he was a Peter Pan in many ways. The boy who doesn't want to grow up and accept responsibility.

As soon as this thought had passed through my head I remembered that Mrs. Simpson had already departed for the train station. Oh golly. She had asked me not to say anything to the prince about her accident, but surely he needed to know, didn't he? It would be much worse for him to show up at the house again, only to find she had escaped to London. Then he'd start to worry that he had offended her in some way.

"I wasn't supposed to tell you this, sir, but I think you ought to know," I said hesitantly. "Mrs. Simpson had a bit of an accident last night and has gone up to London to see her own doctor."

His face turned ashen. "Wallis? An accident? She's hurt? Why on earth didn't she telephone me?"

"I'm afraid there is no telephone here," I said, "besides, she didn't want to worry you."

"What sort of accident? A fall?"

"One of those folding stairs from the attic came down and hit her on the head," I said. "It knocked her out, I'm afraid."

"Oh God. Is she going to be all right?" He looked almost as if he was going to be sick.

"I think so," Lady Aysgarth said. "She was sitting up, quite coherent, soon after. We offered to drive her to the nearest hospital or to summon a doctor, but she wouldn't hear of it. She was afraid the news would get out and there would be bad publicity."

"Silly old thing," he said angrily. "I've told her the British newspapers have made a pact to keep quiet about us. Not like those dreadful foreign rags. But the local people here would have no idea who she was. She'd have been quite safe."

"I still think she preferred her own doctor," Darcy's aunt said.

"She left this morning, did you say?"

I saw him glance at his watch.

"Less than an hour ago, I think."

"And was she being driven to London?"

"The car was taking her to the station, I believe."

"Then I might still have time. There won't be many trains on Boxing Day." He turned to Dickie Altrungham. "Be a good chap, Dickie, and take Georgiana on the ride for me. I've got to try and catch Wallis before she goes to London. She shouldn't be traveling alone if she's ill. She might faint or something on the way." He looked back at Darcy's aunt. "Sorry to dash, but I might still catch her if I get a move on."

He sprinted to the idling motorcar and jumped into the driver's seat. Captain Altrungham and I barely had time to get into our seats before he took off at a great clip.

The mist hung thickly in places as we made our way back and the trees reached ghostly branches over the narrow track. A thin carpet of snow still lay beneath the trees where the sun hadn't found it.

"Damn," David said. "I hope this bloody mist is not going to make it impossible to drive fast."

"There won't be anything on the road on Boxing Day, sir," Dickie said.

"Unless it's my luck that some bloody farmer chooses today to move his cows to a new pasture."

When we came to the open area of lawns around Sandringham House, the lake had completely vanished in the mist and the house itself loomed in the background like an overgrown red dragon. The prince drove around the front of the house and screeched to a halt outside a stable yard. He didn't wait for a second longer. He jumped out of our motor, ran past the outbuildings, and we heard a car's motor revving up then tires screeching on gravel.

Dickie was frowning. "That was a rum thing to happen, wasn't it?" he said. "A staircase to fall precisely at the wrong moment?"

"I thought so too. So did Darcy."

"Is he — looking into it at all, do you think?"

"I'm afraid I don't know what one could exactly look into," I said. "As far as I could tell we were all together in the sitting room when we heard a cry and rushed up the stairs. Only Lady Aysgarth's maid was up there at that time, I believe, and she has

244

been in her service for years." Then I paused, as something crossed my mind. Miss Short. Had she been in the room with us? She was so unobtrusive that it was hard to remember. And she was the one who had supposedly secured those steps. Also I had met her, out in the snow, looking for Lady Aysgarth right after the prince had been shot at. I wondered whether to say something but decided against it. I'd bring up my suspicions to Darcy first and see what he thought. But as my grandfather had once told me, it's often the quiet ones, the ones you'd least suspect. . . .

"You don't believe it was an accident?" I asked him.

"In other circumstances I'd have said yes." He spoke the words slowly. "But there seem to have been too many accidents when the royal family is at Sandringham. My predecessor who fell off his horse and was killed during the hunt last year. I've played polo with him. He was a splendid horseman."

"Surely nobody could arrange for someone to fall off a horse, unless he'd been shot or something?"

"He hadn't. He'd simply fallen off and hit his head on a rock. Another unlucky accident." He saw the hesitation in my face. "But don't worry. We'll take it easy through that part of the ride this morning. No jumping dashed great fences. The prince would never forgive me if I didn't bring you back safe and sound." He sort of raised a challenging eyebrow as he said this.

Was I overreacting or did he manage to give that a double meaning — that he might want to try something with me?

"And old Darcy would probably kill me."

"You know Darcy quite well, I gather?"

"What, old Darcy? Everyone knows your husband, my dear. He's a legend in his own time."

"Really?" I laughed.

He gave me a look of almost pity. "You have no idea of half the things he gets up to. In a professional sense, of course. I didn't mean to imply . . ."

"Naturally. A professional sense," I said, knowing that he had meant to imply that my husband had been a bit of a lad at times. But of course I knew this. I trusted that he had now settled down to just one woman.

We walked together into the stable yard, where three good-looking horses were standing, ready saddled, their bridles held by a stableboy. Dickie looked around, then seemed to find what he was looking for. "Ah good. I thought I left my coffee here earlier. I bet it's stone-cold by now."

He picked up a pottery mug, took a swig, made a face, then put it back again. "Stone-cold," he said. "Right, let's be off. Are you ready for a jolly good gallop?"

"If you give me a mount that can jump and isn't going to try and throw me," I said.

"Absolutely not," Dickie replied. "We have Rani saddled up for you. She's part Arab and very fast, but a smooth ride." I went over to the slender, elegant horse and the stableboy gave me a leg up into the saddle.

"And I'll take Sultan, since the prince isn't here," Dickie Altrungham said. "He's a bit of a challenge but, by God, he can run." Dickie swung himself into the saddle of the large and powerful bay. The horse danced and snorted like a war charger and I was glad I had not been given a similar mount. I'm a good rider, but in the past some horses have simply been too strong for me.

"Ready?" he asked. "Splendid. Let's go."

And he urged his horse out of the stable yard. Mine followed. I sensed immediately that she'd be an easy ride. She responded to the lightest touch on her mouth or a squeeze of my calf. As soon as we were free of the cobbles Dickie urged his mount into a canter. Mine followed suit. We went along a farm track and then into a paddock where patches of grass showed through the melting snow.

"Ready?" Dickie yelled and off we went at a great pace. The wind in my face was icy and took my breath away, but there was that feeling of exhilaration one gets at going fast. The horses' breaths came out like dragon smoke into the cold air. The pounding of the hooves was muffled by the mist that swirled around us. Sometimes the going ahead was clear and then we came to a low-lying patch and Dickie vanished into mist ahead of me. At the end of the field there was a gate. I realized Dickie was not going to slow down for this and we were going to jump it. Dickie's horse took it easily. I worried that my mount was considerably smaller, but she collected herself, then sailed over, almost flying. I gave a little whoop of joy. Then we were going through a woodland on a bridle path that twisted and turned between the trees. Branches reached out to snatch at us. The mist had closed in again. I could no longer see Dickie but I could hear the thud of the horse's hooves ahead of me and the rhythmic chink of the bridle. The snow was deeper in places and my mare stumbled once. I slowed my pace a little until the woods opened up, this time onto a plowed field bordered by a line of stately oak and elm trees. Dickie had now vanished into the mist ahead of me and I urged on the mare to catch him up.

There was a smooth green track under the trees, along the edge of the field, avoiding the uneven clods of soil. I kept the mare to this as she had already stumbled once. Most of the trees were so tall and ancient that their branches would have provided a leafy canopy in summertime, but a few smaller interlopers had sprung up, sticking out twiggy fingers across the path. Still no sign of Dickie and I couldn't even hear the thud of Sultan's hooves. I hoped Dickie would have the sense to wait for me at the end of the field or I would have no idea where to go next.

I saw a large log lying across the path and expected my horse to jump it, but instead she came to a halt so abruptly that I almost went flying over her head.

"It's all right, girl." I leaned forward to pat her flank. "Come on. Let's go."

But she wouldn't move. That was when I realized that what was lying across the path ahead of us was not a log at all. It was a person.

CHAPTER 20

December 26, Boxing Day
At Sandringham House, Norfolk

I am still so shaken I can hardly write this.

I took in the Harris Tweed hacking jacket and above it the blond hair. Two people knocked unconscious within twenty-four hours really was a bit much! I dismounted, leading the mare, as she was trembling and I didn't want her to run for home without me. Going forward cautiously I knelt beside him. He was lying on his side.

"Dickie? Are you all right? Wake up."

I reached out a tentative hand and touched his shoulder, then I moved him onto his back. That was when I saw that his head was at a strange angle, lolling off to one side, and I realized that he had broken his neck. I put my hand to my mouth, fighting back a wave of nausea. How could it possibly have happened? People don't fall off in the middle of a straight gallop and Dickie had already shown he was an excellent horseman. I looked around. He was lying beside a gnarled old oak, with ivy winding up its trunk, and with a large branch jutting over the track. Surely he was not tall enough for that branch to have knocked him from his saddle, and he would certainly have seen it, even through this amount of mist. But I could think of no other explanation.

I searched around for a nearby house, or even smoke from a chimney but all I saw was flat countryside in all directions. I was about to stand up when his eyes fluttered open and he stared straight at me.

"Dickie, it's Georgiana," I whispered. "Don't worry, I'm going to get help."

He frowned as if trying to remember.

"You had a bad fall," I said. "You're going to be all right." Although how that could possibly happen I couldn't say.

He tried to say something. A tiny whisper came out. "Sorry. Ellie." Then a puzzled expression and a whispered word. It sounded like "tapestry," but that couldn't have been right.

"What did you say?" I asked. "I didn't quite hear. . . ."

But his eyes had closed again and I realized he was dead. The only thing to do now was to summon help. I peered into the mist, trying to spot his horse. I didn't think it would have gone on alone, so far from its stable. Taking Rani's bridle I led her around the body and then along the track until I could make out the shape of a horse, standing under another big oak tree. "Hey, Sultan. It's going to be all right." I spoke the words gently, as I went up to him and took his bridle. He followed me willingly.

I had no idea exactly where we were or where I might find the nearest house. We certainly hadn't passed any farmhouses on our ride so far, so this must all be Sandringham land. The other thing to do was to retrace my route. I mounted Rani again, glad that I was on the smaller horse, as it would have been a challenge to mount Sultan without help. I set off at a trot, with Sultan beside me. I had to slow to a walk through the woodland, as the bridle path was not wide enough for two horses. It was a good thing that we were only walking as we came to the gate and neither horse was tempted to jump it. I was able to lean down and open it, then close it again behind us. Across the smoother surface of the paddock I dared to go faster — this was probably a mistake as both horses now sensed they were near their stable and actually went faster than I had planned. But I managed to keep control of both and finally Sandringham House was before us and we were entering the stable yard.

A groom came out at the sound of the hoofs on cobbles.

"You're back quickly, my lady," he said, then he noticed the second horse. "Is something the matter?"

"There was an accident," I said. "Captain Altrungham was knocked off his horse. I'm afraid" — I took a deep breath before I could get the words out — "I'm afraid he's dead."

"Not another one?" The groom blurted out the words, then shook his head. "I'm sorry, my lady. That was an inappropriate thing to say, only it seems just like yesterday that I sent another fine young man off on Sultan — on the very same horse — and I got the same bad bit of news." He paused, breathing hard. "On Boxing Day that was too. One year ago."

"I know," I said. "It seems almost too much to contemplate, doesn't it?"

He nodded. "I don't know what to think. Old Sultan, he's usually as sure-footed as any horse I've come across. And a terrific jumper too. Was it at the same wall that the poor bloke came off?"

"No, it wasn't a wall at all," I replied. "Actually it was a perfectly smooth track beside a field."

"So why the horse should falter twice like this? I must get the vet to check him over and make sure there is nothing wrong with his legs. I do hope we don't have to put him down. I'm fond of that horse."

"I'm sure it wasn't the horse's fault," I said quickly. "It seems that Captain Altrungham might have been knocked off by a low branch across the path. Although I can't understand why he didn't see it. The mist was quite thick, but even through the mist he should have seen that branch across the path. I could and I was following him."

"With another rider I might have said that Sultan ran away with him." The groom sucked through his teeth, shaking his head. "He's a strong horse with a mind of his own. The Prince of Wales likes to ride him — enjoys the challenge, you know. But Captain Altrungham, I understand he was a fine rider. He was described as an outstanding polo player."

"I suppose it's possible that something happened before he was knocked off," I said, my brain racing now. "He had a stroke or a heart attack?"

"Fine young man in the prime of life like he was? It's not likely, is it? Although the doctors will be able to tell us more when they do the autopsy, I've no doubt."

The mist now crept into the stable yard and I found I was shivering. The groom must have noticed this. "But you, my lady. You've had a nasty shock and you were smart enough to bring back both the horses, for which we thank you. I suggest you go inside the big house, tell them what happened and have someone bring you a glass of brandy before they drive you home."

I nodded although I was not anxious to go into Sandringham House, uninvited and probably before any member of the royal family was up and about. What I really wanted to do was to be taken back to where I was staying and be with Darcy. He'd know what to do better than I. But I realized I had an obligation to Mr. Altrungham, so I summoned all my courage and headed toward the house. As I came out of the stable yard someone was coming toward me. It was Major Legge-Horne. He stopped short when he saw me.

"Oh splendid," he said. "I'm not too late after all. Damned alarm clock didn't go off and I only woke when I heard a motorcar outside. You haven't been waiting for me, I hope?"

"No, Major," I said. "But I'm afraid the morning's ride has been abandoned. There has been an accident. The prince's equerry had a fall."

"Dickie Altrungham, you mean? Good chap. Good horseman from what I've seen. Not the sort of chap to take a spill from a horse."

"I'm afraid it was Dickie."

"Good God. Is he going to be all right?"

I shook my head. "He's dead. He broke his neck."

He looked stunned. "I don't know what to say. What an awful thing to happen. Thank God it wasn't the prince, though. I presume he's jolly cut up about it."

"The prince didn't go riding with us," I said. "He changed his mind at the last minute. It was just the equerry and me."

"Tried to jump something too big for the horse, did he?"

I shook my head again. Being questioned about it like this was bringing me close to tears. "It wasn't a jump or anything. It was a flat stretch of track beside a field. He must have been knocked off by a low branch. I can't think of any other explanation."

"Low branch? That doesn't make sense.

Any fool can see a low branch coming, can't they? And if they can't miss it, they duck."

This was quite true. I nodded. "I know. I can't understand it either."

The major must have heard a tremble in my voice. "I say, young lady, this must have been most distressing for you. I have my motorcar right here. Why don't I run you home for a hot bath and a cup of tea."

"I should notify them at Sandringham first," I said.

"Don't worry about that. There's nothing we can do for the poor chap now, is there. I'll drive you home and then I'll come back and sound the alarm at Sandringham. I doubt they'll be able to rouse the local police chappies on Boxing Day, or the doctor. But from what you say everything will be quite straightforward."

I was in no mood to argue. All I wanted was to go straight back to Wymondham and have that bath and a cup of tea. I was feeling that I might be sick any moment and realized, of course, that I hadn't had any breakfast yet. And I felt a profound relief that the major would get things in motion, rather than me. It was only when he climbed into the driver's seat beside me that I remembered he had made unwelcome advances to me in the hallway on the first night. I eyed him nervously, but it seemed that today he had switched into efficient Guard's officer mode. He drove as fast as he dared, given the condition of the road, and got me home in no time at all. As I walked to the front door I heard the car reversing on the gravel before driving off.

I stepped into delightful warmth and the smells of coffee and bacon. No dogs came bounding up to me, tails wagging in greeting as usually happened when a visitor arrived. However, my entry was noticed.

"Welcome back, my lady." Heslop appeared in that uncanny way that butlers have. "I hope you've had a brisk ride."

"Thank you, Heslop," I said. "Is Mr. O'Mara at breakfast?"

"I don't believe he is, my lady. Apart from yourself and the major there has not been much sign of life this morning. Understandable, of course."

As I was about to go up the stairs the front door opened and Lady Aysgarth came in.

"Goodness, but it's raw today, isn't it?" she said. "I thought I'd go and take the usual Christmas box to the gardener's family. Just that short way and I'm frozen to the marrow." She paused, as if thinking. "You're back early from your ride. Didn't you do the whole circuit?"

"No," I said. "We came back early." I hesitated, not sure if I wanted to tell her about the accident, to have to go through those details again.

"Are you all right?" she asked me. "You're as white as a sheet. You look as if you're about to pass out."

"I haven't had breakfast yet. I feel a bit woozy, actually."

"Then my dear girl, come and sit down and have a cup of tea and something to eat. Come on." And I allowed myself to be led through to the dining room.

Mrs. Legge-Horne was there, eating poached egg on toast. Darcy's aunt sat me down, poured me tea with a lot of sugar and then made me a plate of food. I drank the tea willingly but I found that I didn't fancy any of the rich and greasy items on my plate. "Do you think I could have just a poached egg on toast, like Mrs. Legge-Horne?" I asked and the plate was whisked away from me.

"No doubt your husband can finish off this lot," Darcy's aunt said and buttered a slice of toast for me.

I ate, finding it hard to swallow each morsel. I kept seeing Dickie Altrungham's face, that cheeky, flirtatious smile. Whatever kind of man he was, he had been alive and had enjoyed life. And now he was dead. It was hard to comprehend. I was still trying to eat when Darcy came into the room. "You're back already?" he asked, then he took one look at my face. "What happened? Did you fall off? Are you all right?"

I couldn't keep it from him. "I'm all right," I said. "But there was an accident —"

"My husband?" Mrs. Legge-Horne asked, standing up. "He didn't fall off, did he? I told him not to go. He wouldn't listen."

"Your husband arrived too late to go with us," I said. "It was the prince's equerry. . . ."

"Dickie?" Darcy demanded sharply.

"Yes." I took a deep breath. "He was knocked off his horse. He broke his neck, Darcy." And to my shame tears started trickling down my cheeks. Darcy took me into his arms and I sobbed on his shoulder.

"I'll get her some brandy," Lady Aysgarth said. "Terrible thing for a young lady to witness. How did it happen, Georgiana? What do you mean by 'knocked off his horse'?"

"That's just it," I said. "I didn't see anything. He was on a more powerful horse and he had gone on ahead. And the mist was quite thick around there. We were on a grassy track at the side of a plowed field. There were big trees beside us and suddenly my horse stopped so abruptly I was nearly thrown over her head. I thought it was a log across the path, but it was Dickie Altrungham lying there. And he died."

"Then how do you know he got knocked off his horse?" Darcy asked me.

"I couldn't think of any other explanation," I said. "There was an oak tree with a branch reaching over the path, and I suppose his horse was a lot taller than mine, but surely he would have seen it."

"You just said it was very misty," Darcy's aunt reminded me.

"It was, but even in the mist you see shapes ahead of you, don't you? They might be indistinct but surely you'd notice a large tree branch."

"And what happened to his horse?" Lady Aysgarth asked. "Was it possible that it just bucked him off and then bolted?"

"It was standing a few yards away," I said. "It was a big powerful horse, but it seemed to me that Captain Altrungham had complete control of it. I don't know what might have made it suddenly buck someone off in the middle of a gallop."

"A bird flew out suddenly and startled it? A rabbit ran out underfoot? Horses are skittish animals, aren't they?"

"I suppose so," I said.

"Could have been an unlucky combination," Darcy's aunt said. "Rabbit runs out, horse is startled and rears up right where there is an overhanging branch. Dashed bad luck on the poor chap."

"Yes," I said. "Dashed bad luck."

And all I could think was the groom saying, "Not another one? On Boxing Day that was too."

"I think I'm going to be sick," I said and rushed from the room.

CHAPTER 21

December 26, Boxing Day
Wymondham Hall, Norfolk

> What a horrible thing to have happened. It
> has quite spoiled the holiday spirit for
> me. I don't think I'll ever get that sight
> out of my mind.

After that they were most solicitous. I was
led through to the drawing room, which was
unoccupied at that hour of the morning,
and placed in an armchair beside the newly
lit fire. A glass of brandy was brought for
me and I took a tentative sip. I felt the fiery
liquid warming my body and the shivering
subsided.

"Was the Prince of Wales unhurt?" Darcy
asked me.

"He didn't come with us at the last minute," I replied. "I felt I had to tell him about
Mrs. Simpson after he wanted to throw

pebbles at her window. He rushed off immediately to try and catch her at the station before she went to London. So it was just Captain Altrungham and me on the ride."

Darcy was frowning. "Has Sandringham been notified?"

"The major said that he would do it. He was going to drive straight back there." I gave a big sigh. "There's not much anybody can do except recover his body." I paused. "I suppose the doctor will have to verify the cause of death."

Darcy put a hand on my shoulder. "I think I should go over there," he said. "Maybe make a couple of telephone calls as well."

"Darcy, are you thinking that this might not have been an accident?" I voiced the suspicion that had been creeping into the back of my own mind.

"I'm saying that Dickie Altrungham wasn't the sort of chap who would have fallen off his horse for no reason. I've played polo against him. I think I'd like to take a look at the body."

"Meaning?"

"Meaning someone might have made sure he came off his horse. Taken a shot at him first, perhaps."

"I heard no shot," I said. "Besides, why would anybody shoot someone like Captain

Altrungham?"

"He was a retired army man, but I think I mentioned that he was placed with the royal family by the Home Office — for security reasons. Perhaps he had found out something. A plot against the Prince of Wales, maybe. Irish republican terrorists."

"Then if they were going to kill anybody, why not go straight for the prince himself? Why kill the bodyguard?" Then I remembered something that made me go cold all over. "But somebody did take a shot at the prince the other day."

I put my hand to my mouth as the reality of what I had been thinking dawned on me. "It was the Prince of Wales who was supposed to go riding with me this morning. He pulled out at the last minute, so the person might have thought they were killing the Prince of Wales."

Darcy nodded. "That thought did cross my mind too. They were not dissimilar in appearance, were they? And with riding hat on, going fast on a horse in the mist, it would have been hard to tell the difference."

I paused, frowning. "Now it really seems likely that it wasn't an accident that those stairs fell on Mrs. Simpson last night, doesn't it?"

"That also crossed my mind," he said.

"But who could it possibly be? Somebody with a grudge against the royal family? It has to be someone with access to this house if Mrs. Simpson's accident was not an accident. We know everybody here, apart from the major and Mrs. Legge-Horne, and he works for the royal family himself. Oh, and the Americans. But they are friends of Mrs. Simpson. They'd hardly be likely to want to knock her out. And the servants all seem harmless enough, don't they?"

"It would have to be someone who knew those steps could be faulty, if it wasn't indeed an accident and a coincidence," he said.

At that moment the front door opened, there was excited barking, and through the open doorway I saw Miss Short come into the front hall. "Quiet, boys," she said. "You've been for a lovely walk, now behave yourselves."

Darcy and I exchanged a long look.

"She was the last one to fiddle with those steps," I whispered. "And she's the only one who has been out this morning apart from the major and me. But surely — I mean, look at her. A quiet, unobtrusive little mouse. Can you picture her aiming a gun at someone?"

"It's sometimes the quiet ones," Darcy

said, repeating exactly what my grandfather had told me once.

"But that makes no sense. She's been with your aunt for years, hasn't she? The loyal companion. And she's certainly not anti-royal. Look how she spoke up when Mrs. Simpson suggested we could skip listening to the king's speech. Until then she'd hardly said a word."

"Keep an eye on her," Darcy said. "Maybe find a way to chat with her."

"I did, when I gave her a lift after she was out looking for Lady Aysgarth. She told me about the dear little tea shop she used to own before it went under. She seemed most grateful that Lady Aysgarth had rescued her."

"She was out looking for Lady Aysgarth that morning, was she?"

"When someone shot at the prince? Yes, she was. That occurred to me too."

"I'll see if there is any kind of record on her when I make those telephone calls," Darcy said. "Look, I'd better be going. I want to get to the body before it's moved. Go and have a rest. I'll see you later."

I watched him go, then I finished my brandy. It had an immediate effect on me at that early hour and I felt the room swimming around a bit. I had better do as he says and go to lie down, I thought. It seemed like a good idea. I had no wish to repeat my story to all and sundry. I went upstairs, lay on the bed and must have drifted off to sleep.

I awoke with a start to find someone bending over me.

"It's only me," Darcy said. "Are you all right?"

"Yes. The brandy knocked me out, I'm afraid. What time is it?"

"Only about eleven."

I sat up, still feeling the after effects of that strong drink. "You're back from Sandringham, then?"

"I came back to fetch you," he said. "It seems the queen is anxious to speak to you."

"Oh golly. Not again." I stood up. "I'm sure I look a fright."

Darcy looked at me with amusement. I had taken off my jodhpurs, boots and jacket and was now wearing a polo-neck jumper and knickers.

"Well, I would suggest putting on a few more clothes before you venture out," he said.

"So did you manage to find out anything?" I asked as I opened the wardrobe and opted for the same kilt and blouse as the day before.

He sighed. "I got there too late, I'm afraid. By the time I'd managed to follow their directions and found the right field they'd already arrived with a tractor and cart, moved the body, and tramped around all over the place. So I followed them back to Sandringham House and the body is being kept in one of the outbuildings until the doctor arrives. But I didn't see any evidence of foul play. Certainly no gunshot wound. Just a broken neck, which would have undoubtedly come from the fall."

"So no way to prove that anyone helped him to fall off?"

"Not that I can see." He perched on the bed as I sat to brush my hair. "You were close behind him and I gather you couldn't see much in the mist. But did you hear anything?"

"I can't say that I did," I replied. "The mist muffled things. All I heard was the thump of my horse's hooves and the jingle of the bridle. I don't even remember hearing a bird."

"So certainly no cry?"

I shook my head.

"I was thinking if his horse had reared up, or stumbled or he'd hit his head on a branch, there would have been some kind of expression coming from him. That moment when you realize you are going to hit something or fall you usually cry out, don't you?"

"You'd have thought so," I agreed.

"What about after you dismounted and went to look at the body."

"He was actually still alive when I first got there," I said, determined not to cry.

"That must have been horrible for you," Darcy said, "but what I wanted to know was: did you get any sense then that anyone was nearby?"

"I really didn't. Certainly no sense of danger as I have had before in my life when I was in a tricky situation or someone threatening was nearby."

Darcy shook his head. "So frustrating. I also took a look at the horse, wondering if something had possibly been used to trip it, but its legs seemed fine."

"It certainly moved easily enough beside me when I brought it back," I said.

"It makes no sense. A good horseman does not fall off when a horse is cantering down a straight stretch of track with no obstacles. And even if he did lose his balance and fall —" He paused, looking up at me. "You've fallen off horses in your life, haven't you?"

"Several times."

"And hurt yourself badly?"

"Only once, when I was trying to make an old horse jump a fence and he stopped short and I went sailing forward. I broke my arm that time." I thought about it. "But usually you feel that you are about to fall and you sort of brace yourself and roll, don't you?"

He nodded. "That's what I was thinking."

I stared out of the window where the mist was now lifting and a red wintery sun was peeking through. "I suppose we may learn more when the doctor has examined him. It could be possible that someone drugged his morning coffee and that just happened to be the moment when the drug kicked in?"

"That would imply that someone at Sandringham House was involved in this. I spoke to a couple of people there this morning, and to Scotland Yard too, and they seemed to think that the servants have been working for the royal family for years if not generations."

"I wonder if that includes both inside and outside servants. I remember he had a cup of coffee in the stable yard and that would have been easier to meddle with."

Darcy nodded. "I believe, from my conversation, that Scotland Yard will be sending someone up to snoop around a bit. Dickie Altrungham was, after all, given this post to

271

provide security for the prince. The target may have been the prince himself, which I suspect was the case, but it may also have been Dickie, if he had discovered any kind of plot."

I sighed. "Either way it's going to be dashed difficult to prove, isn't it?"

"If he was drugged, the autopsy will show it. Otherwise . . ." He didn't finish the sentence. Otherwise someone might have killed with impunity and be waiting to kill again, I thought.

CHAPTER 22

December 26, Boxing Day
Wymondham Hall and then Sandringham,
Norfolk

I feel terrible. I suppose it must be shock.
All I can think is that somebody around
us has been trying to kill my cousin David.

I finished dressing, brushed my hair and
came down the stairs with Darcy. There was
now chatter going on in the drawing room.
I tried to sneak past, but Mrs. Legge-Horne
saw us.

"Any news?" she called. "Did you happen
to see my husband?"

"I believe he was among those recovering
the body," Darcy said.

"But he's all right?"

"I'm sure he is."

Colonel Huntley stood up. "So tell us —

some poor fellow came off his horse and broke his neck? That's a darned shame." His gaze fell upon me. "And you were with him, little lady?"

I tried to ignore for now that he had called me "little lady." But I wasn't going to forget it. "He had gone on ahead," I said. "I'm afraid I didn't see anything until I came upon his body lying there."

"An awful shock for you, my dear," Lady Aysgarth said. "Why don't you spend the rest of the day in bed? We'll have food sent up to you."

"It's all right, thank you," I said. "I'd rather be up and busy than lying there and thinking. Besides, Darcy tells me the queen wants to speak to me, so we'd better not keep her waiting."

As we headed for the front door I heard Dolly Huntley's voice. "See, what did I tell you? The queen relies on her. They are really good buddies."

This brought an interesting thought into my head. Darcy's aunt Ermintrude had been invited to move down to Sandringham because she had formerly been the queen's confidante. Why then did the queen not want Darcy's aunt at her side right now? Why me? And I suppose I answered my own question. Because she knew that I had been involved in solving several murders before now. I had some experience with crime and evil. I shook my head. She might have thought that, but in truth those crimes had been solved more by luck than anything and I didn't feel in any way competent to solve this, if it was indeed a murder. I really wished she would not place such faith in me.

Darcy and I were silent as we drove along the narrow lane. When our motorcar pulled up outside Sandringham House, there were several other vehicles now in the courtyard. One was a police car, another an ambulance. The latter wouldn't be of much use, I thought.

"I'll be out here, waiting for you," Darcy said.

"Coward!"

"I haven't been summoned to the royal presence." He grinned. "But I'll be working. Having a chat with some of the outdoor staff. Go on. Good luck." He gave my shoulder a reassuring squeeze.

I took a deep breath and went toward the front door. I was received by a footman in splendid livery and expected to have to explain who I was and that the queen had sent for me, but he seemed to know and had been waiting for me.

"Her Majesty is in her private sitting room. Please come this way, my lady," he said and whisked me along the central corridor, where portraits of ancestors, crowned with sprigs of holly, frowned down at me and the decorated Christmas trees now seemed out of place. The footman tapped on a door at the far end of the hallway, opened it and announced "Lady Georgiana, Your Majesty."

This was a very different room from the one I had seen her in a few days ago. It was not an ornate palace room, decorated with chinoiserie or priceless antiques waiting to be knocked over, but a simple country sitting room with comfortable sofas and a blazing fire. Another large Christmas tree stood in front of the window, decorated with hand-carved wooden ornaments from Germany as well as tiny candles in wooden candleholders. The queen, sitting on one of these sofas, looked rather small and frail, her expression unable to hide her worry. She reached out a hand to me. "Georgiana, my dear. Come and sit beside me. So good of you to come when you've had such a shock."

I took the hand and bobbed the usual curtsy before I sat beside her.

"So you were party to the whole thing,"

she said. "Such a senseless thing to happen. His poor little wife will be devastated. So devoted to him, I understand, and a second baby on the way."

It crossed my mind that Dickie had not seemed similarly devoted and had definitely flirted with me. But I nodded. "As you say, ma'am, quite senseless. It wasn't as if we were doing anything dangerous. We had jumped a gate before that but this was an easy gallop beside a field."

"And he just fell off? Or someone mentioned that he hit his head on a low branch extending over the path?"

"That may have been the case, ma'am," I said. "I'm afraid his horse was faster and he disappeared into the mist ahead of me. There was a branch extending over the path but it seemed too high, even given that his horse was several hands taller than mine."

Although her bearing was as usual upright and composed, her fingers toyed nervously with the wool of her skirt. "I would dismiss it as a freak accident were it not that the same thing had happened at the same time last year, and to a similar person. My son's former equerry and now his current equerry. That has to be more than coincidence, doesn't it, Georgiana?"

"It does appear to be that way, ma'am," I agreed.

"Two excellent horsemen. Fit. In the prime of life and suddenly that life is snuffed out. You realize what I have to conclude, don't you?"

She looked up at me and again I was struck with how clear and blue her eyes were. The whole of that family had the bluest eyes. Mine, unfortunately, came more from the Scottish side of the family and were a sort of hazel-green. "I have to conclude," she went on, "that on both occasions this was some sort of plot against the Prince of Wales. The two were riding close together in a similar misty situation last year and my son was supposed to be riding Sultan today. And now the prince is nowhere to be found. I've been sick with worry about him. You don't happen to know where he is, do you?"

"I'm afraid I do, ma'am," I said. "He went to the railway station in King's Lynn to try and stop Mrs. Simpson from taking the train to London."

"And didn't think to notify anybody first? Not even his bodyguard. Not even his family. Usual inconsiderate nonsense from that boy." She sighed. "He always has lived only for himself. Nobody else matters, except for that woman. Does he care if his father is failing fast and any worry might kill him? Of course not." She paused. I couldn't think of anything to add to this and remained wisely silent. Then she started speaking again, "One small glimmer of hope, I suppose, is that she has deserted him to go to London. They might even have quarreled. I knew she took exception to his spending the whole of Christmas with his family. She does like to be the center of attention and he is usually so sickeningly devoted to her."

"I'm afraid there was no quarrel, ma'am," I said. "Mrs. Simpson had a nasty accident the night before. She hit her head and was knocked out. So she decided she must go back to London and see her own doctor."

"An accident? She hit her head? At Ermintrude's house?" Her voice was suddenly sharp.

I nodded.

"It makes one wonder, doesn't it?" she said quietly. "So the evil has stretched out that far."

I met her gaze. "Are you saying that you believe in the curse that the servants have been talking about, or do you think that there is someone actively doing harm?"

She managed the ghost of a smile. "I don't think I'm the sort of person who believes in curses, Georgiana. But I do believe in evil. I told you that I can sense it in this place. I sensed it last year when my son's former equerry was killed. Everyone was saying 'frightful bad luck, the poor chap,' but I felt a terrible uneasiness. And as soon as we arrived here a week ago, the same feeling of dread crept over me."

I thought carefully before saying, "Ma'am, you believe that someone within the Sandringham Estate has evil designs on the Prince of Wales?"

"I find that hard to believe that anyone in our employ is actively working against us," she said. "We are most cautious in the way that we vet our employees and frankly everyone working here at Sandringham has been on the estate for years."

"Since the two accidents happened to men on horseback, one could assume that they were the work of an outsider," I suggested. "It isn't hard to gain access to the estate, is it?"

"Absolutely not. You just cross the fields and there you are. Right next to us. I suppose this will mean bringing in the police and doing a thorough check of the area. How tiresome. We came here for some peace. Until now I've managed to keep all this from the king, except for that first shooting accident that narrowly missed my son. The king witnessed that and was quite upset by it. I simply can't risk letting him hear about anything else that would worry him."

I nodded in sympathy.

"Is there anything I can do, ma'am?" I asked.

"Yes, there is," she said. "You have some experience in these matters, don't you? You discovered that previous plot to assassinate us at the royal garden party."

I didn't want to admit that was mainly by luck. So I said nothing.

She reached out and covered my hand with her own. Her hand was ice-cold and I noticed the blue veins standing up through the white skin. "I want you to get to the bottom of this, Georgiana. Reassure me that we are dealing with freak accidents and not with some kind of anarchist or communist." She paused, then added in a low voice, "or a deranged person."

"I'll do my very best, ma'am," I said.

I was just attempting to stand up to leave when the door was thrown open and the Prince of Wales himself came in.

"Ah, there you are at last," his mother said. "Have you any idea of the worry you have caused us? Disappearing without a word to anyone. Not saying where you were going? Not taking any kind of bodyguard with you?"

The prince crossed the room and bent to kiss her cheek. "Don't be silly, Mother. When have I ever needed a bodyguard? Especially out here in the middle of nowhere."

"You've heard the news, I take it?" she said coldly.

"News, what news? I arrived back to be met by some blathering master of house saying my mother had been worried about me, so I came straight to your side like a dutiful son."

He looked from the queen to me. "Didn't you tell them where I'd gone? Or was it misplaced loyalty that made you keep silent?" He looked amused.

"I never had a chance to tell anyone anything," I said. "They were all too busy. There was an accident, sir. Captain Altrungham was thrown from his horse and killed."

"Dickie?" He looked as if I had slapped his face. "Thrown from his horse? That man could ride any horse ever created. Was he attempting to jump something impossible again? That stone wall with the brook beside it where poor old Jeremy came a cropper last year?"

I shook my head. "No, it was in the middle of a flat field. He may have hit his head on an overhanging branch but I can't see how that happened."

"Good God." He sank down into an armchair facing us and put his head into his hands. "I can't quite believe it," he said. "God, I feel awful. I was supposed to be riding that horse. I asked him to do me a favor and take you out riding."

I stood up, feeling horribly embarrassed. "I should go, ma'am."

She nodded solemnly. "Perhaps you should."

I gave a half curtsy, half bow and backed away as one is supposed to do. As I turned to locate the door she added, "I'm counting on you, my dear."

Oh dear. I wish she hadn't said that.

CHAPTER 23

December 26, Boxing Day
On the Sandringham Estate, Norfolk

This is awful. How can the queen expect
me to solve everything? I have no real
skills, just a modicum of luck. This is a
job for the police. They can ask in local
pubs if any strangers have been seen.
They can question suspicious-looking
people, take casts of footprints. But then
if it was an outsider, how on earth did he
arrange for the stairs to fall on Mrs.
Simpson? How could he even have
known they were loose?

Darcy was waiting for me outside. "You
look whacked," he said. "Did you get a
proper grilling?"

"The queen is worried, Darcy," I said.
"She told me she senses evil around the
place."

"That doesn't sound like her. She's normally the most levelheaded of people. Don't tell me she's a believer in the curse?"

"No, not that. But she did sense that something was about to happen and she fears for her son."

"For the Prince of Wales?"

I nodded.

"So she believes that someone is trying to kill him?"

"She does."

"It sounds so improbable, doesn't it." Darcy looked around him. The estate lay still and pristine under its carpet of snow. "Out here, in the middle of the peaceful countryside. If you were going to kill the prince, there would be easier ways to get at him."

"I think the queen believes that it's someone around her. She speaks of the feeling of evil that she detected when she arrived."

"The boys from Scotland Yard should be here by this afternoon," he said. "They will be able to question everybody."

"The queen says that all the staff have been with them for years and are quite loyal."

Darcy opened the motorcar door for me and I got in.

"It does occur to me that if the intended

targets were the Prince of Wales and Mrs. Simpson, then even a most loyal retainer might have felt that he was doing a service to the monarchy by making sure he never becomes king."

"Crikey," I said, hating myself instantly that these schoolgirlish terms came out under moments of extreme stress. "That is a point, isn't it? But how would you ever prove it?"

"One might think it was someone in my aunt's employ since the person knew about the wonky staircase."

I gave a nervous chuckle. "Oh, Darcy, think of it. Her butler is older than the hills. She has a harmless young local maid and footman, gardener and the gardener's wife comes in to do the laundry and heavy cleaning. Oh, and a cook and lady's maid, also aged."

"And Miss Short," he said.

"Oh." I looked up at him. I had forgotten about her again. She was the sort of person one tended to overlook. "And Miss Short. Yes, she does seem the sort of person who feels strongly about the monarchy and tradition and who would be infuriated by an American interloper. And she was out and about when the prince was shot. So I could, indeed, pin the staircase on her. But knocking someone off his horse? That horse is at least sixteen hands and was moving really fast. She's five foot one at the most. What could she do?"

"I don't know," he said. "But I do think it might help if you became friendly with her. As you say, she's a devoted fan of the monarchy. She'd be honored to talk to you. She might spill out more than she intended."

"I love the way you volunteer me to become friendly with someone who, if we go with your strategy, has killed or tried to kill four people. What if she thinks I'm becoming too snoopy and I'm the next victim?"

"As you said, she's only five foot one. Besides, she has no beef with you."

"Reassuring talk," I said.

Darcy started the motor and we drove out of the forecourt.

"And what did you learn while I was being grilled by the queen?" I asked.

"I went to take a look at the corpse. The doctor had arrived and was all set to pronounce it a broken neck caused by a fall from a horse, sign the death certificate and go back to his Boxing Day celebrations. When I suggested he should do an autopsy to see if anything precipitated the fall, he was quite short with me. However, when I pointed out that he could have had a heart attack or stroke, he did come around and agreed I was quite right. So at least now the autopsy will be done."

"If we are considering Miss Short, then putting poison or even a sleeping draft in a drink would be something she could do fairly easily," I said. "Before we go, we should ask the groom if he saw her this morning."

Darcy gave a pained smile. "She's hardly likely to have come into the stable yard and said, 'Do you mind if I slip something in the prince's coffee cup,' is she?"

"No, but if she was wily enough she could have been a frequent visitor, with a carrot or lump of sugar for the horses, then nobody would even pay attention if she came in, patted a few horses, then dropped something into a mug of coffee." I remembered Dickie Altrungham's coffee cup, but then he'd complained it was cold and only took that one swig. "But of course she wouldn't know whose mug, would she? So that doesn't make sense."

Darcy stopped the car again at the entrance to the stable yard. I followed him in. The horses had now been returned to their stalls and the place had an air of tranquility.

We found the groom rearranging bridles in the tack room. Darcy asked him a couple of questions but got nothing out of him. Nobody else had visited the yard this morning except himself and the stableboy. He certainly hadn't seen any strange women around. And he had saddled up Sultan himself so he knew that nobody had tampered with the saddle and bridle.

"I'd swear that was a good sound horse, just raring to go for a gallop when I sent him out of here," he said. "And the young gentleman — well, he was a proper rider, he was. You could tell by his seat." He took a step closer to us. "The boy here thinks that only something supernatural would have spooked that horse. The curse, you know. A ghost, a demon, whatever. The boy says he's seen things himself, when he goes back to his mum at the cottage. Things lurking in the woods and wafting across the fields. Things that would make your blood run cold."

"Did he see anything this morning on his way to work?" I asked.

The groom shook his head. "He slept here in the stable, with no chance of oversleeping, knowing that the prince wanted to be out bright and early."

So that was that, then. We came away having learned nothing except that there were things that lurked in woods and wafted across fields. Darcy must have been thinking identical thoughts because he turned to me as we walked back to the motorcar. "I think we should take another look at that field, don't you? You have sharp eyes for anything unusual."

"Good idea. Although it was clear to me that the horse had not been spooked by anything. My mare was trembling when she came across the body. But Sultan was standing a few yards away just waiting. If anything had frightened him, he would have been off and gone."

"That's true," Darcy agreed.

"So are you intending to drive to the field?" I asked. "Or do we have to walk several miles through paddocks and woods?"

"You're not up to a good hike?" He smiled.

"If it wasn't so awfully cold, I'd say yes. But I think I'm still in shock. I'm shivering."

He put an arm around me. "Don't worry. They told me the way to get there by car. It's a bit bumpy at the end but at least most of it is by road."

"Thank heavens I'm wearing sensible

brogue shoes this time," I muttered. Even so, I anticipated rather wet and cold feet. So we set off. After a mile or so we left the narrow lane and bumped along a farm track where a tractor had churned up mud from melting snow. Darcy came to a stop. "I think we can leave the vehicle here. There won't be any tractors out on Boxing Day."

"We'll need to have Phipps give the motor a good clean when we get home," I said as I got out. And a feeling of homesickness came over me. Home. Safety. Mrs. Holbrook. Granddad. Why, oh why, hadn't we refused Aunt Ermintrude's invitation and stayed there? But I knew the answer — because the queen had sensed something wrong and wanted me nearby.

Darcy took my hand and helped me over a stile, then we walked through a narrow stand of trees, coming out onto the field where the accident had happened. Mist still lay over the far side, but the path where we had ridden was now clear.

"Which tree was it?" Darcy asked me.

I followed the route we had taken, staring up and examining each of the trees as we passed. It seemed so much longer on foot. Then finally we came to a big oak. Its trunk was wound around with ivy and thick branches reached out in all directions.

"This was it, I'm pretty sure," I said. "Yes. I remember looking for somewhere to tie up my horse and noticing those dead brambles beside it."

Darcy stared up at the big branch that came across the path. Then he shook his head. "You were right. It is too high. Even if he was on the biggest horse he'd have gone under it safely — unless he was standing on the saddle."

"Which I'm sure he wasn't," I replied. "He was in a flat-out gallop, which is how he got so far ahead of me." I stood looking around. The silence was complete except for the cawing of distant rooks. I stared up at the tree. It was an old oak with a huge gnarled trunk — exactly the sort of tree I'd have enjoyed climbing when I was a little girl. So someone could have climbed that tree easily and waited. . . . To do what? To shoot Dickie Altrungham? To waft something that spooked his horse? In which case the person could not have climbed down and got away before I arrived. I tried to remember what I had felt when I dismounted to examine the body. Had I sensed any kind of danger? Any eyes watching me? I shook my head. I had been so intent on trying to help Dickie and then on locating his horse that I hadn't given any thought to my own danger.

"I suppose someone could have positioned themselves on that branch so that they could have flapped a piece of cloth and startled the horse," Darcy said.

"But you said yourself he was a splendid rider. If the horse had reared, he would probably have stayed on, or at the most come off backward. Besides, I told you, the horse was quite calm when I found him. He allowed me to lead him and trotted meekly beside me all the way home."

"And the horse would probably have whinnied and you'd have heard Dickie trying to calm him," Darcy agreed.

I looked up again. "Someone could have dropped down a length of rope, a noose, so that the rider was garroted as he went under the branch." I shuddered as I said the words, picturing someone lurking above, leaning out over that branch and dangling down a rope, waiting. . . .

"Then there would have been rope burns on his neck. Besides, a rider on a fast-moving horse would have yanked anyone off a branch above unless the rope was well secured and I don't see any signs of a rope dangling, do you?"

That was definitely true.

"Something happened here," I said. "So you're sure he wasn't shot?"

"He wasn't shot." Darcy went over to the tree.

"Can one get fingerprints from a tree trunk?" I asked.

"I doubt it. Not an old tree like this with all the ivy." He sounded amused. "Besides, my darling, it is the middle of winter, in case you hadn't noticed. Everyone is wearing gloves."

"Oh. Right." I studied the ground. "And you said you didn't find any useful footprints?"

"Unfortunately by the time I got here there were several farm chaps tramping around, so any footprints would have been obscured."

I went to join him, standing beside the trunk. "And since everyone was probably wearing rubber boots the prints all look the same anyway." Then I saw something interesting. "Look, Darcy, there was a lower branch once. It's been cut down. See — there are a couple of logs lying among the brambles."

"Cut down just now?" He sounded excited.

I peered closer and shook my head. "No, some time ago, I should think. Besides, there is no sign of sawdust."

"No use to us, then." He sighed.

294

I stood staring down at where the body had lain. The grass had been well trampled and it was hard to see exactly how the body had been positioned. Then I remembered what I hadn't mentioned before, having not wanted to share the information in front of anybody else.

"Darcy, I told you he was still alive when I knelt down beside him. He said something. . . ."

Darcy was instantly alert. "What did he say?"

"At first he said 'sorry.' And then 'Ellie.' "

"That's his wife. He wanted to tell her he was sorry if he'd caused her grief."

"Might he have caused her grief?"

"He was a bit of a playboy, you know. You remember those English settlers in Africa and how they behaved when we were there."

"All too well. But surely he wasn't as bad as that?"

"Probably not. But I wouldn't have thought he was the faithful type."

I thought of those flirtatious glances he had given me. Not the faithful type. But then he was the one who had told me that Darcy had been a bit of a lad too. Did Darcy intend to be the faithful type? But this was not the time to bring such matters up.

"He apologized to her. That's all that mattered," I said.

"Did he say anything else?"

"Only one word and I couldn't quite get it," I said. "It sounded like 'tapestry,' Does that mean anything to you?"

" 'Tapestry'?" Darcy frowned. "It means nothing to me. Are you sure that's what he said? Could it have been something else? 'Travesty,' maybe?"

"It's possible. It was the tiniest whisper and his lips hardly moved." I shuddered as the image of Dickie Altrungham, lying there with his head at a strange angle flashed before my eyes.

Darcy put an arm around my shoulder. "Come on. Let's get inside. You're shivering again. I don't want my wife coming down with pneumonia."

We made our way back to the stile. As Darcy helped me over I looked out and saw smoke coming from a chimney, not too far away. "There's a house just on the other side of that wood," I said.

Darcy climbed up to join me. "A farm cottage," he said. "Is this Sandringham land still? I suppose it must be. So they would know who owned the cottage — not that it matters. Everyone is inside on Boxing Day, not working the fields."

"I think I recognize that roof," I said. "It's the gardener's cottage behind Wymondham Hall."

"So it is," Darcy agreed. "So we've actually driven in a big circle to get here. Too bad there's not a road through that piece of woodland. Do you want to take that little path and I'll drive and see who gets home first?"

"I would if it weren't so cold," I said.

It was only as we were driving toward Sandringham that I realized the implication of what we had just seen. Someone could have slipped out of Wymondham Hall and returned without being noticed.

CHAPTER 24

December 26, Boxing Day
Wymondham Hall, Norfolk

Oh dear. Now I'm really confused. Is it possible that we are staying in a house with a murderer? I'd love to go home today but the queen is counting on me. I just wish I felt safe.

We arrived back to find everyone assembled in the drawing room. Lady Aysgarth and Mummy had the chairs beside the fire. The major's wife and the Huntleys occupied the sofa facing the fire. Fig was looking awkward and bored as Addy showed her how she dressed her new doll and Binky was kneeling on the floor in the far corner with Podge while they sent the train around a ring of track. Podge and Addy were dressed again in their party clothes while Nanny sat on a straight-backed chair near the door in case they needed to be whisked away at a moment's notice. The grown-ups were drinking sherry. Conversation stopped as we came in. I saw Mrs. Legge-Horne's worried face look up at me.

"Any news?" she asked.

"Not much to tell," Darcy said. "The poor fellow came off his horse and broke his neck. But we can't tell how or why it happened."

"These things happen, even to the best rider," Colonel Huntley said. "Horse puts his foot into a rabbit hole, stumbles and over you go. It's happened to me before."

That was something we hadn't considered. But then surely Sultan would have been limping and the groom had declared him to be sound afterward.

"I meant about my husband," Mrs. Legge-Horne said. "Is he going to be stuck there all day, do you think?"

"I don't see any reason for him to be kept there," Darcy said. "The doctor is conducting a postmortem on Captain Altrungham but that shouldn't involve your husband. I expect he's on his way back now."

I watched her face, the struggle between worry and disgust. She loved him, I thought. But she also knew that she couldn't trust him, and when he was absent her thoughts always went to the worst possible behavior.

Darcy's aunt was sitting by the fire with a lovely purple and gold angora shawl around her shoulders.

"You must be frozen, my children," she said. "Come and sit and get warm. Oh, and help yourselves to sherry first. Luncheon is ready at any time, but we were waiting for you to return. I suppose we should still wait for the major. He will be back for lunch, do you think?"

"I really couldn't say," Darcy replied. "I didn't notice him when we left, but he could have been out in the gun shed, I suppose."

"Of course. The gun shed." Mrs. Legge-Horne said the words flatly.

Darcy poured me a sherry and I took a sip before I perched on a stool close to the fire. I felt the red glow stinging my frozen cheeks and held out my hands to the flames.

"So did you get to see the queen?" Dolly Huntley asked, leaning toward me with excitement on her face.

"Yes, I did. It turns out she was worried because the Prince of Wales had taken off without telling anyone where he was going. So she feared something terrible had happened. She was most annoyed when she found out that he'd only driven to the station to try and stop Mrs. Simpson from going to London."

"So he didn't succeed in stopping her?" Darcy's aunt asked. "She's not on her way back here?"

"As far as I know she's gone back to her London house," I said. "I suppose she may return after she's seen her doctor."

"It wasn't as if she was actually having a good time with us, was it?" Mummy asked, her eyes twinkling as they usually did when she made mischief. "In fact I can clearly state that she was bored to tears. Obviously we are not up to the standards of repartee of her usual glittering set and our conversation was sadly lacking. None of us was worth bothering with."

"She did have the colonel and myself here," Dolly Huntley said in a voice dripping with sweetness. "We are among her oldest and dearest friends and we came all this way especially to be with her."

"Oh dear, I'm so sorry," Mummy said. "Of course you are. How crass of me. So what will you do now? Go back to London or stay on in the hope that Mrs. Simpson returns?"

"I don't see any reason to go rushing back to London, do you, Homer?" Dolly asked him.

"I think we had better stay until we get

confirmation about what the dear lady wants us to do," Colonel Huntley said. "No sense in rushing back to London to stay at a dreary hotel when it is comfortable here."

"It all depends on whether her desire to be near the prince outweighs the inconvenience and boredom of our company," Lady Aysgarth said, looking a little amused. "I doubt that the prince will be able to leave his father's side. It wouldn't be right, knowing that the end might be near."

"Oh gosh. Do you really think so?" Binky looked up from his position on the floor. "I wonder if I should go and pay my respects to the king. I've got great admiration for him."

"As if he'd want to see you, Binky, when he has his family around him," Fig said in her usual cutting tones.

Binky flushed. "Dash it all, Fig, I am related to the old chap, you know."

"First cousin once removed, isn't it?" she said. "And you've only seen the king a few times in your life, haven't you?"

"When grandfather was alive the king used to come up to Castle Rannoch and shoot with us every autumn," Binky said. "He was always kind to me. He'd give me humbugs he carried in his pocket. I think he was fond of me. And he's certainly fond of Georgie."

He looked across at me for confirmation and I nodded. "But I don't think it would be right to intrude on their family Christmas, do you? We should put off any visit until later."

"Oh, absolutely," he said. "I wasn't meaning today. I was meaning before we go home."

"I'll ask the queen what she feels is right and suitable," I said. "I'll tell her you'd like to pay your respects, Binky. As would I."

"So you'll be seeing her again, then," Dolly asked me. "Any chance you could take a couple of your fellow guests for a visit? I'd sure love to see the inside of a palace and to meet a real queen."

"I'm afraid now is not the best time," I replied, feeling awkward. "I'm sure Captain Altrungham's death has shaken them all up. They will be in mourning, won't they?"

"Don't worry, Dolly. If you wait around long enough, you might find that you know a real queen and you can go to the palace whenever you want," Colonel Huntley said.

There was stony silence in the room as we took in the meaning of this.

"Surely you can't possibly mean that Mrs. Simpson might one day find herself in the position of queen?" The words came from

Miss Short. Nobody had noticed her until now. She had been sitting quietly in the background beside the Christmas tree, but her face was now bright red as everyone turned to look at her.

"Well, my dear," Colonel Huntley said in his slow southern drawl, "if the Prince of Wales becomes king and he marries her, which I'm sure he intends to do when her divorce goes through, won't that make her a queen?"

"Certainly not!" Miss Short said. "A twice-divorced commoner? Unheard of. Impossible. The British people would never stand for it."

Lady Aysgarth tried to smooth things over. "You have to understand, Colonel Huntley, that we feel rather personally about our monarchy. And the truth is that the king is per se head of the Church of England. And the Church does not condone divorce. So for the king to marry a divorced woman in the first place would be a breach of all his position stands for. And to try and make her queen? Well, that simply would not do. Parliament would never allow it."

"But when he's king, can't he just change the law and proclaim her as queen?" Dolly asked. "I know that's what she wants."

"Well, I'm certainly never curtsying to

her," Fig said adamantly. For once I was in complete agreement with her.

"I really think we had better go in to luncheon," Lady Aysgarth said. "We are keeping the kitchen staff from their afternoon off."

I was now feeling jolly hungry, after the scares and shocks of the morning, so was happy when everyone agreed.

"We'll save some for your husband, Mrs. Legge-Horne," Lady Aysgarth said, "in case he doesn't get a bite to eat at the big house."

We went into the dining room in no particular order. Luncheon was a simple affair. It was a large game stew, made from the leftover parts of partridge and turkey, as well as fresh rolls. Very satisfying. Since we were not assigned places, I chose to sit next to Miss Short at the foot of the table. She looked embarrassed as I sat beside her.

"Oh no, Lady Georgiana. You should be sitting among the honored guests, not next to me."

"I don't think we're being very formal this time," I said, giving her an encouraging smile, "and I don't want you to feel you are being left out of the conversation."

"I am only the companion." She blushed bright pink. "In fact I consider myself fortunate that Lady Aysgarth includes me in such a glittering party. I could well picture myself eating on a tray alone in my room. As it is, I've had a splendid Christmas. One of the nicest I remember."

Apart from a man dying and a woman being knocked out, I wanted to say. I certainly didn't want to put her on the defensive.

"It has been really nice," I agreed. "I was rather disappointed not to be spending my first Christmas as a married woman in my own home, but I'm glad I came after all."

"Apart from your horrid shock this morning," she said. "I trust you are now over the worst. Let's hope it won't create nightmares."

"I am over the worst," I said. "Although I feel so bad for that man's family. He leaves a wife and little children, doesn't he?"

"I believe so. I don't think I've ever met him. We do not exactly mingle with the higher echelons at Sandringham House. The prince coming here to visit was a novelty, although Lady Aysgarth usually sees members of the royal household quite regularly, in normal circumstances. This time, with the king being so weak, she has stayed tactfully away, unless summoned."

"You said you've been with Lady Aysgarth for quite a while," I said. "I remember you said you had a little tea shop in Harrow-gate."

Her face flushed again. "How kind of you to remember. Yes indeed. Such a pretty little place it was. How I regretted having to give it up. But I think I can say that I found a position where I could be of use with Lady Aysgarth. I don't believe you ever visited Aysgarth Abbey? It was rather a depressing sort of house and her ladyship was very much alone there. The earl was often away — jaunts to the Continent, you know. Gambling in Monte Carlo, that sort of thing. And he never let her travel with him." She gave me a knowing little look. "He liked to be fancy-free, if you get my meaning."

"So why didn't she travel too? On her own?"

She leaned closer to me. "It's my belief he kept her short of money. Only enough for the housekeeping, and no more."

"So she wasn't too unhappy to leave the place in Yorkshire behind and come here, then?"

"She was thrilled to be asked by the queen, if you must know. And that house was enough to drive anybody to depression. Do you know she used to paint all the time — it was her one outlet. She'd be up in her studio in one of the turrets, painting away, day after day. And since she's come here she's hardly painted a stroke. She feels more positive, you see. Her whole personality has changed. She has turned herself into the image of the person the queen would want her to be. The perfect lady-in-waiting again, just like all those years ago in her youth."

"I wonder if she misses the painting," I suggested.

"I think it was her only means of expression and emotion before. Now she's settled into being an ordinary country woman — visiting the chickens, walking the dogs."

"I thought you walked the dogs," I said.

"Only when she doesn't want to. Usually she's out bright and early every morning with those dogs. Only today she asked me to do it as she wanted to make sure her guests were all taken care of at breakfast. I took them on her usual route — quite heavy going with snow still in places and frozen puddles. The dogs were rather impatient with me and my little legs. I had to watch that they didn't run off. She'd never forgive me if I lost one of them. She adores those animals. Lord Aysgarth did not like dogs and never allowed her to have any."

"How awful. A house needs dogs around, I think. Darcy and I are giving each other a puppy for Christmas."

"That's the ticket." She smiled at me. "Would you like a little more of this delicious stew? You haven't eaten much and it's getting cold."

I was trying to think what else I might want to ask her while I had the chance. "I shouldn't really. I had far too much food yesterday. But let me give you a little more."

"I won't say no. Wonderfully rich and satisfying, isn't it?"

I dug the ladle into the bowl in front of us, searching around for good pieces of meat. Then something strange floated into the bowl. It took me a moment to realize it was a turkey's foot — its nasty clawed toes sticking out of the gravy. Hastily I dropped it onto my own plate. "Ah, here's a nice little wing," I said and put that onto Miss Short's plate. I suspected that the turkey foot had been Queenie's work and hoped I had been the only recipient of one.

"You must enjoy being here rather than in Yorkshire," I went on with my chat.

"Oh yes. So much nicer here. Not nearly as lonely. The weather, the surroundings and the fact that we are close to the royal family at Sandringham. Such an honor. Sometimes we see the little princesses out riding with their groom. Such sweet little girls, and so dignified too. It's my hope that little Elizabeth will be queen someday. I can't see her uncle the Prince of Wales producing a child at his age, even if he does marry that woman. And I'm sure the child would not be deemed a rightful heir."

"One would hope not," I said.

There was an awkward silence, then I asked, "You had no near neighbors at Aysgarth?"

"There were a few cottages down by the ford. Local farming folk, you know. But as for meeting the right sort of people — very rarely. Lord Aysgarth was not what you would call sociable — unless a pretty woman was involved." She gasped as she said this, realizing that she had overstepped the mark and glanced down the table to see if her employer was listening. But Lady Aysgarth was deep in conversation with Colonel Huntley and my mother.

"So how did he die in the end?" I asked. "An accident, someone said?"

She nodded. "He liked to go out walking. It's rugged country in the Dales. He was going through a ravine when a large boulder crashed down onto him."

She tried to look regretful but I thought she found this pleasing.

I wasn't sure what to ask her next when I

heard a knock at the front door, then male voices.

"Ah, my husband is home at last," Mrs. Legge-Horne said.

But instead the butler came into the dining room. "There is a gentleman from Scotland Yard who wishes to speak with Lady Georgiana and Mr. O'Mara."

CHAPTER 25

December 26, Boxing Day
Wymondham Hall, Norfolk

> This is not turning into a merry Christmas
> at all. It is one worry after another. In
> future I will stay home, whoever invites
> me!

The man who stood waiting for us in the
foyer had that typical Scotland Yard detective look I had seen many times before —
and in case you think I've been arrested on
several occasions, let me point out that I
was the one they were asking for help, at
least most of the time. This one was thin,
with a little fawn mustache and sunken
cheeks. He had his collar turned up, was
now clutching a trilby hat and looked frozen
to the marrow.

"Mr. O'Mara?" he asked, still stamping
his feet a little to bring them back to life.

"That's right," Darcy said. "And this is my wife, Lady Georgiana."

"I'm Detective Chief Inspector Broad. How do you do, ma'am." He gave me a nod.

For some reason I found that amusing. A man called Broad when he was clearly so narrow. I tried not to smile.

"Shall we go into the drawing room to talk?" I suggested, as I didn't know what other rooms there might be on the ground floor of the house. "The company is still at luncheon, so we should have some quiet there."

"Somewhere near a fire, if you don't mind," he said. "I've just walked over from Sandringham House."

"That's a good walk in this weather, Detective Chief Inspector," Darcy said.

"Not intentional, I can assure you. I asked where I might find you and was told this place was 'just on the other side of the trees,' We came by train, you see. And in a taxicab."

"Oh goodness." I gave him a friendly smile. "We'll run you back when you are ready, then. But would you like a hot drink? Or something to eat?"

"I wouldn't say no, ma'am," he said.

I considered mentioning that I was normally addressed as "my lady" and not "ma'am," then I realized I was the wife of a mister. Therefore he was probably within his rights to call me "ma'am" now — although I still retained my title.

I rang the bell inside the drawing room. Heslop appeared and I requested a cup of tea, a bowl of soup and a sandwich if possible. Queenie brought them in soon afterward. From the shape of the sandwich I'd say that she'd made it, but at least it didn't have any poultry feet sticking out of it. The inspector seemed grateful and we let him eat and drink before he spoke.

"Mr. O'Mara," he said, "I'm not quite sure why we were summoned here, but I gather you were the one who alerted Scotland Yard, and since the dead man was one of our own, so to speak, and the royal family is involved, I was sent here straightaway. Perhaps you can fill me in on the pertinent details."

Darcy related the facts. Like most policemen I had met, the DCI's expression did not waver. When Darcy had finished, Broad said, "Let me get this straight — a young man falls off his horse and you think it's a job for Scotland Yard?"

"A couple of reasons for bringing you here, Detective Chief Inspector. First, this man was an excellent rider. I have played polo with him on several occasions. And second, I too would have called this a tragic accident if it had been an isolated incident. Unfortunately an identical occurrence happened at this time last year, to another superb rider. Then a few days ago someone happened to graze the Prince of Wales with gunshot." Darcy leaned forward in his chair. "Now, the reason this is worrying to me is that the Prince of Wales was supposed to go riding with my wife, and the dead man rather resembles the prince."

The inspector's face now grew more solemn and intent. "So what you are suggesting, sir, is that someone was trying to kill the prince."

"I fear that may be the case," Darcy said.

DCI Broad now turned to me. "I understand you were the one who was riding with him. Did you actually see him fall?"

I explained about the mist and the fact that his horse was much faster. "I came upon his body lying there across the path," I said. I didn't think it necessary to mention to this man that Dickie had apologized to his wife before he died. "His horse was standing nearby. This makes me feel that the horse had not been spooked in any way. Nor was it injured."

"And did you happen to see anyone else

in the vicinity?"

I shook my head. "Nobody. It was absolutely silent and we were in the middle of fields."

He sighed. "I don't know what anyone thinks I can do."

"You can look into the staff at Sandringham, can't you? See if anyone might have a grudge, or be an Irish republican sympathizer." Darcy grinned. "Yes, I know I sound like an Irishman but I have chosen my British citizenship and I think you'll find I'm known to your boss at the Yard."

"That's true, sir. I was told if you said it was necessary, it probably was." Broad frowned. "You think it could be Irish sympathizers, out here in the middle of nowhere?"

"A good place to ambush a prince with nobody around him, don't you think?"

"I suppose so." He sighed. I've found that policemen sigh a lot. And suck through their teeth in an annoying manner.

"At the very least you could have your men snoop around the neighborhood and see if any strangers stayed at a local pub," Darcy suggested.

I glanced across at Darcy. Was he going to mention what happened to Mrs. Simpson, or that Miss Short had been out with the dogs when the accident happened? Apparently not. I had been mainly silent, unless asked to speak, but suddenly something came to me with remarkable clarity. Major Legge-Horne had been out and about on both occasions. He had been assisting at the king's shoot when the prince was winged. And he had turned up at the stables when I came back with the horses, claiming he had overslept. But now that I came to think about it, he had seemed a little out of breath. And had he actually been in the room when Mrs. Simpson was hit by the stairs? It was hard to remember if anyone wandered in and out.

The only thing against this was that he was a proud former officer in a Guards regiment. The best soldiers and most loyal men to the Crown anywhere. But I supposed what we had surmised about Miss Short might also be true for the major. A great patriot might be disgusted that the future monarch planned to marry such an unsuitable woman. He might have thought, as others had done, that the second son would make a better king and decided to take matters into his own hands. He would know the route we were going to take when we went out riding, because it was the route of the hunt the year before and he had taken part in that — albeit not too successfully.

"What is it, Georgie?" Darcy asked me, sensing my thoughts.

"I was just wondering about Major Legge-Horne," I said. "He was on the spot on every occasion."

"Who is this major?" the DCI asked.

"He's staying here at the house," I said, "and I have no reason to suspect him except that he is the one person who was close to both the crimes, and who knew which route we'd take on our ride." I saw Darcy give me a strange warning look. "As I said, I'm sure he's a true-blue officer of the Guards, but I was just wondering if he might be the sort to take matters into his own hands for the sake of England."

"Meaning what, ma'am?" DCI Broad asked.

"Meaning that the Prince of Wales might not make an entirely suitable monarch."

"And why might that be, ma'am?" He looked puzzled. "I understand he's been a bit of a playboy, but I'd say his heart's in the right place and I'm sure he'll step up to the job when the old king dies."

That's when I realized what a good job the British newspapers were doing. He didn't know about Mrs. Simpson, even if his superiors did!

"We'll take a look at this major, if you

think we should, madam," he said, "but I don't see how we are going to be able to prove anything if a bloke falls off his horse in the middle of nowhere and there are no indications of any injury except for a broken neck from the fall."

"I suggest we wait for the autopsy before we abandon this completely," Darcy said. "If Captain Altrungham had been drugged, for example?"

"For what reason, sir?" The inspector still looked confused. "I mean, why would anyone want to kill him?"

"I couldn't tell you, Detective Chief Inspector. But I do believe, given that this is a repeat of last year's accident, that foul play could have been involved."

"Don't young gentlemen take stupid risks during hunts?" The inspector had that sort of disdainful smirk I'd seen before when talking of the aristocracy.

"We do come off occasionally," Darcy said. "I've taken part in hunts, I've ridden in steeplechases. I've fallen off a few times, but I've never hurt myself seriously and I don't think I've come across anybody who died from a fall until now."

The DCI sighed again. "Well, Mr. O'Mara, I was told by my chief to take you seriously, so that's what I'm doing. I'll have my men look into all those working on the Sandringham Estate. We'll ask around at local pubs as to whether there have been any strangers staying the night and I'll even take a look at the site of the accident — just in case there is any kind of clue."

"We were out there this morning," I said. "The problem is that a group of men with a tractor went out to retrieve the body, so any footprints in places where it's still snowy have been well and truly trampled over." I paused. The inspector was paying attention. I went on, "There was a suggestion that he might have hit an overhanging branch, which of course would have knocked him from his horse. But Mr. O'Mara and I decided the only overhanging branch was far too high above the biggest horse. There had been a lower branch but it had been cut down some time previously, not too recently, I think. Anyway, the pieces of the branch still lying under the tree had traces of snow on them."

"So you saw nothing out of the ordinary?"

"Only that the tree would have been easy to climb. A person could have sat on that branch, waited for the rider and then dropped something onto him. But I arrived soon afterward and there was nobody around, no sign of footprints coming to pick up a large rock or anything heavy."

Detective Chief Inspector Broad shook his head. "What you are suggesting would require enormous precision and a lot of luck. To drop something onto a fast-moving rider so that you knocked him from his saddle and didn't just injure him?"

"I suppose you are right," I said. "And besides, something like that could also have injured the horse and the horse was quite calm and in good health when I retrieved him."

"I'll go and take a look for myself," he said. "Maybe you'd like to come with me, Mr. O'Mara. Show me exactly where it was — and hopefully give me a lift in your vehicle so that I don't have to walk."

"I'll be happy to," Darcy said.

I waited for him to say "Won't you join us, Georgie?" but he didn't. Instead he said, "I'll see you later then, darling."

And off they went, leaving me feeling slightly miffed.

CHAPTER 26

December 26, Boxing Day
Wymondham Hall, Norfolk

> Darcy has gone off without me. Clearly in
> the end I am a mere woman and not a
> member of the boys' club! Still, that does
> not stop me from doing my own investi-
> gations.

I returned to the dining room to find that
the pudding course was finished and the
guests had already gone through to the sitting room for coffee. Faces looked up at me
expectantly as I came in.

"An inspector from Scotland Yard, did you
say?" Aunt Ermintrude asked. "What on
earth could he want?"

"Captain Altrungham's death," I said.
"He's gone with Darcy to see where it happened."

"What for, exactly?"

"I suppose one can't be too careful when the royal family is involved," I said.

"I don't understand," she said, frowning now. "A man falls off his horse. It's not a matter of national security, is it?"

"Well, I think it's because a similar accident happened last year. I think there are people who feel it's too much of a co-incidence."

"Utter rubbish," Darcy's aunt said. "If you're part of a hunt, you take risks and jump things you probably shouldn't jump. And if you go out riding on an icy morning, horses can stumble and throw you. Terribly sad in both cases, I admit, but nothing the police can do anything about."

Colonel Huntley was leaning forward in his chair, his eyes focused on me. "Is there any reason to believe that this wasn't entirely an accident, do you think?"

"How could you possibly tell?" Darcy's aunt said. "And if it were, if someone was hiding behind a tree and leaped out to frighten the horse, there was still no guarantee you'd unseat the rider. Especially not a good rider."

"He wasn't shot or anything, was he?" the colonel asked.

I shook my head. "There was no trace of blood on him. Just an obviously broken neck from the fall."

"Well then, there you are," Darcy's aunt said. "Calling that poor man away from his family on Boxing Day for nothing." She got up. "Does anyone want to take a rest? We can play a game or do a jigsaw puzzle."

"I think Dolly and I will take a little nap," the colonel said.

"I'm up for a card game or a board game," Binky said. "Nothing energetic like sardines after a large meal."

"I'll join you at a board game," Fig said, being remarkably agreeable for once. "It must be ages since we've played anything. What do you have, Lady Aysgarth?"

"There should be some games in the corner cabinet," Darcy's aunt replied. "Snakes and Ladders, that sort of thing."

"Jolly good fun, Snakes and Ladders," Binky said. "Come on, Fig. Going to join us, Lady Aysgarth? Georgie?"

"I think I have had enough excitement for one day," I said.

"I'd go up and have a rest, my dear," Darcy's aunt said kindly. "Shock can be delayed, you know. And finding a dead body — well, that's enough to upset even the strongest of constitutions."

I didn't like to say that I'd come across several dead bodies in recent years. "I think

I'd rather stay with the company until Darcy returns," I said.

"Who'd like to make a fourth?" Binky asked, still with that hopeful and enthusiastic look on his face. "How about you, Mrs. Legge-Horne."

She shook her head. "Oh no, thank you. I couldn't concentrate on anything until my husband returns. I'm worried about him."

"I don't think you've anything to worry about," Lady Aysgarth said. "I'm sure they are all at sixes and sevens at Sandringham now, especially with the arrival of London policemen. He's probably been asked to stay on."

"Yes," Mrs. Legge-Horne said, nodding as if trying to convince herself of this. "Although what he could contribute to anything I've no idea, since he was up too late to join you in the ride."

Did she sound a little too emphatic? Did she, in fact, have suspicions about her husband that were similar to mine?

"I'll be happy to make the fourth," Miss Short said. "It's been ages since Lady Aysgarth and I played a game."

I took a magazine over to the window seat and turned the pages mechanically, half listening to animated voices as the game started. Binky's delighted crow: "Oh, how about that? The biggest ladder, eh, Fig?"

And Fig's equally delighted: "Oh no, Miss Short. You've landed on the snake."

I got up to pour myself a cup of coffee, then seeing Mrs. Legge-Horne sitting alone on a sofa I went to sit beside her. "I'm sure he's all right," I said. "It wasn't as if he came riding with us."

She gave me a tired little smile. "Don't worry, my dear. You wouldn't understand. My husband is not exactly what you might call reliable. I'm often not sure where he is or what he's doing."

I understood that well enough. Off somewhere with a woman, maybe? Flirting, or worse? I was about to change the subject to something harmless when I heard the crunch of tires on gravel. I looked out of the window, hoping it might be Darcy back already, but it was the major himself.

"Here's the major now," I said. "See, you were worrying for nothing."

"That's right. For nothing," she said. She got up and started toward the front door when the major came running up the steps and let himself into the house.

"Where on earth have you been, Reggie?" Mrs. Legge-Horne demanded. "We were all worried sick about you."

"You mean you were worried. I don't suppose anybody else cared," he said and from the aggressiveness in his voice I could tell he had been drinking. "If you really want to know, some of the chaps at Sandringham — the beaters, outside staff — were having their own little Christmas party today and they kindly invited me to join them. It would have been churlish to refuse, so we had a couple of Scotches together. In the Christmas spirit, you know."

"You could have let us know."

"How could I let you know, you silly woman? There's no telephone here. Did you think I was going to drive all the way back just to tell you I wouldn't be back for a while? Use your head, for God's sake."

"I was worried something had happened to you."

"Worried? What on earth could have happened to me? I was at Sandringham bloody House, for God's sake. With the bloody royal family. Did you think I'd be set upon by one of their dogs?"

"A man was killed this morning," she said.

"A chap fell off his horse. And luckily for you I did not go riding."

"Well, remember that you nearly came a cropper on the hunt last year," she said. "On exactly the same route, so I hear."

"I did not come a cropper. The horse

became a bit lame and I had to walk him home through the fields, that's all."

"Not what I heard," she muttered.

"What did you say?"

"Nothing." There was a silence, then she said, "You must be starving. Shall I have some lunch brought to you?"

"Don't fuss, old thing," he said. "I had plenty to keep me going. They had sausage rolls and Scotch eggs — all that sort of thing. I'm well taken care of and now all I need is a little nap. See you later, all right."

And he set off up the stairs, leaving her standing at the doorway to the sitting room. When she came back in, I saw the pain and humiliation on her face. Trying to be tactful I picked up a magazine and appeared to be engrossed in it.

"Your husband finally came home, did he?" Lady Aysgarth asked.

"Yes, thank you." I saw Mrs. Legge-Horne fighting to control her expression. "Apparently he was invited to join the Boxing Day celebration with some of the Sandringham staff and didn't like to refuse."

"Of course not," Lady Aysgarth said. "Better let him sleep it off, then."

She went back to Snakes and Ladders. I kept glancing out of the window, waiting for Darcy to return. In the end I put on my coat and hat and went for a walk. I headed in the direction of the gardener's cottage, thinking I might check in on my puppy — Bubble, or was it Squeak? I changed my mind at the last moment, realizing that Boxing Day was a family celebration and I shouldn't intrude. So I kept going, then came to the edge of a field and stared out, trying to locate the line of trees where the accident had occurred. There was a copse in the way, which blocked a clear view of the actual tree, but I had more or less pinpointed it when I glanced down. There were footprints in the snow heading in that direction. Someone had come this way since the snowfall.

I reasoned that this was Miss Short with the dogs, nothing out of the ordinary. But it would be worth mentioning to Darcy when he came back. I didn't know if there were any distinctive markers on the soles of Wellington boots but he might. A cold wind stung my cheeks. I stuffed my hands into my pockets and headed back to the house.

CHAPTER 27

December 26, Boxing Day
Wymondham Hall, Norfolk

I feel I should be getting somewhere. There is something nagging at the edge of my consciousness — something that should be obvious. I am certain now that Captain Altrungham's death was not an accident. I need to find out more about the major, also Miss Short. It doesn't seem to be turning out to be a restful Christmas!

Darcy arrived home just in time for tea. We were in the sitting room, enjoying slices of the Christmas cake, when he came in. His face lit up, although whether that was from seeing me or the cake I couldn't tell.

"Ah tea. Jolly good," he said. "I had to miss my pudding after luncheon." He helped himself to a large slice of Christmas cake and came to sit beside me on the window seat.

I didn't like to interrupt him while he was eating and I couldn't very well with everyone in the room. "All well here?" he asked at last. "Did the major finally come home?"

"He did. He said he'd been celebrating with the outdoor staff at the big house."

"Oh? Oh, right." He didn't say any more, but I sensed there were things left unsaid. Annoyingly we were not going to change for dinner, as it was to be another cold supper so that the servants could enjoy their day at home if they lived nearby. He was obviously thinking along the same lines as he said, "I couldn't find my fountain pen earlier. Have you seen it? I must have dropped it in the bedroom."

"I'll help you look," I said and we made a graceful exit.

Once upstairs in our own room I burst out, "Well? Did you learn anything?"

"I'm not sure," he said. "It seems that Dickie did communicate with Scotland Yard a few days ago, reporting the attempted shooting of the Prince of Wales and saying that he had some idea who might be responsible."

I thought about this. "So why not just shoot him? Less risky than knocking him off his horse."

"But not as easy to claim as an accident."

"No."

"He had, apparently, been uneasy about last year's fatal accident as well."

"So he had his suspicions but never voiced them?"

"He might have, but apparently nobody listened."

"Pity."

"We went to take another look at the site. There was some evidence of bark being disturbed on the branch above. It's possible someone was up there and able to hit him with something."

I frowned. "It wouldn't be that easy to get down in a hurry and I was only a minute or two later on the scene."

"You don't think anyone could have been hiding up in the tree?"

I considered this. "I suppose it's possible. It is a big tree, after all. And ivy growing on the trunk. I didn't have any sense of danger, but perhaps I was too shocked by what I was seeing. Once I saw he was dead, all I wanted to do was to find his horse and notify everyone."

"Might you have heard anyone breathing?"

I had to laugh at this. "Hardly. We had

two horses who had been galloping flat out. They were both breathing pretty hard." The picture swam into my head of the horses' breaths, puffing out like steam.

Darcy shook his head. "The whole thing is hopeless, unless the police turn up an undesirable anarchist staying at the local inn. They are doing a background check on everyone at Sandringham."

"Speaking of which, I saw your face when I said the major had come home."

"I don't think there was any kind of celebration for the staff at Sandringham," Darcy said. "The moment the death was announced the queen declared the house would be in mourning."

"Oh." We exchanged a long look. "So where do you think he was?"

"At the very best at a pub . . ."

"Are pubs open on Boxing Day?"

"Some might be, especially in the country where things aren't too regulated. He might also have a lady friend nearby."

"Don't tell his wife, will you?" I said.

"I suspect she already knows what he's like."

"By the way," I said, remembering my own little piece of news. "I went for a walk. There were footprints going past the gardener's cottage and out across the field in the direction of Dickie Altrungham's accident. Of course, it could just have been Miss Short walking the dogs, but . . ."

"But worth taking a picture of a print, just in case there is something unique about it," Darcy said.

"What else do we do now?" I asked.

"They've asked me to help out," Darcy said.

I gave him a long, hard stare. Men were asked to help out. But then I remembered that the queen had specifically asked me. "Darcy," I said, "did you ever mention the accident that happened to Mrs. Simpson?"

"I did not. It became quite clear that the rank and file at Scotland Yard does not know about her relationship to the prince and I didn't think it was up to me to inform them."

"So they don't know that someone connected with this house might be a prime suspect?"

"No." He paused. "Let them exhaust their inquiries at Sandringham and in the neighborhood first. And we can keep our eyes open here. Take a look at Miss Short's boots when she goes out next."

"And the major?" I asked.

Darcy frowned. "You think the major might have something to do with it? A major in the Guards?"

"Only because he was at the scene each time. He rode with the hunt last year and was late returning, claiming his horse had gone lame. He was handing out shotguns when the prince was shot, and he showed up at the stables just when I returned with the horses, claiming he'd come too late to join us."

"I see." He looked troubled. "So what would his motive be?"

"Same as Miss Short — he loves his country and he can't abide the thought of an American divorcée marrying the king. He also thinks David is weak and will make a poor monarch."

"I'd hardly say that Bertie is much better," Darcy said. "He has that awful stutter. He's not good in public. He loses his temper."

"But I think he's true-blue, Darcy," I said. "And look how wonderful the Duchess of York is. She's absolutely made him. They know how to behave and they care about the country. And little Lilibet could well be queen someday."

"You have a point there," he said. "So we observe the major, although how we tie him in to a riding accident I have no idea."

We joined the group in the sitting room.

Binky suggested another game, but it was clear that we were rapidly losing interest in the Christmas spirit of togetherness. Lady Aysgarth produced a big jigsaw puzzle, which kept some of the group occupied. Major Legge-Horne reappeared, having slept off whatever he'd been drinking.

"So what is the plan for tomorrow?" Colonel Huntley asked.

"The king has said that he feels well enough for a small shoot," the major said. "I gather the queen is not at all happy about it. The cold weather is bad for his chest; and she doesn't think it's proper with a death in the household but she doesn't want to stop the king from a small pleasure, so we'll be going out around nine."

"Any chance I could join you?" Colonel Huntley asked. "I've done some duck hunting in my time."

"I think that would be acceptable," the major said. "They did mention that I could invite Mr. O'Mara and the Duke of Rannoch, so I presume you could tag along too, although I should warn you there are strict protocols involved in British shoots. If you come, you will have to observe the rules of rank. You only shoot when I tell you to."

"Quite understood," the colonel said. "I'm a military man, don't forget. I know all about rank and protocol."

"Are wives allowed to come along and watch?" Dolly asked excitedly.

"I believe that would be permitted, as long as you stay silent and keep well behind the line of marksmen. They bring chairs and blankets, hot broth — that sort of thing. If you do come, please remember that my reputation is at stake here. I can't afford to have you do anything that would embarrass me, like going over to talk to the royal family without an invitation."

"Oh, I do understand," she said. "I'll be as good as gold. Do you think the little princesses will be there?"

"I'm sure they won't. I believe it will only be the king, the Prince of Wales — maybe the Duke and Duchess of York and the Duke of Gloucester. The Duke of Kent is now with the family, as his wife has a new baby. So will you be joining us, Your Grace? Mr. O'Mara?"

"Oh rather!" Binky said. "I haven't had a decent shoot in ages. Shall you be coming, Fig?"

"Good God, no," Fig replied. "I can't think of anything worse than standing in a freezing meadow waiting for birds to fly past."

"Darcy?" Binky asked.

"I'll come," Darcy said. "And I think Georgie would like to as well."

"Not to shoot," I said. "I'm a poor shot. I'd embarrass you. But I don't mind providing moral support." A shoot involving the Prince of Wales was definitely not something I'd want to miss. I looked across to my mother, who was in the best chair as always. "Do you want to come with us?"

"To watch poor defenseless birds being shot? How absolutely ghastly. I can't think of anything worse, except watching an inferior actor play Hamlet. So thank you, darling, but I'll stay curled up by the fire. I'll see if I can find a good book."

"Shall we join them, Lady Aysgarth?" Miss Short asked.

"You go with them by all means," Darcy's aunt said, "but the thought of standing in the bitter cold watching someone else shooting birds has lost its appeal for me. Too many years of standing there while the earl went shooting."

"I do like a good shoot," Miss Short said, "but I should probably stay and keep you company."

"Oh, don't be such a martyr, Shortie. If you want to go, go."

Miss Short shook her head. "No, I'd only be in the way, I expect. Let's hope it won't decide to snow."

"There is supposed to be a hard frost overnight," Lady Aysgarth said. "That should mean the lake is ready for skating. I think they have extra blades at Sandringham if we want to make a skating party one day."

"Oh God," Fig said again.

With plans for the morning in place we enjoyed our sherry and sausage rolls and then went in to supper. It was another simple meal, this time a big turkey curry with accompaniments. From the way we fell upon it you'd have thought we hadn't eaten for days. It was very tasty and just right for a winter evening. An orange mousse followed and then port for the gentlemen while we returned to the sitting room for coffee. This time nobody seemed in the mood for a game. We listened to a concert on the wireless for a while and eventually went up to bed.

CHAPTER 28

December 27
Wymondham Hall and later on a pheasant
shoot at Sandringham Estate, Norfolk

I am feeling quite queasy this morning.
Queasy and uneasy. And not just the
result of the turkey curry. As if something
is about to happen. I rather wish I hadn't
said I'd attend the shoot. But if something is about to happen, maybe I can
do something to stop it. Miss Short said
she isn't coming, but the major will be
there and it will be up to me to keep an
eye on him.

The day dawned with a red sun rising over
bare trees and frost sparkling on the ground.
"You will be careful, won't you?" I said to
Darcy as we dressed in our bedroom.
"You don't think anyone will mistake me
for the Prince of Wales, do you?" he asked. I

had to smile too. Darcy is almost six feet tall with dark curly hair, and my cousin the prince is short and blond.

"It's just that I have an uneasy feeling in my stomach," I said. "I almost hope the king isn't feeling well enough and they call it off."

But no such message came from Sandringham. We were urged by Lady Aysgarth to eat a hearty breakfast, but I was too tense to eat more than a couple of mouthfuls of scrambled egg and a little Marmite on toast. We had to take two motorcars, Binky in ours and the colonel and his wife with the major and Mrs. Legge-Horne. I realized as I watched that lady getting into their motorcar that nobody had asked her whether she wanted to attend but here she was. Perhaps her husband took it for granted that she'd accompany him.

We set off toward Sandringham House, the tires crackling as we drove through icy puddles. There we were met by men who helped us into waiting shooting brakes and off we bumped to follow the royal party to a copse at the edge of a field. The field had not been plowed and still held dead stubble. The woods behind where the men were taking up position were quite dense with plenty of what looked like rhododendron bushes. We ladies were offered chairs among the bushes, which was good, as it sheltered us from the worst of the bitter wind. Even though I was warmly wrapped in my overcoat, felt hat and woolly scarf as well as tweed trousers, I couldn't stop shivering. My position was behind Darcy and I sat, leaning forward, all senses fine-tuned as the king and his sons, as well as the Duchess of York, were escorted to the prime places. Major Legge-Horne was moving among the beaters, keepers and gundog handlers in that slightly too officious way of his. I watched the dogs, sitting still, but eager and ready beside their handlers.

Major Legge-Horne called out the rules. Numbering from left to right. King first. Make sure you finish off a bird with the second barrel. Loaded guns were handed to the participants. The beaters moved off to do their job. We heard the crunch of dry grass as they moved through the stubble. Suddenly there was the beat of wings and birds rose awkwardly into the air. As they came over in front of us there was a burst of gunfire. Several birds fell. Dogs rushed out to retrieve them. I really dislike killing things but I always seem to find this exciting. I suppose it's in my blood. More birds were flushed, from a different angle this time. Guns crackled. Birds dropped. My gaze moved up and down the line of marksmen. I noticed the king had trouble raising his shotgun and had to be assisted. My gaze focused on the Prince of Wales. He seemed to have lost interest and was standing back for a cigarette. The other royals were still enthusiastically accepting newly loaded guns. I saw that Darcy had hit both of his birds. So had Binky. My brother was actually a good shot. I turned to look at the other women. Because of the thick nature of the woodland I couldn't see any of them properly — only a hat with a feather in it here and Dolly Huntley's unsuitable red hat just on the other side of a bush. At least she was behaving herself and not upsetting anyone with loud stage whispers of excitement.

I was tempted to stand up for a better look at everything, but that wouldn't have been right. We were supposed to sit still and not move. Finally the Prince of Wales said, "I think His Majesty has had enough. Ready to call it a day, Father?"

"I think so, my boy," the king said. "Not as fit as I used to be. Either that or the damned guns are getting heavier." He came stomping back toward us. "But we got ourselves a fine bag, didn't we? The keepers did a good job of raising the birds this year.

You must tell them that, Major. Give them a bottle of Scotch each, eh?" Then he looked around. "Where has the damned fellow got to? Skulking off again?"

The loaders looked around. "He was here not too long ago, Your Majesty," one of them said. "He scolded me for dropping shot on the ground."

"Well, he's not here now," the Prince of Wales said. "We'll probably find him in the gun room with the whiskey."

He assisted the king back to the nearest shooting brake. The rest of the royal party followed while the loaders collected spent shot and stacked the guns to be transported back to the house. The dogs were leashed and loaded into a shooting brake, until one of them pulled at the leash and started barking. He dragged his handler to a bushy area, not far from where I had been sitting, and that was when we noticed a foot sticking out from under a bush.

CHAPTER 29

December 27
On the Sandringham Estate and then back at
  Wymondham Hall, Norfolk

Oh no. How could I have got everything
so wrong? The queen is right. There is
evil present, but how can I ever find out
where it hides?

It was hard to tell, at first, that it was Major
Legge-Horne who lay half hidden under a
rhododendron bush, among the bracken.
He had been shot from behind at very close
range and his head had been destroyed
beyond recognition. Dolly Huntley had to
be led away in hysterics. I was glad the royal
party had already departed. Mrs. Legge-
Horne just stood like a statue, staring in
disbelief, her hand over her mouth.

"Not Reggie," she whispered. "It can't be
Reggie."

I put a hand around her shoulder. "Come away. It will only cause you more grief to stay now."

"How could anything cause me more grief?" she said in a choked voice. "I've lost my husband. Someone has killed my husband and I want justice."

"I'm sure we'll find out who did this," I said. "Why don't you let us take you back to the house and have a nice hot cup of tea."

"A brandy would be a better idea for her," Darcy said, coming up behind me. "I've sent one of the men in the shooting brake to bring the Scotland Yard boys here. As soon as they come, you can take Mrs. Legge-Horne and the Huntleys home. I need to stay on. I want to have a good look around for myself. See if I can find out what bore of shotgun did this and who was shooting with one."

"But it can't have been one of the shooters," I said. "They were all out in front, in the field. I was watching them. Someone came up behind him, through the bushes." I thought about this. "They must have waited until the birds were released and there was a volley of gunfire. Nobody would have noticed one extra shot."

Darcy took my arm and led me off to one side. "I was out there with my back to the major," he said. "Did you happen to see him?"

"I did," I said, not wanting his wife to hear that I had suspected him of being the killer. "He walked up and down, making sure the loaders were doing their job, and then, when the loaded guns had been handed to the shooting party, he stepped back, out of the way of the action."

"So he'd have been standing by the bush where he was shot?"

"Probably," I said. "I believe he went a few steps into the woodland a couple of times. Maybe for a smoke?"

"More likely a swig from a flask," Darcy said.

I glanced around to see if Mrs. Legge-Horne could overhear. But she was still standing like a statue, staring out across the bleak fields.

"And who might have been standing near him?"

I frowned, thinking. "The loaders were in front of him too. And they were pretty busy, reloading the next round of shotguns. Whoever shot him came up behind him."

"Unless there was some kind of plot," Darcy said. "Someone called his name. He turned around and one of the loaders had a chance to shoot him."

I shook my head. "I would have noticed." I paused. "Of course, I don't know if I'd have noticed if one of them sneaked off into the woods while there was action on the field. We all watched while the birds were actually falling. I presume the police are conducting their background checks at the moment. Because all of these tragedies happened outside, so it could very well be a member of the Sandringham outside staff. Someone who got himself hired for that very reason." I wagged a finger excitedly. "And the major found out. That's why he was late yesterday. He did some snooping of his own and found out who killed Captain Altrungham and aimed at the prince. Perhaps he confronted that person so he had to be killed as soon as possible."

Darcy nodded. "You may be right. Let's hope Scotland Yard has come up with something. Let's hope they get here soon. I'd like the rest of these people out of the way so they don't disturb the crime scene."

It seemed a long cold few minutes until the sound of a vehicle could be heard coming toward us. The shooting brake appeared, containing the Scotland Yard detective chief inspector and two uniformed coppers. Darcy went to intercept them and there was a long, low conversation that I was not able

348

to overhear. Darcy came back to me immediately afterward.

"You'll take Mrs. Legge-Horne home and look after her, won't you, Georgie? Tell my aunt what has happened."

"But what about you?" I asked. "How will I know when to come and fetch you?"

"I can make my own way home. Don't worry about me," he said.

"But it's too far to walk from Sandringham."

"The inspector did it. Besides, I can easily cut across the fields from here. See? We're only one field away from where Dickie met his end."

He pointed out the oak trees and I recognized the twisted shape of the gnarled trunk with the overhanging branch. This made me realize something. I had ruled out Miss Short because she had chosen to stay home. But this threw a different light on things. I remember her saying that she liked a good shoot, but then turning down the chance to come, deciding to stay with Lady Aysgarth. Besides, this didn't fit with the pattern of my reasoning at all. I could understand Miss Short trying to get rid of the Prince of Wales and Mrs. Simpson, as they might disgrace the monarchy. But what could she have against the major? Of course then I realized a possible answer to this: because he had been doing his own investigation and found out she was the culprit.

I evaluated this as the shooting brake bumped us back along the frozen track to where our motorcars were waiting at the back of Sandringham House. There was no sign of the royal party. They had already gone inside and probably knew nothing of the most recent tragedy. I wondered if I should have a word with the queen, but Darcy had asked me to look after Mrs. Legge-Horne.

"Would you want to drive your own motorcar or have one of us drive it?" I asked.

She shook her head. "Reggie never let me drive. I wouldn't know how. He made me take the bus, even when the motor was sitting in the garage. He said he didn't trust a woman with a machine."

There was an awkward silence, then she gave an embarrassed little laugh. "Well, I suppose now I'll have to learn, won't I?"

"You'd better come with me," I said. "Binky, why don't you drive the Huntleys in the major's motor?"

I escorted her over to my Bentley. She didn't say a word as I opened the passenger door and helped her inside. A strange idea had come into my head. What if Mrs.

Legge-Horne had shot her husband? He was a domineering bully and a womanizer. In many ways she'd be well rid of him. But then she had seemed so worried when he hadn't returned yesterday and then displayed the sort of anger that comes from worry.

"I don't know what I'm going to do," she said quietly as we drove away. "We live in a grace-and-favor house, so I'll have to vacate that."

"You have sons, you said?"

"I do. But one is in the army and currently in India. I wouldn't want to go out to him. The other lives in army quarters at Aldershot. It's a tiny house and they have four children. No room for a granny."

"I wouldn't even think about it now," I said. "I'm sure you must be feeling quite numb at the moment."

"That's it," she said. "Quite numb. It doesn't seem real really." She turned to look at me. "Who do you think could have wanted my husband dead? It doesn't make any sense. Reggie was very much a man's man. Other men thought he was a good chap. He got along with all of them."

Not with Colonel Huntley, I thought. I remembered how the colonel had demanded to take precedence. But then the colonel was a visitor from abroad. A friend of Mrs. Simpson, invited only to help her feel more at home at this house party. I dismissed him from my mind.

We arrived back at Wymondham Hall and I took Darcy's aunt aside to tell her what had happened. She stared in disbelief. "Killed? The major? Did he get in the line of fire by mistake like the prince did?"

"No. He was found among the bushes at the edge of the field."

"Not shot then. How was he killed?"

"He was shot, actually. At very close range. It was horrible." I closed my eyes, trying to obliterate what I had just seen.

"Unbelievable," Darcy's aunt said. "Shot among the bushes? What was he doing in the bushes in the first place, eh? Are the men from Scotland Yard still around? Are they investigating?"

"They are. Darcy stayed on to help them."

"Darcy? Why would they want Darcy helping them?"

"He's quite good at this sort of thing, apparently," I said.

"Darcy? He's not working for the police now, is he?"

"Not exactly," I said. "But he does undertake some assignments from time to time."

"Does he, by Jove. I always thought of him

as the ultimate playboy."

"I believe he might have been before we married." I glanced back at the foyer. "We should take care of Mrs. Legge-Horne," I said. "She's had an awful shock."

"I should have thought she'd be dancing for joy to be rid of that dreadful man."

"I don't suppose we choose who we fall in love with," I said. "She seems devastated."

"Poor woman. Maybe you could take her up to her room and we'll send up some hot milk with brandy in it."

"Very well," I said. "And some luncheon, do you think? Although she may not feel like eating."

"I've ordered a simple luncheon anyway. A clear consommé and then boiled ham with a parsley sauce. Neither Miss Short nor I have been feeling too well. I think there was something about that turkey curry. We've both been having a lie down all morning, which is unusual for someone energetic like me."

"I haven't been feeling too wonderful either," I said. "I thought it was just the worry over what has happened here."

"I agree, it is worrying," she said. "And now the major. Let's hope they find some damned anarchist or communist soon and life can return to normal."

I went down to join Binky, Fig, Mummy, and the Huntleys, where conversation was definitely strained.

"Dolly thinks we should just pack up and go," Colonel Huntley said.

"I don't want to stay with a murderer loose in the neighborhood," Dolly said. "We'll all end up murdered in our beds, likely as not."

"Oh, I don't think so," Binky said.

"I can't say I'm too happy about it either," Fig said. "That Simpson woman knocked out. Then a man killed falling off his horse. And now this. It's not natural, is it? Someone around here has a grudge. Or is completely insane. Binky, you're not to let Podge and Addy go out to play until this is solved."

"Oh, right," he said. "Can't be too careful, I suppose."

We were glad when luncheon was announced. Miss Short joined us, looking, I had to agree, rather pale. But then I suppose the strain of shooting a major at close range would make anyone look a little sick. She certainly only picked at her food. I found my appetite had come back and actually had a second helping of the ham and scalloped potatoes. It was followed by apple dumplings and custard. Also delicious.

The others announced they were going to

have a rest after lunch, so I decided I might do the same. It had been a very trying morning. I went up to my room and lay on the bed with the covers over me, as the room was decidedly chilly. I wondered when Darcy would return, whether he might be in any kind of danger. It hadn't struck me until now that he could be facing a dangerous situation. What if it was a group of anarchists? What if they fought back when cornered?

Sleep absolutely wouldn't come. I sat up, looked around the room and found I was staring up at that picture on the wall — one of Aunt Ermintrude's ghastly creations. It was quite as bad as the one she had given us. A large green toad about to eat a house. And suddenly I realized: she had called the distant cousin who inherited Aysgarth Abbey a toady person. A toad, swallowing Aysgarth Abbey. The picture had a meaning. She was painting from her own life, her own feelings.

CHAPTER 30

December 27
Wymondham Hall, Norfolk

I don't know what to think. Today has been quite surreal so far.

I couldn't wait for Darcy to return to point this out to him. Were all of Aunt Ermintrude's paintings based on real experiences? I wondered. I came downstairs to find her in the sitting room, reading the newspaper. She was alone except for Miss Short, who sat on the window seat, staring out.

"No mention of the death of Captain Altrungham, thank heavens." Darcy's aunt looked up from her newspaper. "I would hate for the royal family to have bad publicity at this moment. They've been through enough and will go through more when the prince presents Mrs. Simpson to the nation."

She had scarcely finished speaking when Colonel and Mrs. Huntley came down the stairs. "I hope you won't think that we are being rude, but Dolly insists that we go back to London. She says she doesn't feel safe any longer and I have to admit that I agree with her."

"That poor major was standing only a few feet away from me most of the time," Dolly said. "Who could have done such an awful thing?"

"Let's hope that the police will find out soon," I said. "By the way, you didn't notice anything, did you? As you say, the major was quite close to you. Did you sense any movement behind you?"

"I can't say that I did," Dolly said. "I was so entranced with watching the king and the princes and wishing that I had brought my camera with me to show the girls back home what I'd been doing that I really didn't notice what might have gone on behind me."

"You didn't hear a shot behind you?"

Dolly shook her head. "It was so loud when they started shooting, one after the other, that my ears were ringing. Although, come to think of it, I did notice that the shots were out of order once. You know how they went down the line, starting with the king, then the princes — well, I heard a shot to my right when I expected one on the left side of the line. But then I dismissed it as just an echo." She paused. "Sorry I can't help you more."

"I'm sorry to see you go, Colonel Huntley, but I do understand completely," Darcy's aunt said. "I hope you will not think badly of England. This sort of thing is not the norm, you know."

"Of course, I know that," the colonel said. "There are troublemakers in every society. I expect you'll find it was Bolsheviks."

"Or Irish republicans," Miss Short said.

"Do you wish to leave now, or wait until the morning?" Darcy's aunt asked.

"I'm not sure how one summons a taxi, since you have no telephone," the colonel replied.

I wasn't too keen to volunteer to drive them to the train, since it hadn't been easy to find the way here in the first place. Also it was about to get dark. Luckily Dolly said, "I think we'd better wait until the morning. I presume there is a telephone at Sandringham House and they can call for a taxi from there." She glanced at her husband. "I take it we'll be safe enough in our own beds — although poor Wallis was knocked unconscious in this house."

"You can't believe that was anything more than an accident." Lady Aysgarth sounded horrified. "The floors in these old houses vibrate as you walk on them. It could easily have set off a catch that wasn't secured properly."

"I'm sure I secured the catch perfectly well," Miss Short said angrily. "Lady Georgiana was with me. She saw, didn't you?"

I didn't like to say that I hadn't seen. I had been standing back in semidarkness and she had been between me and the catch for the staircase. "I'm sure you thought you'd secured it perfectly," I said. "But as Lady Aysgarth says, things move in these old houses. I know we have the same problems at Castle Rannoch."

"What problems do we have at Castle Rannoch?" Fig demanded, entering the sitting room with Binky behind her, a child holding either hand. "Are you giving away family secrets, Georgiana?"

"Not at all," I replied. "I was saying that we too have creaking floorboards."

"Oh, we certainly have that," Fig agreed. "And howling gales down the corridors because Binky will insist on keeping windows open."

"Fresh air never hurt anyone, Fig," Binky said. "Come on, Podge. Let's set out your train again."

With Mummy's uncanny homing in on food she arrived just as tea was being served. It was accompanied with freshly baked scones with jam, brandy snaps and mince pies and was devoured by all. Except me. I was still too shaken to want to look at food. I got up. "Perhaps I should take a plate and a cup of tea up to Mrs. Legge-Horne," I suggested.

"I can have Annie do it, my dear," Lady Aysgarth said. "No need for you to go running around."

"I was just thinking she might rather see a friendly face right now," I said. "And I don't mind. I've nothing else to do."

I poured a cup of tea, added a lot of sugar and put a scone and a mince pie on a plate before going up the stairs. I tapped on the Legge-Hornes' door then let myself in. Mrs. Legge-Horne was lying there, staring at the ceiling. It was quite clear that she had been crying.

"I thought you might want a bite to eat," I said, putting the items on the table beside her.

"Thank you but I don't feel I could eat ever again," she said. "It's still not quite real." She looked at me suddenly. "They will find who did it, won't they? They will make them pay?"

"I'm sure the police will do their best," I said.

I left her and tiptoed down the stairs again. I was about to join the party in the sitting room when I had a thought. Aunt Ermintrude's other paintings. In the library, she had said. She had stored them away in case they offended the royal guests. And I had a good excuse — Mummy had said she needed a good book to keep her occupied. So I crept down the hall and started opening doors until I found the library at the back of the house. It was a dark and gloomy room, with leather-bound books on shelves reaching up to the ceiling. The lamp hanging from the ceiling threw out only an anemic pool of light. I found a lamp on the mantelpiece and switched it on, but it didn't do much to illuminate a room of that size. There was no fire in the hearth and the room had a damp, cold feel to it, enhanced by the musty smell of old books. I shivered, feeling suddenly alone and cut off. I went across and closed the door behind me. Then I looked for the paintings. They were stacked against the center table, some of them quite large, as was the one we had been given as a wedding present. I examined them one by one. They were all rather disturbing: a mountain scene with what looked like a landslide going into a stream with arms and legs floating down it and a tiny woman dancing on a mountaintop. A group of cancan dancers with a distorted male figure ogling them through unnaturally large eyes. As I went on looking, a strange cold feeling crept over me. Now that I had seen a meaning in that first painting I could interpret what the others might be saying: what if that stream with waterfalls was Aysgarth Falls and the arms and legs were the former earl, crushed by rocks — and the woman dancing was Ermintrude?

I put my hand involuntarily to my mouth as my thoughts started running wild. Had she killed him? Started the landslide that crushed him? I looked back at the other paintings. Some were complicated with strange crisscrossing lines, floating women, flying darts. They all seemed to have one theme — men ogling women. Men coming to horrible ends. I wished that Darcy would come back so that I could show him and see what he thought. I put the paintings back exactly as they had been stacked and was just examining the books, trying to find something my mother might want to read, when the door behind me opened abruptly and Aunt Ermintrude stood there.

"Oh hello, Aunt Ermintrude," I said, putting on a big bright smile. "I hope you don't mind. Mummy said that she wanted something to read and one of the servants told me where the library was. I don't suppose you have any romantic novels? That's the sort of thing I imagine my mother would like."

"I don't go in for romance much personally," she said. I noticed her eyes strayed to the paintings, and was relieved that I had replaced them properly. "I've found that romance is overrated personally. A silly chemical reaction in the brain."

"Oh, I hope not," I said. "I'm in love with Darcy and I think he's in love with me."

"Just wait," she said. "I've found that the male sex is inherently incapable of being faithful to one woman for more than ten minutes."

"What about detective novels?" I said, moving away from this subject. "Do you have any of those? I think she likes Agatha Christie."

"I do enjoy a good detective novel," she said. "There are some over here."

I duly selected a random couple of novels and gave her another big smile. "Thank you," I said. "I'm trying to find a way to keep my mother occupied. I think she's rather bored."

"It hasn't exactly turned out as we hoped, has it?" she said, following me to the door. "At least we had a decent sort of Christmas Day, didn't we? Just how it should be."

"It was lovely," I said. "Absolutely perfect."

She put a hand on my shoulder. "You're a sweet little thing, aren't you? You see the good in everything. I hope you don't end up being disillusioned like the rest of us."

CHAPTER 31

December 27
Wymondham Hall, Norfolk

Oh dear. I keep hoping I am wrong.

Darcy did not return until just before dinner. I had grown more and more worried about him and was relieved when I heard the sound of a motorcar, pulled back the curtains and saw Darcy step out of a Sandringham Estate car. I went into the foyer to meet him.

"There you are at last. I've been worried about you," I said.

"Nothing to worry about. I can take care of myself." He gave me a kiss. His lips were ice-cold. "I felt I should stay on to see if I could be of help."

"And were you?"

"Probably not. We are not much the wiser. The police checked out nearby pubs and haven't come up with any lurking strangers. They have questioned the outdoor workers at Sandringham and, again, most of the men have been on the estate all their lives. We did find a spent cartridge that didn't match the bore of the shotguns that were used. But nothing else."

"Come upstairs and change for dinner," I said. "We are dining properly tonight again."

"How is Mrs. Legge-Horne taking it?" he asked as we mounted the stairs together.

"Quite devastated," I said. "Doesn't know what she'll do without him."

"It's strange, isn't it?" He slipped his arm around my shoulders. "He treats her badly, womanizes, drinks and yet she still loved him."

"You're right. We women sometimes fall in love with the strangest men." I looked up at him. "Aunt Ermintrude is worried that you were a playboy and you won't change."

He flashed me that cheeky smile. "What do you think?" he asked.

I pushed him ahead of me into our room. He grabbed me, drew me to him, ready for a tussle. "But you liked the fact that I was a little bit dangerous, didn't you? You'd have hated a meek little chap who told you how much he adored you and followed you around."

I held him off. "Listen, Darcy. I want to be serious now. It's important."

"You want a divorce already?" He was still in a teasing mood.

I put my finger to my lips, closed the door behind us. "It's about your aunt. Take a look at that painting on the wall there."

"Oh God — you didn't say you liked it, did you? She hasn't given it to us?"

I shook my head. "What do you think it's about?"

"It looks like a giant frog eating a house."

"It's a toad," I replied. "And what do you think it means?"

"Means?" He looked puzzled now. "Do Aunt Ermintrude's crazy paintings ever have a sane meaning?"

"I believe they do," I said. "You remember she called her cousin who inherited the house a toady person? It's a toad. A toad devouring her home."

He frowned, staring at it harder now. "It does have a kind of resemblance to Aysgarth Abbey. The tower on the right . . . How interesting. How clever of you to figure that out."

"I went to take a look at her other paintings," I said.

"Are they all of toads eating houses?" He was still looking amused.

"No. One is of a rockfall and body parts in a torrent while a woman dances on a hillside above."

There was a silence. "Are you trying to suggest that that was her husband's death? She's happy he was crushed by a rock?"

"I'm suggesting that she started the rockfall. That she killed him."

"Crikey. Isn't that going a bit far, Georgie?"

I paused. "Darcy, did you know anything about the man who was killed last year during the hunt? Jeremy something?"

"Jeremy Hastings? I'd run into him a few times at social functions."

"He was the sort who liked to attend your kind of social functions?"

"Meaning what?"

"Parties? Gambling? High society life?"

"I wouldn't count myself as high society," he said. "I do — I mean did — have a few friends who move in those circles. Friends like Zou Zou."

"So what do you know about Jeremy Whatsit?"

"A good chap, I'd say. Good sportsman. Held his liquor well. Loved to laugh . . ."

"Loved to flirt?"

He smiled. "He did have an eye for the ladies."

"Married?"

"Yes. There was a rumor he was having an affair with —" He broke off, looking at me. "What are you saying now?"

"That we might have got this whole thing wrong. These murders might not have been attempts to kill the Prince of Wales. They were all men who were unfaithful to their wives."

"And you think that my aunt Ermintrude . . ." he began slowly.

"It makes sense, doesn't it?" I asked. "You said yourself that the accidents happened not too far from the house. She knows the countryside well."

He ran his fingers through his hair, something, I had noticed, he did when uncomfortable. "Georgie, what you are suggesting is — unthinkable. She's my aunt, for God's sake. My mother's oldest sister."

"I know. But you have to admit it all ties together, doesn't it?"

"Can you really see my aunt sitting up in a tree and clobbering a bloke as he rode past? Can you see her climbing that tree in the first place, and then shimming down in a hurry?"

"It does seem unlikely," I said.

"Then let's suggest that she felt hostility to men who behaved like her husband but she took out that aggression in her paintings, not in real life. That painting of the man crushed by rocks — perhaps that was her fantasy. And she was indeed delighted when it happened, but she didn't cause it."

He paced up and down the room. "My money would still be on Miss Short, except for the fact that she is so small. However, maybe that was to her advantage. Possibly she wasn't visible up on that big tree limb. Whereas my aunt, a large woman — a large and rather clumsy sort of woman, I would have said — would have been most noticeable sitting there as a rider galloped toward her." He paused in mid pace, and turned back to face me. "He'd have seen her. I know there was a mist, but he would have seen a person above him and pulled up the horse."

"Perhaps he did," I said. "Perhaps he looked up and the person dropped something heavy onto him."

"Risky," Darcy said. "Because if he had only been knocked out and not killed, he could have identified his assailant."

"Do you think Miss Short could have shot the major?" I asked. "Can you see her staggering around with a big shotgun? Where would she get such a gun from in the first place?"

"I'm sure Aunt Ermintrude has a gun or two."

"Aha!" I wagged a finger at him. "And besides, Miss Short was not feeling well and took to her bed for the morning." I didn't add that Darcy's aunt had also claimed to have rested all morning. But then how easy it would have been to have slipped out. Mummy had remained at home. So had Fig. They might have seen her go. Or she could have taken a servants' entrance.

Darcy still looked highly uncomfortable. "If what you suggest is true, why on earth did she invite us to stay? Why not have the major and his wife here alone?"

"Because the prince pressured her to host Mrs. Simpson and her friends and she couldn't very well say no. Also we might all provide her with an alibi if she needed one. Oh yes, we had seen her around at breakfast time. And she had taken to her bed today, saying she didn't feel well."

"And how would you ever prove any of this?" He still sounded defensive, I could tell. I understood. She was, as he had said, his beloved mother's sister. In a way it was insulting the memory of his mother.

"I have no idea," I said. "Unless we could match a footprint near the tree to her boots, or a small piece of fabric from an item of clothing was caught on that tree."

"We'll go and take another look tomorrow," he said. "And try to examine the soles of her boots, in case there is any kind of anomaly. Also Miss Short's boots."

"That's something to consider," I said as the thought struck me. "They may be in this together. Miss Short has a grudge against society that she was cheated out of her tea shop. And she seems quite devoted to your aunt. Perhaps they planned to kill the earl together, and now Miss Short is in too deep to back out."

"I still can't accept this," Darcy said. "Doesn't it occur to you that my aunt is considerably worse off now that her husband is dead. She has lost her position in society, her house and estate and is now living quite frugally and humbly."

"But not cut off from the world. Not wondering who her husband was with tonight and when he'd be home again. Perhaps she saw this as a good trade. Perhaps she never thought that the heir would treat her so poorly."

Darcy slumped onto the bed. "I don't like this, Georgie. I can't see how we'd ever find proof."

"But if we go home, what's to say she won't find another man to dispatch? Perhaps she sees it as her mission now. You always did describe her as 'quite batty' after all. Most of our kind of families have some kind of batty family member, don't they?"

"Maybe an aunt who keeps imaginary cats or an uncle who thinks he is Napoleon, but not one who makes a habit of killing people."

I stood staring at that picture, then I came to sit beside Darcy on the bed. "There might be a way to prove it," I said.

"What would that be?"

"We set a trap. We use you as bait."

"What?" He looked startled now.

"She believes you might still be a playboy. What if I secretly tell her how worried I am that you won't stay faithful to me?"

"And let me get my head blown off to prove the point?"

"I'd keep a close eye on you. But it's worth a try, isn't it?"

"It's bloody stupid, if you ask me," he said, then he managed a smile. "But as you say, it's worth a try."

CHAPTER 32

December 27
Wymondham Hall, Norfolk, and then out and
about

I have never felt so nervous in my life.
Why, oh why, did I suggest this lunatic
scheme. If anything happens to Darcy
I'll die.

We dressed for dinner and went downstairs
to join the rest of the group. Binky and Fig
were there, as were Mummy and the Americans. No sign of Miss Short, nor of Mrs.
Legge-Horne.

"You two were gone a long time," Darcy's
aunt said.

"They are still newlyweds. Of course they
were gone a long time." Mummy gave a
throaty chuckle and winked at me. I had
the grace to blush.

"Need to keep my hand in," Darcy said,

"for the New Year's parties. You never know who you might bump into. Old flames . . ."

"Darcy, you are terrible," I said. "How am I ever going to rein you in?"

"A chap needs a bit of freedom," he said. "I'll always come home to you."

There was an embarrassed silence. Mummy gave a bright smile. "At least you have something to occupy you. I've been bored to tears all day. I'm simply not designed for life in the country. I'm beginning to think that a few days with the Goebbels might have been preferable."

"Christmas among those Nazis would have been preferable?" Fig blurted out. "How could you possibly say that, Claire?"

"You're right, Fig darling. Don't mind me. I'm only having a little moan. I like to be active, you see. Lots of people around me, noise, music, fun. I suppose I'm essentially a city girl."

"You could have joined in the shoot today," Binky said. "That was jolly good fun — until the major got shot, that is."

"I don't shoot things," Mummy said. "Never learned to appreciate the thrill of killing defenseless creatures."

"But pheasants are bred on the estate to be shot," Lady Aysgarth said. "And I notice you ate your share of the turkey that had also been bred for your table."

"Oh, I don't mind eating things as long as somebody else kills them first and I don't have to watch," Mummy said, giving us her sweetest smile. "Yes, I know, I'm a hypocrite and proud of it. So what time is dinner?"

Darcy and I exchanged a grin. Miss Short appeared soon afterward, saying she'd been checking on the dinner arrangements.

"Is everything all right?" Lady Aysgarth asked.

"Oh yes, nothing to worry about at all." She sounded distracted.

This immediately made me worry what Queenie had done wrong this time.

"Will Mrs. Legge-Horne be joining us for dinner?" Darcy asked. "Or should we have food sent up to her?"

"I think that might be wise," Lady Aysgarth said. "She let me know that she will be sending a telegram to her son tomorrow in the hope that he will come and fetch her. That's a good idea, don't you think? However crowded a house may be, it's better to be with family at a time like this."

"I'll go and tell Cook to have a tray sent up for her," Miss Short said. "And I'm sure Heslop will be coming in to announce dinner shortly."

He arrived just as she finished speaking. I

376

have always suspected that butlers have supernatural powers and can hear their name whispered from the other end of the house.

"Dinner is served, my lady," he said, "and should I open more of the champagne, seeing that there was another tragedy in the house today?"

"Why not?" Lady Aysgarth said. "The O'Maras brought the stuff to be drunk. Let's enjoy ourselves. After all, the Huntleys will be leaving tomorrow, and Mrs. Legge-Horne."

"We seem to be dropping like flies," Mummy said, then gave an embarrassed little titter. "Oh dear, that wasn't exactly the right thing to say, was it?"

We got up and were about to process in to dinner when there came an unearthly cry from upstairs. Darcy and Binky sprinted for the staircase with the rest of us following. At least Fig, the Huntleys and I were following. I think Mummy stayed put. The cry had come from our corridor and a door was half open with light spilling onto the wooden floorboards. As Darcy pushed inside, ahead of me I heard a familiar voice saying, "I'm so sorry, missus. I caught my foot on the edge of the carpet, see."

I entered the room to see Mrs. Legge-

Horne sitting up in bed, liberally covered with lamb gravy and brussels sprouts, while an upturned plate lay on the white counterpane.

"This damned woman just threw food at me," Mrs. Legge-Horne shouted. "It's a mercy I wasn't badly scalded."

"I said I was sorry." Queenie shot an appealing look in my direction. "Like I said, I was carrying the bloomin' tray and didn't see the edge of the carpet so I caught my foot."

"Go and get something to clear this mess up, Queenie," I said. Darcy had already gone across to the washbasin, wetted a towel and started to wipe gravy off the unfortunate woman.

"Is nothing safe in this cursed house?" she demanded. "I knew we shouldn't have come here. I didn't want to in the first place. Reggie insisted. He wanted to be back among the royals where he felt important. But now look what's happened."

"Was he not employed by the royal family at the moment, then?" I asked.

She shook her head. "He was in semi-retirement, I suppose you could say. He'd had a couple of health problems."

"But they invited him back for this Christmas?"

"I believe it was Lady Aysgarth who invited us, mentioning that Queen Mary would really like an old hand to keep an eye on the king when he went out shooting."

"I see." So she had lured him here. Deliberately.

The men were sent downstairs. Annie arrived with fresh bedding, soap and towels, with a subdued-looking Queenie behind her, and we helped Mrs. Legge-Horne while Annie quickly changed the bedclothes. When things were back to normal, I led Queenie out of the room.

"I'm sorry, missus, I really am," she said. "I didn't half give myself a fright too. I thought I was going to fall on me face."

"It could have been worse," I said. "Speaking of which, did something happen in the kitchen earlier?"

" 'Aappen? What sort of 'appen?" she asked innocently.

"You know, some small glitch in the kitchen?"

"A witch in the kitchen?"

I wasn't sure if she was just playing dumb or not. "A glitch, Queenie. A minor disaster?"

"Not really a disaster, miss. It was them ruddy pancakes. Cook said we'd have to flambé them before we carried them through and I had never flambéed anything before. So she said I'd better try it before dinner, and how was I to know that a good splash of Cointreau could make such a big flame, and it was unfortunate that the tea towel was hanging right above the stove. But no harm done, really. We put it out and it was only one tea towel gone, oh, and the wall a bit black. But nobody hurt."

"Queenie, what am I going to do with you?" I asked.

"It could have happened to anyone," she said defensively.

I told myself for the umpteenth time that she was never going to learn or improve, even if her cooking was a redeeming feature.

A new meal was brought up to Mrs. Legge-Horne, not by Queenie this time.

Finally we reassembled in the sitting room and went in to dinner, the rigid pecking order not being observed, as if these strange happenings had thrown our society out of kilter. Miss Short had seen that the proprieties were observed at table with place cards putting Binky next to our hostess and Mummy on her other side. I was next to Binky, Fig next to Darcy, then the Huntleys and Miss Short at the nonaristocratic end of the table. A splendid meal followed: a cream of parsnip soup, roast leg of lamb with all the trimmings and then little pancakes with a Grand Marnier sauce. Finally there were anchovies on toast to go with the port. It felt strange to be sitting at a good meal, making acceptable conversation, knowing what I had just found out. I tried not to look at Darcy's aunt in case my expression might give me away.

"So how long do you think you'll be staying?" Darcy's aunt asked. "Not deserting me after all this nonsense?"

"We'll stick around as long as you want, Aunt," Darcy said. "We're having a good time, aren't we, Georgie?"

"Oh, rather," I said. I hoped it didn't sound a little too enthusiastic.

We enjoyed coffee and liqueurs by the fire, along with some decadent chocolates, then went up to bed.

"Golly, that was a strain, wasn't it?" I said as soon as we had safely closed the door. "I don't think I can take more unpleasant surprises." I glanced up at him. "You did well with your playboy hints. I wonder if your aunt will take the bait."

"I still can't believe she is responsible," Darcy said.

"She did invite the major," I said.

"And she invited us," he pointed out. We stared at each other, taking this in.

"Perhaps we should go home. The sooner the better." Then I remembered. "Although I did promise the queen I would do what I could and the police will no doubt continue to want you. I'm surprised they didn't come to get a statement from us today."

"I described who everybody was and where they were standing," Darcy said. "I expect they'll want an official statement tomorrow."

"And you and I should go and look at that tree again," I said. "See how an elderly woman could possibly have knocked a man off his speeding horse."

"I really hope they come up with the true killer," Darcy said.

I stayed silent.

CHAPTER 33

Saturday, December 28
Wymondham Hall, Norfolk

I am hoping and praying we can bring this to some kind of resolution. Of course, for Darcy's sake, I hope we prove that his aunt was not involved in any way. He adored his dead mother and I think he sees this as an affront on his family. But if it was his aunt and we have sort of put him as bait . . . golly. It doesn't bear thinking about. I shall follow him like a hawk.

We awoke to another frosty morning with a red sun rising over bare trees. We didn't speak much as we went down to breakfast. Again I felt so nervous that it was hard to eat. Before other guests had appeared we put on coats, hats and boots and started in the direction of the big oak tree where

Dickie Altrungham had met his death. As we walked past the gardener's cottage a bonfire was piled high with dead leaves, twigs and various pieces of household rubbish. And near the top was a rope. I pointed to it.

"What do you think?" I asked.

"What do you mean?"

"That piece of rope? Could it be in any way significant?"

"You believe she swung down from the tree like Tarzan and caught him with her feet?" he asked.

I glared at him. "You are determined not to take this seriously, aren't you?"

"Oh, I take the death of a good chap very seriously," he said. "It's just that I find it hard to believe my own aunt could be involved."

We walked on. I noticed the trail of footprints across the field but didn't say anything. At least one person had come this way before — but big Wellington boot prints all look much the same. We came at last to the stile. I climbed over and walked up to the oak tree, staring up at that branch and trying to picture Darcy's aunt Ermintrude climbing up there, then leaning down to knock a rider off his horse. It would be precarious and risky in the extreme.

"What if somebody had tied that rope to a branch so that it would have caught a rider?" I asked.

Darcy was pacing around the tree, staring up, frowning. "If it was tied to the branch and hung down, don't you think Dickie would have seen it? And if he didn't and it managed to unseat him, how could anyone have untied it and climbed down the tree before you arrived?"

I shrugged.

"Furthermore," he continued, "a rope noose would have caught him from the front and jerked him off backward. He would have hit the back of his head, which he didn't."

"Oh." I felt defeated and frustrated. "So we're none the wiser."

"Afraid not. Too many people have tramped around here to find any meaningful footprints."

We walked around the tree once more, noting that the ivy on it had been disturbed, but then the police would have been up in the tree, looking for evidence. Feeling frustrated we trudged back across the field.

"Ah, there you are. I wondered where you had got to. Been out for an early morning walk, children?" Aunt Ermintrude appeared as we stepped into the warmth of the foyer.

"That's the ticket. Good to stay healthy. I always take a morning walk myself and I'm as fit as a fiddle. Have you had breakfast?"

"Thank you, we have," I replied.

"That's good because a message was just delivered from the big house. Her Majesty is requesting that you pay her a visit this morning, Georgie."

"Oh golly," I said. "I suppose I'd better change out of these trousers and then go."

"It was quite convenient, actually. One of the policemen came with the driver and got statements from everyone about yesterday's little incident. Then the Huntleys were able to be driven back to Sandringham where they could telephone for a car. They sent their regards to you."

So the Huntleys had escaped. "And what about Mrs. Legge-Horne?"

"She gave them her son's address and they will send a telegram, asking him to come and fetch her. She's staying in her room, poor dear."

I went up to change and then Darcy drove me to Sandringham.

"You won't tell the queen your suspicions about my aunt, will you?" he said as we drove through the trees.

"You don't think it's wise, at this stage?"

"I'd rather you didn't. My aunt has been

an old and loyal friend to the queen, and even if she is later proven innocent that friendship will have been shaken."

"You're right," I said. "After all, my hunch is only a hunch at this point."

We drove into the forecourt of Sandringham House.

"Will you wait for me?" I asked.

He grinned. "What do you think? I'd let you walk all the way back?" He stroked my cheek. "I'll be chatting to the Scotland Yard men in one of the outbuildings. I want to see if they've come up with anything since yesterday. Send someone to fetch me when you have finished."

"Will you mention my suspicion to them?"

"I'll tread carefully," Darcy said. He helped me out of the motorcar.

"You don't know how lucky you are not to be put through this." I gave him a look as I stepped onto the frosty gravel. "A royal grilling is not exactly fun. Especially not now when I have nothing to tell her."

"You'll manage. You always do." He bent to give my forehead a little kiss.

As I walked toward the house the door opened and the two princesses came out, closely followed by their governess.

"Hello, Georgie," Margaret called to me. "Guess what? We're going to go skating tomorrow."

"We're going to have a proper skating party. They said the lake should be properly frozen after one more cold day," Elizabeth added. "Will you come and join us?"

"I don't own any skates," I said.

"Oh, I think there will be plenty. We don't own skates either, but Daddy said they would find small ones for us. You strap them to the bottom of your boots."

"It should be fun." I smiled at their eager little faces. "Are you going for a walk? There's not enough snow left to play in, is there?"

"Oh, we're going to see the horses." Elizabeth's face lit up. "Crawfie has carrots we can give them. Come on, Crawfie."

They skipped off beside their governess, two ordinary little girls going to do their favorite thing.

I went into the house, where a footman approached me.

"Please follow me, your ladyship. I'm afraid there will be a slight delay. The doctor has arrived to examine His Majesty, so naturally Her Majesty wants to be present. If you would take a seat here, she should return shortly. May I bring you a cup of tea or coffee?"

"No, thank you," I said, although a cup of

tea sounded like a good idea. I always avoided anything that could be spilled if possible when visiting royal relatives. I sat on the chair in the wide central hallway, beside one of the many Christmas trees that now decorated it. The sweet smell of spruce and lingering candle smoke drifted toward me. I examined delicate ornaments and still the queen did not appear. I worried that the king had taken a turn for the worse and wondered if I should not wait for her at this moment. The house was quite still, apart from the sonorous ticking of a grandfather clock somewhere farther down the hall. My gaze swept the carved ceiling and then the great paintings on the walls. Opposite me was not a painting at all but a large medieval tapestry, depicting the siege of a castle. It was rather violent with arrows flying, boiling oil being poured and men at the castle gates charging forward with a battering ram.

Then I remembered. As Dickie lay dying he had murmured "tapestry." He too had sat in this very spot, waiting to be summoned to a royal room. And I realized how someone might have killed Dickie Altrungham.

CHAPTER 34

December 28
Sandringham House, Norfolk

I think we are finally getting somewhere,
but I'm not sure where we go from here.

I was still staring at that tapestry, picturing
the dying man and the big oak tree, when a
voice made me jump.

"Her Majesty is ready to receive you now,
Lady Georgiana. If you would follow me."

I was taken down the long hallway to the
private sitting room I had visited before.
The queen, upright and stoic as always, was
sitting by the fire and nodded graciously as
I entered and curtsied.

"Come and sit beside me, my dear. It's so
cold and bleak today, isn't it?"

I obeyed. "Is His Majesty not well? I
understand that a doctor has been to visit."
Too late I remembered that one does not

initiate a conversation with a royal person. But she didn't seem to mind.

"More precautionary than anything. He was naturally shocked by the brutal death of an old retainer yesterday." She reached out a slim white hand to me. "Another murder, Georgiana. What are we going to do? The police are here and they have bullied and upset all the staff, but they seem quite lost. Do you have any idea what is behind this outrage?"

"I think I might have some idea, ma'am, but at the moment it is all supposition. I have no proof, and until then I'm afraid I can't share my suspicions."

"Is it someone under this roof? Answer me that much."

"I think I can say that it's not."

"Oh, thank goodness for that. If one of our trusted servants had turned against us, it would be more than the king could bear at this moment. But answer me this: if these have been attempts on my son's life, then why was the major killed? Had he found out who might be guilty and confronted them?"

"That is possible," I said, not wanting to reveal what I had come to believe.

"Shall we know soon, do you think? Before there is another death?"

"I really hope so," I said. "I shall do my best."

"I'm sure you will, my dear. I have great faith in you." She squeezed my hand now. "And you will keep me up-to-date with everything that is going on?"

"I will, ma'am."

Her face softened. "Have you seen the granddaughters today?"

"I have. They were on their way to feed carrots to the horses."

"Those girls are horse mad. It's all they live for. Elizabeth told me she wants to marry a farmer and keep lots of animals." She gave me a sad smile. "Poor little thing. She doesn't realize yet what her future will be."

"I gather they are to have a skating party tomorrow, if the ice is thick enough and the weather holds," I said.

"They are. You and your husband must come and join us. And the rest of the house party, if they feel like it. I expect you all need cheering up after these grim events."

"Thank you, ma'am. I'll pass along your invitation."

"How is dear Ermintrude holding up?" she asked. "She has not been used to entertaining as of late."

"She's doing splendidly," I replied. "We've

been looked after well."

"I'm so glad. She has had a rather tragic life, I feel. So cut off. It makes one retreat into a shell."

I nodded, then stood up, realizing this was breaking protocol. "If that is all for the moment, ma'am, may I be excused? I have Darcy waiting outside for me."

"Of course. We will see you tomorrow, then, unless you have any news before?"

I curtsied and backed from the room, successfully avoiding objects on tables.

Darcy was sitting in the motor. He got out and came around to open my door. "You were gone a long time. Was it a thorough grilling?"

"No. I had to wait because a doctor was examining the king."

"Bad news?"

"No, more precautionary, I gather. But, Darcy, listen to this . . ." I waited until he got into the driver's seat and closed his door. "I think I know how Captain Altrungham was knocked from his horse. Let's go and take another look at that tree."

Darcy gave me a questioning look but drove down the bumpy track until we reached the field. We entered at the gate and walked toward the tree. I went ahead and looked around among the brambles and dead bracken.

"Well?" Darcy said.

"Yes," I said. "I should think this was the one." I pointed down to a log lying there. It was about two feet long and, unlike the others, had no traces of snow on it.

"Well?" Darcy said again, a trifle more impatiently this time.

"When Captain Altrungham was dying he whispered what sounded like 'tapestry.' I saw that tapestry today. It was a medieval castle being besieged and they were using a battering ram."

"And?" Darcy was still frowning.

I pointed down at the log. "This has been moved recently. What if a rope was wound around the big branch and one end was tied around that log. Someone hides among the ivy in the tree. The horse comes galloping up. When it's level she launches the log. It swings out and catches the rider on the side of the head, knocking him off sideways. She lets go. Log falls, rope falls. She unties log. Gathers up rope. Disappears behind the tree as she hears me coming."

Darcy was not looking impressed and excited as I hoped he would. "Sounds bloody stupid to me," he said. "I can't see . . ."

"Let's give it a try," I said. "Go across the

field to the bonfire and bring back the rope."

"Why don't you?"

"I've had a grilling from a queen today."

He smiled. "All right. Anything to humor my wife."

I watched him go, hoping and praying that I had got it right and wouldn't look like a fool when he returned. He came back quickly with the rope, then scrambled up the tree to wind it once around the branch.

"It's certainly easy enough to climb," he called down. "What makes you think this will work?"

"Because she had something similar to this in one of her paintings. You know how she had lots of lines and pulleys and things in the painting we have? She must have played with this sort of thing in her head. Perhaps when she was planning to kill her husband."

Darcy shook his head, but retrieved the log from the frozen bracken. Then we tied on the rope, measuring the height needed for a man on a big horse. The first couple of times the log fell, but the third we got it just right. I shouted "now" and he launched it. It swung out perfectly, he let go of the rope and the whole thing came tumbling down.

"Out of the corner of his eye what Dickie

Altrungham sees looks like that battering ram coming at him," I said.

Darcy stared at it for a moment. "Yes, that would have the force to unseat a rider," he said. "But whoever it was took a big risk. What if you'd been together at that point? What if it had been the Prince of Wales and not Dickie?"

"Then she would have waited for another day, although she knew the prince had gone after Mrs. Simpson." I thought for a moment. "Unless she also wanted to eliminate the Prince of Wales."

"He isn't a cheating husband."

"But he's not going to be a suitable king, is he? And Mrs. Simpson is a cheating wife."

Darcy shook his head. "This whole thing is still conjecture. I can't show this to Scotland Yard without some kind of proof."

"You can suggest the method. You don't have to name the perpetrator."

" 'Perpetrator'? Where did you get a word like that?"

"Experience in the field," I said, giving him a triumphant little smile.

We drove back to Sandringham, where Darcy disappeared for a word with the inspector. I watched the princesses coming back with Crawfie. How happy and carefree they seemed, while so much darkness surrounded them.

We arrived back at Wymondham Hall to find domestic tranquility reigning. Mummy reading by the fire, Binky and Fig playing cards with Darcy's aunt and Miss Short. Mrs. Legge-Horne sat in the other chair by the fire, a rug over her knees, nursing a cup of hot cocoa.

"What news?" Binky asked. "You saw Her Majesty?"

I saw Darcy's aunt's face and read conflicting emotions. "I did. The king was naturally upset by the death of Major Legge-Horne. Apparently he had high regard for the major." This hadn't actually been said, but I wanted to say something nice for Mrs. Legge-Horne.

She nodded. "Yes, he often made use of my husband's expertise with weapons and knowledge of birds. So ironic that it was one of those weapons that ended his life."

I was glad when it was time for sherry and luncheon — today grilled plaice followed by a hearty Lancashire hot pot and then meringues with cream. Darcy and I went up for a rest after the meal. I was actually feeling tired for once and slept for an hour before we joined everyone at tea and played with the children.

Dinner passed smoothly and I began to

wonder whether we would go home with nothing settled, and eventually more men would die. We sat around the fire after dinner, playing charades until we all agreed an early night was a good idea. I had just gone up to our room when Darcy came in, holding a piece of paper. "It appears a note has been delivered for me from the inspector," he said. "It seems they've uncovered hints of a plot to sabotage tomorrow's skating party," he said. "He wants me to meet him at the lake."

"Now?"

He nodded. "They want to catch the person or persons red-handed. I may be gone for a while."

"I'll come too," I said.

He shook his head. "Absolutely not. This is police work. You may have got everything wrong and this could be an Irish plot or an anarchist plot all along. I never believed it could be my aunt." He kissed me. "I'll get changed and be off, then."

"Be careful," I said.

I watched him walk down the hall to the loo. Then I sprinted down the stairs, hastily putting on my coat and muffler before I went out into the night. I climbed into the motorcar, hid on the floor beside the backseat and draped the motoring rug over me.

I just prayed I wouldn't sneeze. No sooner was I settled than Darcy arrived, started up the motor and off we went. The drive over the bumpy track seemed to take longer than I had remembered. I suppose I was bursting with tension. He pulled up and got out. I waited until he had moved off, then came from my hiding place. A pale sliver of moon gave just enough light to let me see that we were indeed beside the lake. The dark shape of Sandringham House loomed on the far side with light twinkling from windows. I could just make out the figure of a man standing out on the ice. He beckoned Darcy. "Over here," I heard him call. Darcy stepped out gingerly across the ice. I opened the car door and crept out, keeping the car between me and the two men.

"What is it? What have you found?" Darcy asked.

"Someone cut a hole in the ice," the other voice said. "Right here." The tone was muffled, coming through the large scarf wrapped around his face and throat.

Darcy moved cautiously forward. Then he stopped. "Wait. You're not Broad."

There was a throaty laugh that I suddenly recognized. "Actually I've been told that I'm quite broad. My late husband made jokes about my figure regularly."

"Aunt Ermintrude?" I heard the shock in his voice. "What on earth are you doing here? You saw the note, I suppose. But this is a police matter."

"Not a police matter. I wrote the note, silly boy. I wanted to make sure I got you alone."

"What for?"

"What for? I should have thought that might be obvious. I wanted to make sure that sweet bride of yours doesn't have to go through a marriage wondering in whose bed you'll end up every night."

"So it was you," he said. "Georgie was right all along. You did find ways to kill those men."

"And more that nobody knows about. The clever ones passed as accidents — like last year's hunting incident. I must say I have enjoyed plotting out new and different methods. They haven't all worked, of course. But the ones that have — most satisfying."

"And what do you plan to do now?" he asked. "You don't seem to have a weapon with you. And in case you haven't noticed, I'm bigger and stronger than you are. Also I'm not over sixty."

"But you are standing on ice." She laughed again. "And if you take one step forward . . ."

She did not need to finish the sentence. Of course he had been taking a step forward. The ice where Darcy was standing gave way, and he slid into the dark water. I didn't wait a second longer. I ran out across the ice toward them, slithering and stumbling as I went. Darcy's aunt turned at the sound of my approach. I wasn't quite sure what I was going to do, or whether she was armed, but it was decided for me. As I came up to her, I lost my footing, pitched forward and brought her down in a perfect rugby tackle. She fell backward, landing on the ice with the breath knocked out of her. I staggered to my feet, breathing heavily. Darcy's head and shoulders were just visible above the ice. As he tried to haul himself out, the edge of the ice gave way with a crack.

"Georgie, take off your coat." He brought out the words between gasps. "I haven't got long at this temperature."

"What do you want me to do?" I obeyed, feeling the icy blast hit me as I removed the coat.

"Lay it next to me so I have some traction."

I did so. He managed, with difficulty, to free his arms, leaned on the coat and tried to hoist himself up. I grabbed desperately at his coat and pulled with all my might. I heard the ice crumbling as he struggled. It seemed like a hopeless cause. His overcoat was waterlogged and heavy, the hole not much bigger than Darcy. What's more, Aunt Ermintrude had recovered enough to stagger to her feet. "Good luck with that," she said. "You'll not manage to pull him out, you know. But your loyalty is touching. Misplaced, but touching."

She started to walk away. "Luckily I brought the shotgun in the car. Just in case, you know."

"What car?" I asked.

"I borrowed the major's, of course. Stupid man. Deserved to die."

"And the latch on the stairs? That was you?"

"Well, we can't have the heir to the throne marrying someone like that, can we? A disgrace to the British monarchy."

She started off across the lake. I noticed that she had tied rags around her feet and was walking quite easily. The wind was snatching at my scarf. I unwound it and passed Darcy one end. "Hold on to this."

"I don't want to pull you in too."

"Take it!" I shouted. "Now kick as hard as you can."

We tried. And tried again. Darcy slumped back. "It's no good."

"You have to do this," I shouted. "We can't let that evil woman win. I won't let you die. Now. Give it all you've got. As if you're swimming in a race. As if you're a porpoise."

His torso rose up. I pulled as hard as I could, and fell over backward as he came slithering out of the water, lying on the ice, gasping like a beached fish. At that moment the moon went behind a cloud, plunging us into total darkness. There were still pinpoints of light coming from Sandringham House across the lake but not enough to see where Aunt Ermintrude was now.

"We must get you back to the car as quickly as possible," I said. "Take off that wet coat." I struggled with icy fingers to pull it off him as he lay shivering and gasping. "Put mine around you. At least the inside isn't wet." I sat him up and wrapped the coat around him. Then I helped him to his feet.

"Which direction is the car in?" he asked, his teeth chattering alarmingly.

"The other side from the house, I think. Come on. Before she comes back. At least she won't be able to find us in the dark."

I half dragged him as he stumbled forward, one ear listening for approaching footsteps, half expecting to hear the sound of a shotgun. Then the moon came out again. I thought I saw reeds and bushes ahead. We had reached the edge.

"Only a few more steps," I said, then heard the ice around us give an ominous creak. At that moment a shot rang out, echoing across the frozen lake. Darcy pulled me down as the shot whizzed over our heads.

"Crawl," he commanded. "We're almost there."

I glanced back. I could see her now. She was coming toward us across the lake with determined strides, the shotgun under her arm and ready. Suddenly there was a cracking sound. She gave a gasp as the ice gave way and in she went. "Help!" she yelled. "Help!"

Darcy and I reached the bank and stood, staring back at her.

"It could be a trap," I said. "We go to help her and she blasts our heads off."

"But she'll die if we don't go."

I was trying to think clearly, horrified at what was going through my mind. My heart was racing so fast that I could hardly speak. I grabbed at his arm. "Darcy, I know she's your aunt, but isn't this the best way? There would be a trial. Either she'd hang or be put in a mental institution."

He was still breathing heavily and shivering. "She is my aunt," he said. "And I understand what you're saying but . . ."

"I'm more concerned that you survive right now," I said. "Your own aunt tried to kill you. Would have killed you if I hadn't decided to come along. And she would have shot us both."

"You're not going to come, are you, Darcy?" came the voice, sounding angry now. "Of course you're not. You've never cared about your family. We've meant nothing to you."

Darcy started forward again.

"Don't." I grabbed at him. "If the ice was thin enough there for her to fall through, then you might do the same. We'll go to the big house and get help."

"You deserved to die, not me, Darcy," came the voice, weaker now and interspersed with gasps. "Men like you should be eradicated from the world. You'll only make that poor girl suffer the way I did. I'm just sorry I won't be around to have another chance. . . ."

Darcy stared out across the ice, then back at me and nodded. "We'll go to the big house and get help."

We reached the car, drove around the lake and woke the outside servants in the cottages. They set out with lanterns and a ladder. By the time they reached the spot there was no sign of her. She had sunk beneath the ice.

Meanwhile we had been taken in, had Darcy's wet garments removed and placed him beside a fire, wrapped in blankets. We were both given cups of tea. It tasted wonderful. I didn't realize until I was holding the cup that I was shivering too. Mostly from shock, I suppose.

"It was the best thing, wasn't it?" I said as we finally drove home much later. "She was a proud woman. We spared her from a much worse end. At least this was quick."

"I know," he said. "My head tells me this was the right thing, but I keep wondering if my mother would have wanted us to save her." He turned to me. "The important thing is that you saved me. If you hadn't come, you'd be a widow by now. You were very brave. And the way you tackled her — you'd have been a star on the rugby pitch."

"All by accident, I assure you," I said. "I lost my footing, pitched forward and grabbed at her. She lost her footing too and over we went."

"Like I said, most impressive." He leaned toward me and planted icy lips on mine. "And one thing I promise you — I will never be the kind of man she thought I was. Wherever I am in the world, you can trust me."

I wrapped my arms around his neck and the kiss this time was warm and passionate.

CHAPTER 35

December 29
Sandringham House, Norfolk, and later back
  home at Eynsleigh, Sussex

I am still shaken by what happened and
how close Darcy came to dying last
night. Such a horrible scene — I don't
think I'll ever get it from my mind. At the
time of writing this they still haven't
recovered her body. Perhaps they will
have to wait for the spring thaw.

Needless to say there was a lot of explaining
to do the next day. Statements to the police,
sharing what we knew with the crowd at
Wymondham Hall.

"You suspected she was a murderer but
you let us go on staying here," Fig demanded. "How could you, Georgiana?"

"I thought you'd be perfectly safe," I said,
thinking that nobody would ever mistake

Binky for a playboy womanizer. "And besides, I wasn't sure. You can't make accusations without proof. So Darcy became bait. I just didn't think it would happen like that and so soon."

"You were jolly lucky," Binky added.

"So that seems to be the end of the house party," Mummy said. "Now do you think we can go home? I've a great desire for your lovely house and Mrs. McPherson's cooking."

Only Miss Short said nothing. Her face was white and stoic and I wondered how much she knew or suspected about her employer. I realized that she'd have to find a new position and start all over again. This was on my mind when I went to tell the queen what had happened. I was dreading doing so, but it had to be done and it was only right that it came from me.

It seemed that she had been apprised of some of the details. Her face was grave as she held out her hands to me. "Georgiana, my dear. What a frightful experience for you. They say you saved your husband from drowning, but poor Ermintrude wasn't so lucky."

I nodded, wondering how much of the truth I should tell her. Should I let her go on thinking that her friend had met a tragic death? But as I sat beside her she said, "Poor Ermintrude. I had worried for her for some time now. She was slipping into madness, wasn't she? I feared as much, which was why I brought her here. I thought she'd buck up and snap out of it if she had people around her. That Aysgarth place was enough to drive anyone insane. Dark, remote and husband gone most of the time."

I nodded, not quite knowing what to say.

She sighed. "I suspected she killed her husband from something she said once. Not that I blamed her, horrible man. But then, when other accidents started happening, I did wonder." She was still holding my hands. "That's why I sent for you. I thought that Georgiana could get to the bottom of it, if anyone could."

"I'm flattered that you have such confidence in me, ma'am."

"I was proven right, wasn't I?" She sighed again. "It was sheer luck that my son wanted an excuse to have his paramour nearby and therefore a house party was arranged. It was easy enough to suggest she invite her nephew and his new bride. I thought the Prince of Wales was in danger, you see. I suspected Ermintrude did not approve of a future queen with an American accent."

"That might have been true," I said, "but

we now think her real motive was to do away with men who were unfaithful to their wives."

"Ah, yes." She nodded. "That makes sense." She stared past me out across the grounds. There were still men out on the lake, presumably trying to retrieve the body. Poor little princesses, I thought. Their skating party now wouldn't happen.

"You'll go home, I presume? I doubt you'd want to stay here with no hostess."

"Of course, ma'am. We'll go home today," I said. "The others are anxious to get away after everything that has happened."

"I'll miss our little chats," she said. "You and your husband could come back and stay in the new year, if you'd like to. After the rest of the family has departed. The king likes to remain in Norfolk until at least the end of February."

"That's very kind of you, ma'am. If the king is well enough to receive visitors."

"I'm hopeful he's on the mend. It does wonders for his spirit to be in a place he loves."

I was about to make a graceful exit when I remembered something. "Ma'am, there is one small favor I'd like to ask. Lady Aysgarth had a companion who really has nobody in the world and nowhere to go now. I wondered if you might think of a position she could fill. She seems efficient and willing."

"Educated woman, is she?"

"Not upper-class but refined."

"I'll speak to the master of house and give it some thought," she said. "You can send her over to us. We'll try to fit her in somewhere. And I was thinking of offering Wymondham to my youngest son, George. So the servants could stay on."

"That is good news," I said. "Thank you, ma'am."

"No, Georgiana dear. Thank you."

I curtsied. "Please give my very best regards to His Majesty and the rest of your family. I do hope you have some enjoyable days ahead now that this is over."

"I'm sure we shall, my dear." She gave me a warm smile.

I had reached the door when another thought occurred to me. "Lady Aysgarth's dogs. I do hope someone on your estate can find good homes for them."

She was still smiling. "I don't see any problem with that. One can never have too many dogs in the country."

As I went back to Darcy I was still thinking about our puppies. They should not be removed from their mother yet. And then my thoughts turned to the mother herself. The sweetest nature, the gardener's wife had said.

"Darcy," I began as we drove away from Sandringham House, "I think we have to leave our puppies with their mother for another week or so, don't you?"

He nodded. "We can arrange to have them delivered to us, I'm sure."

"And then there is their mother. Tilly. Now that her mistress is no more, I'd want her to go to a good home."

"I'm sure she will," he replied.

"What I'm suggesting is that we can give her a good home," I went on. "And our little dears can be with their mother a lot longer."

He gave me a wary glance. "I suppose so," he said. "It is your house, after all. You are free to do what you like with it."

"It's our house, Darcy. And I know three dogs are a bit much but I'd hate it if she was sent somewhere where she wasn't loved and housed in a kennel. . . ."

Darcy patted my hand. "It's all right, old thing. Don't worry. We'll let them know that we're taking the mother too. But not the rest of the eight puppies, okay? Enough is enough."

"I promise not all eight puppies," I said, laughing.

■ ■ ■ ■

We left Norfolk that afternoon. We made the arrangements from Sandringham and the car arrived to take the servants to the station, then Binky and family back to our house.

"I hope you won't mind if we don't stay on at Eynsleigh," Fig said. "Just long enough to gather the servants and ship them to the London house. But frankly my nerves are in tatters and I just want peace and safety in my own home."

I couldn't bring myself to say I was sorry to see them go.

Before we left I met with Miss Short and told her that I had asked the queen to find her a suitable job. She was most touched. "I can't thank you enough. To tell you the truth, my lady, I lay awake all last night, wondering what might become of me. I'm not young anymore." I looked at her with sympathy. I had never exactly been in her position but I had felt unwanted at my brother's house before I took my life into my own hands. Thank heavens I did, or I'd never have met Darcy!

We drove home, and arrived at Eynsleigh at

the dinner hour. We had stopped in King's Lynn to warn Mrs. Holbrook of our arrival. She sounded most flustered. "There is no suitable food in the house, your ladyship. Only for the staff. We didn't expect you back for a few more days, and it's Sunday. The shops won't be open."

"Don't worry about it, Mrs. Holbrook," I said. "Any simple meal will do. We left in a hurry, you see. But we are bringing some supplies with us." Darcy had recovered enough to purloin the rest of our champagne, as well as half a dozen pheasants, plus the smoked salmon, caviar and other goodies we had brought in our hamper. He was remarkably silent on the way home, and not just because the road was icy and treacherous in places. I think he was still suffering from shock that one of his family members had behaved in that way. I could certainly understand his feelings. I remembered the shock I had felt when I had discovered that my father had another family in the South of France — betrayed and vulnerable.

"It's easy to understand what pushed your aunt over the edge," I said quietly when the silence threatened to become overwhelming. Mummy, as usual, was asleep in the backseat. "Married off too young to know what she was getting into, then living alone in gloomy isolation, knowing her husband was philandering."

He nodded. "All the same, it is not pleasant to know that one might have insanity in the family."

"It happens in the best of families," I said. "Look at King George III."

He turned to me and smiled then. "I never really thanked you for saving my life, did I?"

"I wouldn't want to live without you."

He reached across and squeezed my hand.

"How many aunts do you have exactly?" I asked Darcy as we negotiated the London traffic.

"On my mother's side, you mean?"

"Yes."

"My mother was the youngest of five sisters. Ermintrude was the oldest. My aunt Hawse-Gorzley was in the middle."

"Don't let's have any more Christmases with your aunts, Darcy," I said. "Too many unfortunate things happen."

"Don't worry. Aunt Prunella is a spinster and keeps cats, I seem to remember, and Aunt Josephine married beneath her and was cut off from the family."

"How horrid."

"I know. But I think she was the one who cut herself off. I believe he owns a shop or

416

something."

"Darcy, don't be so snobbish," I said. "He might be perfectly nice."

"But you wouldn't want to spend Christmas above a shop."

"Probably not." I returned his smile.

After a silence he gave a sigh. "I suppose it has hit me so hard because she was one of my few connections to my mother. I adored her, you know. She was a wonderful person. Everybody loved her. And she died when I was away at school, so I couldn't even say goodbye."

I reached out and covered his hand with my own.

We arrived home to a warm house and warm welcome. Granddad looked very well and delighted to see us. Mrs. Holbrook apologized that the best cook could do was a big chicken soup and sliced ham with baked potatoes. It sounded like heaven. I realized I hadn't felt like eating much since Dickie Altrungham came off his horse.

Mummy came down to dinner, looking rather pleased with herself. "Look what was waiting for me. Three telegrams from Max. He says he is devastated without me. He can't live another moment without me. He's coming over to London to kidnap me. I'm to meet him at the Dorchester."

So at least Mummy was happy again. After dinner I sat with Granddad by the fire. "Have you had a good time?" I asked him.

"The very best," he said. "It turns out that Hamilton likes cribbage, so we've played many a hand. And Mrs. Holbrook and Mrs. McPherson have spoiled me rotten with good food. All in all a satisfying Christmas. I'll need to take plenty of walks to lose all those pounds. How about you? Was it a good old blowout?" He used the Cockney term for a feast, but it was horribly near to the truth.

"I'm afraid it was rather awful," I said. "Some upsetting things happened. I wish we'd stayed here."

He put his big meaty hand over mine. "I've no doubt you'll tell me about them when the moment is right," he said, "but I can't tell you what a treat it is to have you home again. Smashing. Absolutely smashing, it is."

I squeezed his hand with mine. All was right with the world.

The next morning I woke up feeling unwell.

"I don't think that the meal agreed with me last night," I said.

"I think it's more likely to be delayed shock," Darcy said. "You have been through an awful lot. But I'll give the doctor a ring and see if he can come over to take a look at you."

"Oh, I don't think that's necessary," I said. "I'm sure I'll be right as rain with a cup of Bovril and some toast."

"All the same," Darcy said. "You have been looking a bit peaky for the past few days now. You've said you haven't been feeling well on several occasions. Maybe he can prescribe an iron tonic."

When I tried to get up, he told me to stay in bed. Take it easy for once. I didn't see any reason to resist and Maisie brought up a tray with a boiled egg, toast spread with Bovril and a cup of tea. They went down quite well, so I was tempted to get up, when the doctor arrived.

"I happened to be making a home visit at a farm in the area, your ladyship," he said. "Now let's take a look at you."

He noticed how I winced when he ran the stethoscope over my chest. "Have you noticed any tenderness here?" he asked.

"Oh. As a matter of fact," I began. "Is that serious?"

He gave me a knowing smile. "And it hasn't occurred to you that you might be pregnant?" he asked.

I felt my jaw drop open. "Golly. I never

thought about it. We were so busy, you see. So worried about other things."

"Then let's make a more thorough exam."

At the end he gave me an encouraging grin. "About two months along, I'd say."

"Really?" I could hardly get the word out.

"Congratulations, my lady. Take care of yourself. Eat plenty of good food and everything should progress splendidly. I'll be keeping an eye on you."

Darcy came into the room as soon as the doctor left. "Well?" he said as he sat on the bed beside me. "What did the old boy say? I asked him and he said I'd better hear it coming from you. It's not bad news, is it?"

"Quite the opposite," I said. "It seems there is a future Lord Kilhenny on the way."

Darcy's face lit up. "You're expecting?"

I nodded. He swept me into his arms, hugging me tightly, then released me. "Oh, I'm sorry. Was that too hard an embrace? I've got to take care of you from now on."

I looked at his face with love. "Darcy, I'm not made of porcelain suddenly. You can hug me as hard as you like."

"I can't believe it." He was still beaming. "We're going to have a baby. And we'll have our dogs to keep you occupied until it arrives. What could be more perfect?"

What indeed.

POSTSCRIPT

Fig, Binky and retinue departed the next morning. I was sorry to lose Mrs. McPherson and to once again be relegated to Queenie's cooking. Granddad was sorry to see Hamilton go.

Binky hugged me and told me what a splendid time he'd had with us. Addy cried and didn't want to leave Auntie Georgie. Podge looked as if he was about to cry too.

"Don't worry. I'll come up to London and see where you've set up your train set," I said.

And so they left. Mummy departed the next day, promising to come back to be an adoring grandmother. Granddad didn't need much persuading to stay on. I was really glad.

It was lucky that our neighbors thought we'd be away for New Year's Eve, as I gather we managed to escape a really raucous party. Instead we spent it at home, just the three of us at table with the last of the champagne. It felt just right.

Toward the end of January, Darcy and I made plans to drive up to Sandringham to collect the dogs. Darcy thought we should send Phipps, our footman/chauffeur to do it, but I wanted to make sure they were well looked after all the way home, and to thank the gardener's wife properly for taking good care of them. I wasn't quite sure what to give her. Money seemed crass.

"Aunt Ermintrude's painting?" Darcy suggested, getting a slap on the hand from me.

In the end I decided on some chocolates plus good cologne and soap. I didn't think people like her had many luxuries.

I was wondering whether we should pay our respects to the king and queen, or whether the rest of the royal family was still in residence and they would prefer not to be disturbed. As we drove onto the estate I was surprised to see a host of vehicles parked around the house.

Darcy wound down the window as a man passed us, carrying a camera on a tripod.

"What's going on?" he asked.

"It's the king," the man replied. "He died in his sleep this morning."

We drove on in silence.

"So that's the end of an era," Darcy said. "Your cousin David is now king. I wonder what name he'll choose?" He paused, then reconsidered. "I wonder how he'll handle introducing Mrs. Simpson to the people and how they'll take it." He sighed. "I'm worried for our country, Georgie."

"He'll be all right. You'll see," I said. "He was brought up to do the right thing."

"I admire your optimism." He turned to look at me. "At least I can be optimistic about our own little world, can't I? A baby in the summer. What could be more perfect?"

"As long as you don't go rushing off on assignment at the wrong moment," I said.

Darcy laughed.

HISTORICAL NOTE

This is, of course, a work of fiction but I tried to stay close to the facts where the royal family is concerned.

King George V was very fond of Sandringham House and always spent a month or more there at Christmastime. His whole family came to join him for the celebration and they all walked together to the small church on the estate.

The Prince of Wales and Mrs. Simpson had been skiing in Switzerland and returned grudgingly when told of the king's declining health. However, I have stretched a couple of facts — she did not apply for the divorce until later in the year (and Mr. Simpson agreed to plead guilty!). And there may be plenty of hunts on Boxing Day but not usually on the Sandringham Estate. I've made mine a paper chase, an informal sort of hunt, not the real thing. Boxing Day is normally reserved for the shoot, but in my story it takes place the day after.

The amazing truth is that the British public knew nothing of Mrs. Simpson at that time. The newspapers agreed not to mention her, although she was certainly fodder for the foreign press. Can you imagine today all the newspapers agreeing not to embarrass the Prince of Wales by mentioning his lady friend?

As well as the main house there are several residences on Sandringham Estate (the Duke of Cambridge has one these days); however, Wymondham Hall (pronounced Wyndham) is fictitious.

ABOUT THE AUTHOR

Rhys Bowen, a *New York Times* bestselling author, has been nominated for every major award in mystery writing, including the Edgar®, and has won many, including both the Agatha and Anthony awards. She is also the author of the Molly Murphy Mysteries, set in turn-of-the-century New York, and the Constable Evans Mysteries, set in Wales as well as two internationally bestselling stand alone novels. She was born in England and now divides her time between Northern California and Arizona.